# TAKING CONTROL

# TAKING CONTROL

## Part Two in the
## Starchild Series

BOBBIE FALIN

Bobbie Falin

# Contents

To Sam

# I

# PROLOGUE

Two worlds, their fates entwined for ages beyond memory in ways their peoples cannot imagine. One, known to the Ly Kai as the Homeworld, rich in history, fallen in glory, yet comfortable, its people wielding the power of the stars. The other, the dwelling place of the Goddess Kep, its people divided into her First and Second Children. The First Children, the Eldren, possess their own forms of power, which they use to isolate themselves from the Geffitzi, the Goddess' newer, troublesome Second Children. But ties hidden by the dust of ages are still ties that exist to keen-eyed seekers of power, who will to do anything to seize and rule.

***

Horrified to discover the Ly Kai refugees lied about her Birth-star, telling her she was born to Freya, a weaker star in the Hierarch of Power, instead of mighty Arylla, that powered their exile on this alien world, young Kaphri flees the tower of Kryie Karth. Fearing she is destined to evil, she vows never to use her star power again and sets out with her tiny dragon companion, Gemma, to find a new home on a hostile planet.

The Ly Kai, however, do not belong on this world. Lured by a promise of a new, exciting life over their luxurious but dull Homeworld, they followed Arylla-born Araxis through a gateway between worlds Then, when Araxis sought set himself up as their supreme leader, they rejected him. When he threatened to close the way back to the Homeworld, his terrified followers combined their star power against him. The battle escalated until they were forced to destroy him. Almost. They succeeded in destroying his physical form, but his life essence escaped. And in that last second before he severed from his body he struck a terrible blow, killing all the Ly Kai women and children...except one...an infant niece born to the same star as he. If he can find her and lure her into desiring the power of her Birthstar, Araxis can possess Kaphri's physical form and rise again.

When Kaphri encounters three angry Geffitz warriors, Frax, Uri, and Tobin, they demand she remove the barrier Araxis created to keep their people from returning to their homelands in the south, where he planned to create his empire. The Ly Kai, however, hating and fearing her as the surviving child, refused to share details of that time with Kaphri. All she knows is they fled north in fear of Araxis. Now a strange force is driving her back toward the feared south and she dares not reveal it to these warriors. For, if they discover the link between her and the evil that forced her to run from Kryie Karth, they will kill her.

And then Gemma tells them Kaphri may be their only hope of reclaiming their lands...

With help from Frax, she escapes Araxis' grasp, but their flight takes them through the heart of an evil power and traps them all on the southern side of Araxis' barrier.

Now Kaphri, Gemma, and her Geffitzi captors find themselves

trapped in the south. Worse, they've added two more war-riors—blood enemies to her own companions—to their number. They must find a way to unite their forces and fight their way for-ward.

But, as Uri warns, "The Evil One will not let this little one go so easily."

# 31

## A New Day

Kaphri woke to the sounds of a rustling breeze and birdsong.

Confused, she pulled to a sitting position and looked about. Sunlight glinted through a canopy of newly unfurled spring leaves.

Uri glanced up at her from where he sat, his back propped against the trunk of a nearby tree. The rest of the warriors were nowhere in sight. *"Welcome back among the living. How do you feel?"*

She rubbed at her temples. *"My head hurts. How...?"*

*"You fell asleep on your feet, so Frax carried you. He said he had plenty of practice lately."* Uri's broad grin caused the color in her face to deepen.

She thought back to the warm, soft darkness of the previous night. Despite the horrors of escaping Araxis and his forces in the tower the warriors called Maugrock, a strange sort of bliss had settled over her as she walked through the late-spring night. It was the first time in many days that she was dry, warm, and without immediate danger hanging over her head. It would have been easy for her to think she was in another time and place. The stars were a glorious blaze she no longer needed to fear. She could have danced for joy, or just lain in the grass and stared at them in rapture. But that was not possible. Frax had been ruthlessly determined to put as much distance between them and their pursuit as he could. Wrapped in their private thoughts after coming to a tense truce among themselves, the warriors walked swiftly and silently with their long-legged, ground-eating gait.

As usual, Kaphri had found herself scrambling to keep pace until, fighting weariness and pain, everything had become a fog. She vaguely remembered the feel of hands upon her, struggling in protest, and a sense of Frax's irritation, but little more.

But, that was last night. Now the sun was shining gloriously and she was hungry.

Uri had anticipated that. Using his uninjured arm, he pitched her several soft, round, reddish fruits. She caught them gratefully and bit into one, savoring the sweetness as it broke beneath her teeth.

*"How is your shoulder?"*

*"I'll live."* Uri smiled.

*"Where are the others? Where is Gemma?"* She twisted about, looking for her little golden dragon companion.

*"She agreed—as it appears we are all going to survive in spite of our wounds—that it can do no harm if she seeks an herb I requested. The rest are off to scout the countryside. It's been a while since the Children of Kep walked in this land. We would not like any unpleasant surprises. It was ours, and we don't think any of our people survived the attack of your Evil One, but something may have come here in the twenty years of our absence. Meanwhile, we—you and I—are to rest, so we're ready to go when they get back. When you're done eating, bring your arm over here and let me check it."*

She did not find the idea of the two new warriors wandering

around freely very comforting, especially since her companions considered them enemies. She searched for a way to approach Uri about them.

With him, a direct question seemed best. *"Uri, who are those two, Seuliac and Velacy Aedec?"*

His gaze locked on her, his mood becoming serious. *"Trouble that we didn't need, Willow."* He called her by the name he'd given her in the dark zone, Omurda.

*"They prefer to speak aloud."* The two appeared to favor speaking over the telepathy her original three companions used.

*"Yes, their clan usually does. Why?"*

She mulled her response for a moment, and then decided to voice her concern. *"The Ly Kai speak aloud when they do not wish someone to know their true thoughts."*

*"Really?"* He grinned. *"They can't hide their true thoughts if they use telepathy?"*

*"One cannot lie in a sending."*

Uri's eyes sharpened beneath the humor. *"You honestly believe that?"*

*"We mindspeak. Can you not tell?"*

He appeared taken aback by the question. *"Well, first, I could never accept that premise. I don't think any Geffitz would. It's just not..."* His curiosity overcame him. *"May I?"* When she nodded, he lightly touched her mind. His humor vanished. *"You really do believe that!"*

*"Because it is true."*

*"Interesting. I'm not sure that holds true for Geffitzi. It wouldn't be a strong argument for using telepathy, and you certainly wouldn't find people ready to admit to skill in lying."* He gave a short, ironic laugh. *"Actually, mindspeak isn't equally distributed in my people, Willow. It's traditionally stronger in the southern and the western clans. Those from the north and east are much weaker. Being less proficient, they are also more suspicious of the ability. Many of the rural populace never use it at all. Not that it*

*doesn't exist; you will find it in use in any holdhall, though some users try to hide their ability. Intrigue works best if it is not overheard. Do the Ly Kai ever speak aloud?"*

She took another bite of fruit to mask the twinge of pain his question caused. *"They did to me."*

*"Why?"*

*"It was my choice. They saw no reason to hide their true feelings of anger and resentment from me when they sent, so we did not mindspeak."*

*"Were they cruel to you?"*

*"I did not say that,"* she responded stiffly. The Ly Kai survivors in the tower of Kryie Karth had hidden many things from her, but most of those things had been based on a fear of what she might become. Their anger and resentment came from the things they had lost with her uncles' betrayal.

*"No. No, you didn't."*

*"I think speaking aloud is kinder, in a way."*

Uri shook his head. *"Kinder? Maybe. But who speaks for the purpose of kindness? I think speaking aloud is sometimes dangerous: one can never be sure what the listener hears. Words are too open to interpretation. And, as you say, who can judge the truth in it? But sending is dangerous, too, especially if you believe it's always true, Willow. A skillful sender can twist or disguise a lie, particularly if one doesn't even think to question it."*

That was an interesting idea. *"Perhaps you are right. Rath spoke aloud, but I always believed he spoke true. I never suspected he acted for a purpose other than his own."*

*"Trust like that would get you killed in some Geffitz holdhalls."*

*"Are they truly so dangerous?"*

*"Things are not as bad as they used to be, but yes, lust for power breeds treachery. I must warn you: don't let the Aedecs fool you. Caer Rhynog, the holdhall of our new guests, is historically one of the most treacherous. Traditionally they may not be as telepathically strong as the Kitahns, but*

they have their skills. And they don't make the identities of the people who possess those skills common knowledge."

"But you trust them to wander about."

"Yes. Why?"

"They...hate..." she tapered off, reluctant to say more for fear he might ask how she knew their feelings. Frax had warned her in Omurda never to use that part of her mental skills on a Geffitz. She did not think he would discriminate in that crime between an ally and an enemy.

Uri nodded. "Yes. They're Aedecs." He said it as if it explained everything.

"So I have heard," she murmured, looking down at the fruit in her hand. The Aedec name held a significance that was beyond her.

She felt the touch of Uri's humor again. "Yes. Well." He paused for a moment in thought, and then he was back. "Once you named your titles to us. You called yourself a Daughter of the First House of Dolphere." She nodded. "I'm sure to your people there is great significance in that, based on...?" He looked at her, waiting for her to finish the statement.

"Based on our bloodline and the power we wield. The position of our family Birthstars has always been high in the Hierarch of the Ly Kai. The Dolphere family has long ranked high in the governing of the Ly Kai Home-world."

He nodded. "We have something similar here. Two ancient houses have ranked higher and longer than all the other families. One is the Aedec family of Caer Rhynog. The other is the Kitahn family of Caer Cadarn. Two families so old and powerful— and stubbornly proud—will, inevitably develop a few interests at cross-purposes. And sometimes family and blood take precedence with them over good sense or common purpose."

"They feud?"

"Blood feud."

"Recently?"

"Yes, since the beginning of our history."

"Oh." Kaphri digested the information for a moment, the agreement of a truce between their feuding houses coming back to her. "*Frax trusts their word?*"

"*He knows how far to trust their word. There is a difference.*"

"*How far is that?*"

"*For as long as they believe it suits their purpose. So, Frax must think ahead of them.*"

"*Can he do that?*"

"*Frax?*" Uri smiled with hard satisfaction. "*The Aedecs have reason not to trust the Kitahns, too, Willow.*"

She could understand that. Memory of Frax's latest bits of manipulation to discover what drove her southward stung her afresh.

"*And you, Uri?*" She remembered the sense of surprise she had felt in the Aedec warriors on seeing Uri wearing the red and green of Kitahn. "*Seuliac does not react toward you in the same way as he does Frax and Tobin. What of you?*"

"*Enough Kitahni blood flows in my veins to make an Aedec touch his blade when I enter a room, Willow, but I am Caspani, and we have our own interests to guard. The interests of Rhynog and Cadarn are not always those of the rest of our people. But, just as I wear the tabard of Cadarn because the colors protect better in this terrain, in this matter I also stand with Frax. Seuliac Aedec can be trusted not to act until he is sure of exactly what is transpiring around him. Hopefully, by then, reason will prevail and our new friends will see the need to stand with us in this.*" Once again, the touch of Uri's subtle humor lightened the seriousness of their conversation. "*Seuliac is the Warlord of Rhynog, commander of the Aedec family's land forces. As self-serving as he appears, he does have a reputation of good sense. He won't do anything that might harm Rhynog, and everything that will advance its cause. Velacy,*" he shrugged slightly, wincing as the movement pained his shoulder, "*is second in line as an heir to the Lordship of Rhynog. He is young, proud, and as belligerent as an*"

*Aedec could possibly be, but he is not reputed to be a complete fool. Now, finish your fruit, then come here."*

The fruit was good, and she wanted to savor its fresh taste after so many days of dried roots and worse, so she took the third piece with her as she walked over to sit in front of him. The Geffitz's big hands were light as he unwound the cloth that bound her outstretched arm. He grunted with satisfaction and turned it so she could see it clearly. All the infection had disappeared, leaving the knife cut dry and scabbed.

*"It heals well, but there'll be a scar. You begin to accumulate warrior's badges, Willow."*

Kaphri looked up at him with a mental frown, not understanding the reference. His mouth curved. *"Badges. Marks of battle, like this."* He twisted to show her a long silvery scar that ran over the skin of his ribcage from his left breast to his lower back. Remembering the slash marks on her shoulder, left by plain cat's claws, her eyes widened at the thought of the injury that had left such a mark on him.

Something else caught her attention. His shirt was gone! He wore only the burgundy and green-trimmed tabard, and it was clean. And he had bathed.

She was abruptly aware of how dirty, as well as blood-smeared, she was after her fall down the mountainside.

Uri saw her look down at her clothing. *"You can bathe later, when the others return. We wouldn't want you slipping under a rock again, unsupervised, would we?"*

Kaphri ducked her head, avoiding his eyes while she watched him smear a salve on her arm from a small vial he carried in a beltpouch.

Her curiosity drew her back into their exchange. Warrior's badges. What a strange idea. She asked him what it meant.

*"Wounds earned in battle,"* he explained.

*"I am no warrior."* A touch of bitterness that she would have

rather kept hidden crept into her sending. She did not do battle. She ran.

Uri held her gaze steadily. "*Don't judge yourself too harshly: you're braver than you credit yourself. You had the warrior mind-set at the barrier. I touched it in you, and so did the others.*"

Memory of the mental brushes she'd experienced at the barrier came back to her. The Geffitz seemed to sense her perplexity. "*It's the warrior's way of determining truth and protecting ourselves from treachery, by touching on another's true intentions. There is no honor in dying from foolish, blind trust, Willow. A warrior does not shield; his motives can withstand the examination of his fellows. You were ready to die for what you believed was right. That's all anyone can ask of a warrior.*"

The discussion of motives and honor was leading in a painful direction she did not wish to pursue. She'd been trying desperately to escape from them when she fell captive to Araxis' winged forces in the shadows of Omurda.

She might be forced to try again.

But she never wanted them to come to harm because of her. "*I am sorry I caused you injury, Uri. I really am.*"

His hands stopped their light work. He studied her closely. "*My wound is not your fault. We all realize there is risk in what we do. A Geffitz warrior does what is necessary.*"

"*Why? Why did you risk your safety to come to that tower? It was dangerous.*"

"*We must know what threatens us from the Maugrock, so we can prepare to defend against it. To protect the others, the ones we leave behind, so they, and we, too, can live in safety. I wouldn't hold much honor if I didn't do everything possible to ensure the safety of the ones less able to defend themselves.*"

She searched his face. "*You left ones you care about behind?*"

He nodded. "*Family, friends. A female, soon to be my lifemate.*"

"*What is she like?*"

Uri looked surprised.

"*This female...?*"

"*Ladrienca.*"

"*Ladrienca. What is she like?*"

Uri smiled. "*Laddy? Like the touch of the hot summer sun on your face, or a summer storm at night, fierce and warm in its intensity, but cooling to the spirit. Sweet as indrum fruit as it bursts on the tongue, clearminded as the sky after the snow. Fair and soft as tamsin flowers as they fall in the spring.*"

His eyes took on a distant look and Kaphri caught the image of a pert, smiling face, similar to the warrior before her, but more delicate in its features. A deep longing ran through Uri's sending and Kaphri shifted uncomfortably, trying to move away from it without being obvious.

Such fondness and need! She had not known such feelings were possible.

Uri broke the sending with a sheepish grin. "*Sorry. I got a little lost in my thoughts there.*"

For a moment, they sat in silence while she tried to sort through the baffling emotions she'd just gotten from the big warrior. They left her feeling awkward, but she decided she must pursue the subject further.

"*There is a fondness in you for this female. This separation is painful. You...choose...to experience these feelings? Why?*"

"The feelings and time shared are worth the sadness of the separation. And the return will just be the sweeter." Uri studied her, bemused. "Willow, don't you know anything about love? What of your mother and father?"

"My mother died in the betrayal, when I was two years old. My father—is still in the north."

It was Uri's turn to look discomfited. "Ah. Perhaps your people don't..."

"They were lifemates," she said stiffly. "I am aware of the joining between male and female. I learned the rituals of binding, so, as High One, I could conduct the ceremony." Hredroth knew whatever for; all the survivors in Kryie Karth were old men, except for her.

But she had touched feelings similar to the ones they were discussing. They came from every one of the men in Kryie Karth when they longed for those they had lost in the betrayal. Longing, laced with a bitter anger toward her.

Sudden fury at herself lashed through her. How foolish she was to have pursued this conversation.

"Willow? Hey, Willow Wand—" Uri's mental touch was full of concern.

Kaphri dodged it, suddenly wanting to be alone. But before she could scramble to her feet, a glimmer of gold flitting between the trees caught her eye.

"*Gemma!*" Joy shot through her, washing away the horrible sense of desolation with a flood of warmth. She eagerly stretched out her arm and the winged dragon fluttered onto it with a mental brush of pleasure.

As the little dragon slipped up on her shoulder, Kaphri gave Uri a guilty glance of apology for severing their conversation so abruptly.

He was settling back against the tree, his expression thoughtful as he observed them. She caught the barely perceptible wag of his head that told her it was of no consequence. That he understood her slip in mindspeaking her companion against Frax's ban, and she relaxed back down into the spot where she had been sitting.

"*Give these to the Geffitz. Unpleasant as they are, you may share them.*"

Kaphri held out her hand and Gemma dropped some shriveled orange berries into it. She looked at them doubtfully but Uri acted pleased to see them.

"*You have my thanks.*" He nodded his head at the little companion.

Despite a mental sniff of irritation from Gemma, Kaphri sensed his reaction pleased her.

He handed one of the berries back to her. *"Eat it."* He gave a grimace. *"Don't worry about washing it; it'll kill whatever would ail you. Swallow fast."* He winked as he tossed one into his own mouth, clenched his teeth, then swallowed it with a shudder.

She understood what he meant the next moment as the horrible bitterness of the berry flooded her mouth. Gagging, she swallowed.

Uri had his waterbag ready for her.

Seconds later a noise behind them drew their attention. Tobin had returned. Kaphri turned away as he suspended the two dead animals he carried from the low branch of a nearby tree and came over to lay several withered plants next to Uri.

The other Geffitz nodded his thanks again.

The scout stood for a moment, looking at the three of them, then, surprisingly, sat down. Kaphri realized his silence was tightly suppressed excitement.

*"Well?"* Uri had noticed it, too.

*"Game is everywhere! They're so tame they would come up and eat from your hand. Nothing has hunted here in twenty years. If we could re-claim this land..."* He was mindspeaking Uri without shields, something he rarely did in her presence.

As the warriors continued their exchange on hunting, Kaphri took Gemma from her shoulder and set her in her lap so she could look into her green eyes while she stroked the line of her ridged backbone. There was so much to tell her. Tobin and Uri appeared to be absorbed in their conversation, but the girl knew it was not the way of these warriors to drop their guard. They would instantly be aware if she mindspoke. But refusing to allow her to communicate with Gemma, after Kaphri's captivity in the tower, would be most cruel. She decided to try speaking quietly, with shields down. At this point, all the Geffitzi would do was order her to stop.

*"Gemma, I missed you so much."* She wanted to immerse herself in the dragon, but she also had to be sensitive to any reaction coming from her two companions. *"What happened to you?"*

It was no surprise when Uri blinked. His brow furrowed and there was the barest passing of withdrawal before he centered his attention back on Tobin.

He was going to let her communication pass. A tension drained from her that she hadn't even realized she felt.

Gemma had held her reply, waiting for the Geffitzi reaction. *"The gray ones fly swiftly and my wings are not so large. It was at least four days flight for me from the Taprock River to the Maugrock."*

*"I didn't know. I was so scared. They made me breathe something that caused me to lose my senses when they took me. And,"* she added, *"I was very ill. Frax used a poisoned dart on me. He said the Balandra drew out the poison and kept me from dying."* She closed her eyes for a moment. *"They carried me to a horrible place and chained me in a room high in a tower. It was terrible—so cold and dark. And when I finally came to, five of them came in with a bowl and a knife..."*

# 32

## The Crystal

Uri and Tobin's exchange stopped.

She looked up to find them listening to her. Uri lifted a brow as their eyes met and Tobin shifted to a more comfortable position. They waited in expectant silence, so she resumed her sending, sharing the story with the three of them now.

Shortly afterwards the two Aedec warriors wandered back into camp. Seuliac was palely sporting a nasty bruise on his forehead but otherwise appeared none the worse for wear. At first, they hung back, as if they thought Uri might stop her narrative in their presence. When that did not happen, they came over and settled on the ground to listen, too.

Her story became long in the telling. Occasionally Uri or Tobin would break in with a pointed question. Even Velacy overcame his obvious distrust of her enough to raise a question or two. Seuliac merely listened, his eyes fastened on her, his attention like a sharp blade.

Some of the details, like the force in the central core, brought a reaction of strong dismay or interest. It didn't seem prudent to tell them she had pushed Frax into the shaft, despite Uri's puzzlement over the other warrior's quick acceptance of such an unknown element.

Kaphri's mindspeak was a sharing of words, impressions, and detailed memory images. Uri and Tobin were familiar with the tower, having trained there as young warriors. They were almost with her as she desperately counted off the passages. And they were all as shaken as she was at the sight of Ving in the vast chamber, with the sound of hundreds of unseen wings rustling in the darkness. They snarled rage at his threat against the Geffitzi clans and shared Frax's shocked dismay at finding the debris that blocked the stairwell missing. Their awe and fear at the sight of the temple, deep in the rock below the Maugrock, was immense, and even Gemma grew distressed when she described moving across the rune circles, the serpent searching through the images in her memory with an uncharacteristic feverishness. Tobin ran through the children's rhyme when she stumbled in her recitation, half, she thought, to reassure himself he would have known the words too, if he was there instead of Frax. The rest of the details beyond that point Uri and Tobin knew, and she was reluctant to discuss her second attempt at escape except for a brief mention of her removal of the bloody sign on her forehead.

To her surprise, both Gemma and Uri reacted to the last bit of information with agitation.

Uri caught her right hand and turned her fingers up to study them intently. "*You didn't just wash the sign off. That was bad magic! What did you do?*"

Gemma moved on her shoulder, tiny claws digging into the muscles of her right arm as she leaned forward. Kaphri went over her actions again with as much detail as she could remember.

"*Something that looked like blood.*" He snatched her words. "*Kep, you* were a mess when Frax brought you in—blood all over your face and shirt and breeches. Blood on your hand. Where would the blood on your hand come from?" He lifted her arm, studying the remnants of her soiled sleeve, trying to see some reason in the motion. "Frax wasn't injured, so he's not the source." He was thinking rapidly, with an urgency that alarmed her. "Your leg? But you said they chained your hands upwards. Where would you get blood—or something else—on your hands? Think!"

She shook her head, unable to answer.

He weighed her hand in his as he studied her thoughtfully. "Blood. Or something. Sweat? Is not dark. Your clothes. You didn't wash them yet."

She gave him a reproachful look. How could he ask such a question? Her clothing was filthy.

He dropped her hand, watching it fall to brush her breeches.

"What the...?" His big hand caught her right leg above the knee and rolled it inward, almost throwing her over before she could catch herself. Gemma dug claws to maintain balance as Uri stared at a dark, caked smear high on the cloth of her outer thigh. He looked up, his eyes fastening on her face. "Where did this come from?"

She started to shake her head again, then stopped, memory of a sensation of stickiness and her reaction of dismay tugging at her. Things felt clouded and dark in her mind as she struggled to remember. "From the..."

"There's something there!" Tobin reached forward.

"No!" Uri caught his wrist and held his hand away from her leg. His attention came back to her. He repeated his question. "Where did this come from?"

"Down there, in the circle. I..." Vague memories flickered in her mind. In the temple. She was looking at the runes in the center of the rings. She wanted to see them, but something blocked her view. When she reached down to brush it away, something dark, thick and warm clung to her skin.

Such sadness. Her breath caught in her throat as the memory rushed over her now. She had wiped her hand on her breeches to break with the sensation, then Frax was there, slapping the canna disk away before she could look at the inner ring, breaking the spell the circle worked on her. He was dragging her away, over to the altar... The details were still obscured and clouded in her memory, as if something, or someone, had willed she should forget them.

She glanced at the dark blotch on her breeches with fear now, remembering the thread that tangled in her fingers and the round shape that hung from it. The smear had cracked, separating along a definite edge.

Uri drew one of the thin-bladed boot knives the warriors kept so readily at hand and slipped the point of the blade beneath the break, lifting gently. A twisted, tangled mass caked with dried darkness came away. Uri held it up and they all stared.

*"Kep, what is that?"*

*"Let's find out. Waterbag, Tobin."* Uri laid the thing on the ground and carefully poured water over it. The stuff softened and flowed, dark and red. *"That's dried blood! But whose?"* Uri poked the mess with the blade and a glint of warm, golden metal resolved through the crimson. Using the knife again, he caught it in a notch in the blade and lifted it to reveal a delicate gold chain. From a loop, still caked with blood, hung the bauble she'd seen in the temple.

*"What the hell is this?"* Uri poured more water over the chain and lifted it again. The water ran down the strand in dark droplets to gather on the charm at its end.

They all watched in stunned silence as a drop fell from it—and disappeared in the air.

*"Holy Kep! Tobin! Take this!"* Uri thrust the knife handle into his companion's reluctant hand as he fumbled about for a leaf and a twig. But as he reached out to capture some of the dark crust still

caked on her breeches leg, the stuff was blackening and crumbling to a fine powder that fell away without leaving a trace.

Uri drew back with an expression of bafflement and disappointment. *"Damn,"* he swore. *"If I could have caught some of that..."*

"Take this!" Tobin spoke aloud, but it was not hard to catch his meaning as he shoved the weapon with the chain back into Uri's grip. He scrambled to his feet and took a step back.

The chain gleamed cleanly now in the shadowy forest light, with no trace of stain remaining. Uri raised it to eye-level so he could take a closer look, but Kaphri noted none of the warriors were eager to touch it. Uri studied the bauble for a moment then held it out for her to see.

There was something at the crystal's center.

*"What is that, Gemma?"* Kaphri leaned forward to peer at it. There was a tiny golden sphere encased in the ball of clear crystal.

*"A remnant of ancient power,"* the serpent replied.

*"Ancient,"* Uri glanced at Gemma. *"And to what leanings? Good or evil?"*

With a swipe of his hand, he cleared the leaves on the forest floor to expose a small patch of soil. Quickly he drew some dried leaves from a pouch at his belt and crushed them between his fingers to form a small pile of pale powder in the dirt.

A clean, fragrant smell brushed Kaphri's senses. A strange, brief stab of loss ran through her, quickening her heartbeat for a breath before fading. The scent had been the touch of something rare, good and pure.

*"Sevil,"* Gemma murmured with approval and Kaphri realized she was identifying the leaves.

Tobin hovered beside them, as reluctantly fascinated as the rest of them, while Uri traced symbols at four points around the powder, naming each as he went: earth, wind, fire and water. Then he drew two lines, one above and one below the symbols, and broke them in half with two shorter ones above and below the dust. That completed, he suspended the crystal over the sevil by the chain and spoke several words aloud with quiet but firm resonance.

He was working some type of spelling, that was simple to see, but Kaphri didn't think he was prepared for the response he received. The powder beneath the crystal flared in a clear, white glow, like the blaze of a tiny sun, then died away, leaving no ash or waste behind.

A stunned silence hung over them all.

"*Perhaps,*" Uri looked up to search her face, "*you should tell me, in detail, how this came to you.*"

"*Why? Is it evil?*" A blaze of panic shot through her.

"*No.*" he said, taking a deep breath. "*It may have come from the temple, but it's not evil.*"

"*Then what is it?*"

"*My knowledge is limited. An ancient working. Possibly a talisman of safe passage or guardianship. The intent is pure; you saw what it did under a spell of testing.*"

"*Well, it wasn't a safe talisman for someone,*" Tobin observed sharply.

"*No,*" Uri conceded. "*Whoever carried the thing appears to have lost it in the heart of evil's stronghold, along with a lot of blood. But it appears to hold power against that evil. The blood on her hands and clothes must have held the crystal's power in suspension.*"

"*But it was warm,*" she protested.

"*And wet. And now it's dried and crumbled beyond dust. Now, tell me.*"

She went over her passage through the temple again, seeking in her memory for any elusive details of those moments in the vast darkness, when rising fear that she was alone in the blackness had prompted her to increase the light of the canna disk. All too clearly, she remembered the scent of ancient dust, the feel of an ominous, gathering presence, and the sensation of immense structure around her. But her actions felt veiled. Through a fog, she saw the vague shapes laid into the floor inside their great circles, and the dark smear that obscured the central pattern. The recall of heavy, warm stickiness, now caused her to mentally recoil, but Uri would not let her break the memory chain. He pressed her onward like a firm hand. The terrible sorrow snatched at her again, shaking her to her very roots, before giving way to a faint, tingling recollection of rising demand. Of a powerful external force urging her to wipe the stain away, to see the shapes hidden beneath. Then the vagueness gave way to the memory of Frax glaring down at her in fury and the lick of hot purple—

She broke her recall, pulling herself back to the present. Her hands shook when she raised them to her forehead.

Gemma moved on her shoulder, her quick mental touch reassuring.

Uri studied Kaphri solemnly. "*It would seem the amulet, and Frax, made timely appearances. Perhaps you haven't realized yet, but the presence in the temple is a remnant of a dark and malevolent force that nearly destroyed our world before we defeated and drove it out ages ago.*" His expression tightened with dismay. "*The place where you stood is known as the Goroth M'nget, the Circle of Sacrifice. Legend says the runes there hold a terrible power that can ensnare the unwary with just a look. Judging from that, and the images you've shown us, I would say this crystal must have been working to protect you, even before you picked it up.*"

"*I don't know anything about this object, but I know the thing in the darkness is evil,*" she told him. "*I think Araxis used it in Kryie Karth when he tried to ensnare me.*"

Uri raised a hand to stop her, his face suddenly pale. "*Wait. You think he's using it?*"

"*I think he tried to. But he wasn't successful. It's not the same as the power of the Ly Kai,*" she hastened to add, "*even if it does lurk inside the barrier.*"

"*Now, there's something else I don't understand,*" Uri said. "*You told us it grabbed you at the barrier. If it's the same force, why didn't it react to your presence when you were right on top of it in the temple?"*

How had she passed through the heart of its power in the temple without the evil force reacting more strongly? What had made that different? It was difficult to recall small details: during most of her passage across the vast floor she had been tired and in pain, her mind drifting...

Her heart gave a painful thump. Her mind had been drifting because of the reversed symbol the Balandra had painted on her brow. It had locked all her power away from her. Had it also isolated her from the very thing that would mark her presence in the darkness?

*"Severing you from your power might have hidden your presence in the temple,"* Uri gave voice to her thoughts.

*"The ultimate question is,"* a familiar mental voice broke in calmly as a hand reached down between them and lifted the chain from the notch in the blade, *"is she to use this thing, or is it to use her?"* Frax raised the strand, the crystal glinting brightly, to study it in the light. *"How long would you say it's been lost to this world, Uri? How many hundreds of years?"*

*"Even the serpent observes it's ancient."* Uri answered, a trace of uneasiness in his tone.

*"Just a little something this one seems able to walk around our world and pick up."* Kaphri bristled, the earlier animosity at the barrier crackling between her and the Geffitz leader as their eyes met, but she bit back any response as he continued. *"Whatever this is, it was serving some purpose down there."*

*"Yes."*

*"And now it's not."* He gave her another glare before he shifted attention back to Uri.

*"No, it's not."* Uri's response was quiet and unhappy. *"But,"* his sending picked up some urgency, *"it must have been working to aid her. It had to be the source of the blood on her hands that helped remove the*

*symbol from her forehead. And look. This is where it clung to her clothing! Up on the mountainside, when she turned toward the serpent,"* the flat of Uri's hand brushed the side of her thigh where the dried blood had caked, *"it would have come in contact with the barrier. It could be what opened it."*

*"In other words,"* with a quick movement of his hand, Frax caught the crystal up, clasping it, chain and all, tightly in his fist. His knuckles whitened. *"This little trinket has worked to make us prisoners here, on this side of the barrier?"*

Uri heaved a sigh. *"Well, maybe. There does seem to be some force at work here. It's as if the thing was waiting for her to find it. I wonder if she could have come through the barrier without its help."*

*"Force?"* A curl of angry frustration ran through Frax's sending. *"Almost as if? Uri, I don't think we begin to have any idea of the forces at work here, manipulating us."* His eyes locked back on Kaphri with a hard, angry glitter as he considered her from behind a shielded mind.

***

For the first time, Frax Kitahn allowed the possibility he was not quite in control of their situation. In fact, things had taken on a monstrous life of their own. What had he gotten them into when he insisted on taking the girl captive in Omurda? Where, of all things, he had listened to the words of a Guardian! At every turn, this girl seemed to be moved along by forces beyond her control, and now, they, with her. And, of all the things she had revealed to be working on her at the barrier, they had just added another to the list. The small crystal dug into the skin of his hand as he clenched it tighter.

Well, he was not ready to relinquish his hold, real or imagined, on his fate, just yet. *"Uri, you're the one best schooled in the lore of our world. What is your counsel on this?"*

Uri turned his attention on her with a thoughtful expression. To-bin was already glaring at her darkly, not to mention the wary regard of the Aedecs. It was a tribute to her fortitude that she did not writhe beneath the intense, piercing glare of five pairs of gray Geffitzi eyes.

Uri replied cautiously. "*The Evil One has stirred powers from the past with some success, Frax. The most recent evidence: the return of the Balandra. Something is happening. Something significant and not, I fear, in the best interests of the Children of Kep. But you saw the testing. This thing does not carry evil. It already protected her, if not us, too. It came to her. It isn't evil.*" He frowned. "*I fear its removal from its resting place may have serious repercussions, but, considering what we know, I don't think it would be wise to take it from her.*"

Frax nodded. He opened his hand to let the necklet dangle from one finger before her eyes. "*Put it on.*"

Kaphri drew back with a quick glance at Uri.

The sandy-haired Geffitz gave her a nod. "*It came to you. Its power may yet serve you in some way.*"

Serve her? She did not want anything of its power. She didn't want anything from this world. Kaphri made no move to take the thing from the Geffitz leader's hand.

Frax's mouth tightened. Impatiently he separated the strands of the chain with his fingers and reached down to drop it over her head, pulling the collar of her shirt away from her neck so the small ball dropped coolly between her breasts before she could protest.

"*You found it, Priestess, you wear it.*"

# 33

## Strategy

"If you're so sure that damn thing put us here, why not use it to pass back over," Tobin snapped. "There must be a way."

Uri shook his head. "Taking either her or the crystal back would only invite disaster, Tobin. We know what will happen if the Evil One captures her."

"So what are we supposed to do?" Tobin sat back down beside Uri, his frustration obvious.

"She wants to go south. We'll take her south."

All their attention locked on the Geffitz leader. For a moment it appeared Frax was lost in thought and had absently spoken aloud. Then he looked around, his gaze sweeping over them as he weighed their individual reactions. Tobin's expression was startled, Uri's, guardedly receptive. The two Aedecs were stonily wary. The girl's expression, as usual, was emotionless, though he did catch a tiny flicker of mental dismay at his words.

He could guess what her thoughts had been. Did she honestly think he would consider a parting of their ways now that the barrier trapped them in the south? She was the key to this whole mess, and he did not intend to let her out of his grasp.

"And why would we do that?" Tobin's question broke the silence. "We have orders, Frax, and they don't include her."

"Our mission didn't end when the barrier broke, Tobin. It changed." Frax gave him a glare that brooked no argument when the younger Geffitz began to protest. "We're cut off from the north, caught in a new situation, but we will not be bystanders. Far from it. We have what the Evil One wants. What Uri said last night is true: he will come after her. He'll find a way to breech his barrier, and when he does, he'll bring his forces with him, shifting them from the north. That will reduce the threat to the clans. So, even if we can't be there, we can influence the battle to our people's benefit.

"That includes keeping her out of his hands. Leaving us with two options: kill her and remain on this side of the barrier—I don't think we'll get back through on our own—or help her and draw off his attention away from the north. Personally, I want a shot at doing something about that barrier." He took in the cautious nods of agreement. "We all share the same problem: the Evil One. He drove us from our lands and put up a barrier to stop our return, and he's a threat to her continued existence. Someone has to stop him. Neither of us, her people nor ours, alone, succeeded at putting an end to him. Together we might have a chance."

He turned to Kaphri. "*We'll help you get wherever this geas draws you, Priestess, because it's the only thing we can act on right now. Just remember; it's not a guarantee of your life. If things look like they're going bad in any way...*" She knew how to finish the statement. They would kill her. "*In return we want the barrier to our lands removed. You will make that happen. Agreed?*"

She had no choice but to agree, though she had no idea how, or if she could accomplish his goals. Araxis truly was a problem they both had in common. She would never be safe with him in pursuit of her.

"*Geas? What's this about a geas?*" Uri's tone sharpened.

The corners of Frax's mouth tightened. "*Another little bit of information I picked up from her at the barrier, Uri.*"

The other warrior's expression was grave. "*Where there's a geas there's someone else's purpose.*" He shifted his attention to Kaphri. "*Whose? What does this thing bid you do?*"

"*All I know is that it drives me southward.*" She looked away.

"*It gives you no specific sense of purpose?*"

"*No.*"

Exhaling loudly, the big warrior withdrew into troubled thought.

Frax continued. "*I doubt we can fight all the forces we'll draw away from the Maugrock, so, we'll go dark and avoid them. Later we can take up resistance tactics. The first question: how much of a head start can we get before they come through the barrier? It's been two days since I hit Araxis with the poison dart. You're certain he's not dead? That you'd know if he was?*" All eyes were on Kaphri. She nodded. "*Then the Balandra saved him, just as they saved you. Still, he'll be ill, and it'll take some time to gather his strength. The next question: can you tell when he breaks the barrier?*"

She shook her head. "*I don't know, especially if we move away from it. In his present form, however, he doesn't possess the power that he used to create it.*"

"*Are you saying he can't come through?*" Tobin asked.

No matter how she wished she could tell Tobin that was true, she knew better: Araxis would stop at nothing to attain what he desired. "*No. He may destroy Ving's body in the process, but he will find a way to come through. I just can't say I'll sense when he does.*"

Frax shrugged. "*Then we must wait and see.*"

"*We can run up and down the length of the land indefinitely, striking here and there, but even if we destroy his forces, it won't solve the problem of him or her. What's the point? How is this supposed to end?"* Tobin persisted.

All attention focused back on her.

*"I'm being drawn somewhere, perhaps to the gate the Ly Kai used to enter your world."* The survivors memories had revealed that much to her. Perhaps she might find something there to help her along the Paths of Power. To help her attain the full potential of the starpower the Twenty-five had denied her in Kryie Karth. *"Perhaps I will find something there to help me,"* she offered lamely.

Velacy made a startled, angry exclamation, and she realized much of what their two Aedec companions were hearing was new information for them. Frax, Uri and Tobin were already aware of her helplessness. She was sure they did not want to share how her mindblocks hampered the full use of her starpower, or her absence of knowledge, in front of these new warriors.

"And where is this gate?" Tobin demanded.

She had never gleaned the slightest image, much less the location, of the place where the Ly Kai entered this world. Her sense of ineptitude stung her.

*"Are there any landmarks? What did the land around it look like? Were there mountains? Plains? Forests? The Great Water? A river close by?"* Tobin's impatience grew each time she was unable to reply.

"Kep, I don't believe this!" He sprang to his feet in disgust, only to sink back down at Frax's impatient gesture. *"Do you realize how big this land is, girl?"* he flared.

*"Whatever draws me, I will find it."* Kaphri looked at him with a calmness she did not feel. *"The geas didn't let go when I passed the barrier. Even as we speak it pulls at me."* That was true; the geas was beginning to insinuate a rising need to move while she sat there. But now a small tingle of panic edged it. Her passing through the barrier seemed to have strengthened its urgency.

"Well, Kitahn," Seuliac Aedec finally spoke up with a short, harsh laugh. "You have many pieces of this puzzle, but not enough. So, what's your plan?"

"The Balandra prefer to fly at night, so we'll travel during the day and shelter at dark. Speed is important, but making it our first consideration would be reckless. We'll go to where she is drawn, but not in a direct line. On this side of the continent, we'll move slightly westward."

"*No.*"

"*No?*" Frax made the word sound as quietly dangerous as the look he shot her.

"*I told you, I can't go westward. I will not go westward.*" It was as if a sudden torrent broke loose inside her. Everything, from her ignorance of her Birthpower, to her total ignorance of where she was going, surged up inside her. And here was this Geffitz, trying to direct her future. Again. Did he think she was so helpless she was unable to take any action on her own? She lashed out in defiance. "*And I will not be treated as a prisoner any longer!*"

"*Prisoner, hold-guest, slave,*" Frax shrugged, "*they're only words. What you choose to call yourself is unimportant. But you will do as you're told, Priestess.*"

From the corner of her eye, Kaphri saw Tobin nudge Uri, a slight, mocking grin quirking his mouth.

His amusement fired her frustration further. "*Why? What are you—*" she was forced to pause a moment. Standing, she was more than a head shorter than he; sitting while he towered over her was even more ridiculous. She got to her feet, drawing herself up as tall as she could in defiance. "*going to do? You will not kill me. You can't kill me! As you say, without me, you have no hope of destroying the barrier.*"

Frax took a step forward so he stared down at her with the barest space between them. Kaphri would have gladly taken a step back, but defiance would not let her. She held her ground, refusing to show any reaction as she glared up into his stormy gray eyes.

*"Oh, we're all too conscious of that, Priestess,"* His sending was a furious hiss. *"But it won't give you the tiniest bit of leverage. If you want to play difficult, I'll play difficult, and, serpent or no serpent, I will make you squirm. But you will cooperate. If you try to sneak off again I'll track you down and drag you back, and if you're thinking of attacking us, now that you feel comfortable with your power again, you better be sure to finish it all in one try. I told you, you're too dangerous to wander freely on my world. I will not allow it. We'll help you, and you'll help us in return. In between, things will be done my way."*

What choice did she have? She was much better off with these warriors, insufferable as they were, than on her own. Grudgingly Kaphri gave a slight sending of assent.

*"It's settled, then. Sit down. Now."*

They continued to glare at each other.

*"Why does he put up with that?"* She heard Tobin mutter in an impatient aside to Uri. *"She's nothing but a little slip of thistle. I would..."* She saw him make an abrupt crushing gesture with his hand.

*"Did you ever grab a handful of thistle, Tobin?"* Uri gave a mental chuckle. *"Some have nasty, sharp little barbs hidden within."*

Tobin gave a snort of irritation and flopped onto his back.

Velacy seemed to agree with Tobin. He shifted his position restlessly. Seuliac Aedec, however, was watching their exchange with intense interest. It crossed Kaphri's mind that, like Tobin, he was also wondering why Frax bothered to argue with her. A chill of resentment ran over her. Why, indeed? In the end, she could do little against anything the Geffitz leader decided to do with, or about, her.

But Seuliac did not know that. For all the two new warriors knew, she could burn them all to cinders with a glance as Frax had suggested. He had done nothing to dissuade them of the idea.

She knew he read the spark of realization in her eyes. *"Not another word, Priestess. Sit down now."* The words were a sizzle of warning in her head, meant only for her. There was a hardness there—a warning that he would not be thwarted in this. She had agreed and he considered the matter ended.

She opened her mouth. Closed it again, teeth clenched.

*"This bickering isn't getting us anywhere,"* Uri observed.

*"True. We waste time."* Frax shifted attention back to the others, leaving her to stand there, still mutinous and resentful, but alone. The moment of contesting wills had passed.

Gemma's mind gently touched hers, and Kaphri reached to stroke her as she sat back down.

*"Tobin, what's your memory on the maps of the land?"*

Staring up at the sky, Tobin made a short, mockingly magnanimous gesture with his hand. For a second a sense of blankness emanated from him, then the image of a hand-drawn map blossomed in their minds, adjusting details as the scout checked his recall.

Kaphri's anger dissolved into wonder. So this was what Frax had meant when he spoke of Tobin's special talents! Here was the southern continent of this world, laid out in amazing detail for them to view.

Stricken by its beauty, she scanned over the image.

The flowing, long-lined writing on the map was indecipherable to her, but she could pick out the carefully rendered symbol of Maugrock, sitting on its sheer precipice at the southern edge of the dark band that was Omurda. From there the land stretched down in all directions with the curved markings of hills and mountains, winding rivers and dark lakes. The line of the western Great Water was distant from their current point, but curved inward, cutting deep into the land below them. In that area the markings were numerous, but they were also lighter, as if Tobin purposely avoided any attention to them beyond their mere existence. A large block of lettering in the space near the Great Water, however, showed that, at some point, someone certainly had a lot to say about the piece of dimly etched land. She turned her attention away from it, seeking directly below them. There was an abundance of forests and hills, and several rivers cut the land, flowing west. To their east, a chain of jagged mountains broadened and ran south. East of that ridge lay a huge, flat expanse with more markings for what she supposed were cities, or the things the warriors called 'caers'. So much space! Why would Araxis have felt the need to take it all for himself?

She noticed Frax had inserted a line, running down from where they must be toward the vague, many-lettered area Tobin was avoiding.

"...toward the coastal marshes. The Balandra have good reason to avoid the area..." he was saying.

"The Palenquemas?" Tobin jerked to a sitting position. The image of the map blurred with his distress. "Frax, that's insane! No one in their right mind would go near the Palenquemas. No one disturbs the Wyxa. Even this Araxis didn't disturb the Wyxa!"

"You listen to too many old wives tales, Tobin," Frax growled. "The warriors of Cadarn have always moved around the swamp as they pleased. Besides, I didn't suggest entering the Palenquemas. We'll just use its proximity to discourage pursuit. It should be the last place the Balandra want to approach."

"And it should be the same for us! There's truth to glean from old wives tales, Frax. Why not go east over the Myginau Pass?"

"Because it's early spring, Tobin, and Myginau Major's impassable for at least another month. This way we can go south into the Llowlech, and cut through below the Yerebetan Ridge. Those passes will be clear."

She could see Frax's arguments were not persuading Tobin. Hastily she tried to fix the map in her mind before the young warrior's dismay erased it.

"You may fear the western marshes, Kitahn," Velacy broke in.

"But Rhynog walks where it chooses and let all others beware." He cast Tobin a scornful glance.

Tobin blazed with instant fury. "It's easy to speak boldly when you don't know what you're talking about, Aedec. You all quake in your boots enough from fear of the Eldren Races in other places."

"*You....!*" The mental flash of Velacy's temper was dizzying.

The map vanished.

"Enough!" Frax said. "This isn't a test of foolhardiness or bravery. We have more pressing matters at hand."

"Nothing could be so pressing as dispatching this Aedec fool, Frax," Tobin sprang to his feet.

"For once we agree, in principle at least." Velacy was on his feet too, his hand hovering over the knife at his belt as he squared off against the Kitahni scout. "Come, Kitahn, meet your death."

"Sit down, both of you. Now." Frax's quiet tone caused the younger warriors to glance at him. The light of cold fury in his eyes sent a chill through Kaphri. It proved enough to cool the heat in Tobin and Velacy, as well. Slowly they sank back down, although they continued to exchange silent, angry glares.

"*Priestess,*" Frax leaned forward, ignoring the younger warriors now the moment of direct confrontation had passed. "*Did you see anything on the map you recognized? Anything to tell us where you might be drawn?*"

Something about the lower end of the eastern plateau had momentarily tugged at her attention—a chain of mountains that curved back up along the Great Water on that side, but it had not stirred the sort of response she suspect he was asking for. She shook her head.

"*Seuliac, what do you say?*"

"*About using the Palenquemas as cover?*" Seuliac studied Frax as if he were trying to discern the Kitahni leader's motive for asking his opinion. He shrugged. "*We must go south anyway. If the Balandra really* fear the place enough to avoid it, and, based on history, they should, then the reasoning's solid."

"You would side with Cadarn in this?" Tobin looked at the white-locked warrior in disbelief. "Then it must be the wrong choice..."

"I've had those winged hounds of hell on my tail once." Seuliac reminded him coldly. "Anything that lessens the possibility of that happening again is welcome to me."

Frax nodded and glanced at Uri. "Uri?"

"We're not talking about entering the place. I think skirting the edge could work to our advantage." The Caspani Geffitz was cautious.

"Or our undoing," Tobin protested furiously.

His uneasiness over Frax's plan was not doing anything to ease Kaphri's fears, and Uri was not particularly enthusiastic with the idea either. Perhaps she should be concerned, too. Who, or what, was the Wyxa?"

"What is this place you speak of?" she broke in.

"An immense marsh known as the Palenquemas runs along the western coast," Frax replied. "An ancient race called the Wyxa, live there."

"I thought you said Araxis drove all the peoples out of the south." Kaphri gave a mental frown of confusion.

"The Wyxa aren't people; they're bugs! And nothing with the intelligence beyond a plant would disturb them." Tobin shot Frax a meaningful look.

"The Wyxa are one of the Eldren Races, left over from a age before our own. They've lived in the swamps since the beginning of time as we know it," Frax explained calmly, ignoring Tobin. "Legend says they once interacted with the other creatures of this world, but at the time of the Great Cataclysm, two-thousand years ago, they withdrew into solitude. Now they live deep in the swamp. It would be extremely difficult for us to find them, even if we set out with that purpose."

"Why would Araxis leave them?"

"We don't know he did. He may have sent his disease upon them, too.

*But none of them came north, and there are—other—things that might make destroying them difficult."*

She did not like the sense of caution behind his sending. *"Such as?"* It was better to know it all now.

The commander studied her in thoughtful silence. He was taking more time to answer than she found comfortable, when Tobin exploded fiercely.

*"Your Araxis is nothing compared to the Wyxa! It would've been merciful for the rest of us if he'd been stupid enough to take them on. But he probably didn't realize they existed, and they were happy to leave it that way. They didn't help us."* He got up and walked away, snatching the dead game off the branch as he passed it. Frax watched him go without comment.

Kaphri looked at Uri. *"I don't understand."*

Frax nodded for Uri to explain.

*"The dark power under the Maugrock is a remnant of something which almost destroyed our world a long time ago. It, or he, was called Bithzielp, and his power was foul and cruel, spoiling everything it touched with hatred, pain, and death. He tried to spread that foulness throughout this world. He came close to succeeding. You see, we are not the first peoples of our world. Races we call the Eldren: the Wyxa, the Mijadi, others, some still here and some gone, existed before us."* He shrugged. *"Our history tells of a great civilization of winged beings. A powerful priest cult, devoted to the worship of this Bithzielp, rose up among them and spread throughout their cities. Soon those cities began to vie with each other for the Foul One's attention by perpetuating his evil. They enslaved other races of this world and used them mercilessly to build temples and monuments to his foulness, and to offer as blood sacrifices. It was a black, terrible time. The Wyxa, alone, remained untouched and unaffected by his power.*

*"One day the priests of the city-temple Geron Maed—the place where your people fled—decided to honor Bithzielp's supreme rule over this world by changing the position of Kep's eldest daughter, the large moon , Twyfel, .*

Hearing this, the priests dwelling in the Black Tower of the Maugrock grew more ambitious, deciding to thwart their competitors' attempt and move all three of the moons to a position of their choosing first."

"But this world only has one moon," Kaphri protested.

"Now. But then..." Uri held up a finger for her silence. "The stories say that upon hearing rumor of their plans, the Wyxa sent an envoy to the Maugrock to warn them that such attempts would bring disastrous results to our world. The priests heard the Wyxan envoy's words and laughed. They sent him back to his people and continued with their preparations to move the three moons of the world, racing against the priests of the lake towers. Again, the Wyxa sent the envoy, and again they laughed and sent him away while the priests carried on with their plans. They began to work their sorcery to move the moon. The priests in the northern tower, furious, fought back, attempting to wrest control and move Twyfel to their place of choosing. The land began to tremble and the Great Waters roiled. They tossed and fled, withdrawing from the lands of the Wyxa, leaving them dry and thirsty. Again, the Wyxan kingdom sent its messenger. But this time the priests, seeking to accomplish their purpose ahead of their rivals, took the envoy and sacrificed him to Bithzielp instead of sending him away. The Wyxa rose up in wrath at the death of one of their own. They struck out in vengeance, causing the priests to lose control of their sorcery. Pulled out of their paths and suddenly unguided, two of the moons collided, crushing themselves to pieces. The third, the smallest of Kep's daughters, escaped, as you see it today, while the two destroyed moons slowly spread their debris to form the ring that gives us Omurda, the Dark Zone.

"Kep's sorrow at the loss of her daughters nearly destroyed her. In the cataclysm after the collision, tears of fire rained from the sky and her flesh tore and twisted in massive rifts. Her waters devoured portions of the land and vomited other bits from her depths. Some parts of the world, once fruitful, were scoured lifeless, cursed by the Goddess' wrath." Kaphri remembered the horrible desolation of the mountain ring around Kryie Karth with renewed awe. "Many of the peoples living on our world died in the cataclysm and the remainder scattered, losing much of the knowledge of their time. The Wyxa, whether from anger, shame, guilt or indifference, withdrew into what remained of their swamp kingdom, choosing not to mix with the other survivors. Before they went, however, they put a curse on the surviving worshippers of Bithzielp. The Wyxa took away all their beauty and cursed them with the twisted ugliness of their hearts. Then they drove Bithzielp and all his followers out of our world through the Goroth M'nget, the circle of runes in the Black Temple, and they sealed it against his return."

"The Balandra," Kaphri gasped. "But Uri, how can that be? I saw a statue in the temple—" she was stricken with horror at the differences between the beautiful creature caught in first flight and the ugly gray creatures that had held her captive.

"They look as if something sucked all the life out of them, yes." Uri nodded. "The Wyxa did that to them when they drove them out of our world. And now, somehow, the Balandra are returning, and bringing their evil with them again."

"A story to curl Tobin's hair, Uri." Frax grinned at the Caspani Geffitz, but his sending was heavy with tension. Uri gave a short, uneasy laugh.

"Folktales," Velacy muttered in scorn.

"Creatures from folktales you've seen with your own eyes, Velacy."

Unable to argue with Uri's comment, Velacy scowled.

Kaphri shuddered. If the Wyxa had done such a horrendous thing to the Balandra, perhaps Tobin had good reason for his dismay at approaching their stronghold.

"And you think the Evil One, this Araxis, is responsible for the Balandra now slipping back through?" Seuliac leaned forward, his eyes flicking from Uri to Frax. "That he aided them in opening the way between the worlds? Why? For what reason?"

"This Araxis commands the Balandra in the tower. I saw him. And she says he used the dark power that lurks beneath the Maugrock in an effort to trap her."

"He has power of his own—enough to take our lands. He's proven that already. What does he want from the Maugrock?" Seuliac's expression was tight with anger. "Does he seek to take more from us? And why does he want this girl?"

"Apparently his power is greatly diminished."

Greatly diminished? That was an understatement. Kaphri looked at Frax.

"How so?" Seuliac was on the statement so swiftly it made her blink.

The commander shrugged. "According to the Priestess, he suffered a debilitating blow at the hands of his own people after he brought them here. One from which he's never completely recovered. He needs her assistance to restore his health."

Such a brazen manipulation of information! But, Uri had told her Frax knew how much to trust these new warriors who were his ancient enemies. Still, she was not used to such a blatant twisting of facts. She reached a hand to stroke Gemma, lying so still on her shoulder through this whole exchange.

"Is this true, girl?" She was not surprised when the warlord's question dropped into her head.

Frax had severely edited the information, but he had not lied. "Yes," she sent firmly.

"Then he must be destroyed."

"Agreed. And it will be up to us, and her, to see it done." Frax turned his attention to Uri. "I want to brief these two a bit more on our situation while Tobin cooks those rabbits. Would you take the Priestess to the stream and let her clean up? Don't linger too long. We should make the most of the remaining daylight after we eat. And," he focused a stern glare on her, "don't you dare pick up anything, not even a rock!"

# 34

## Windmer

"*I don't like this, Willow. A constant headache is not normal, no matter who, or what, you are.*" Uri handed her two doxentler leaves from his beltpouch.

"*It comes and goes, Uri.*" She tried to sound bright and unconcerned, "*It's nothing. Really.*"

He snorted disbelief as he watched her put the leaves in her mouth.

She chewed slowly so as not to appear too eager for the relief she knew they would give. She could send Gemma out into the forest to get them, bypassing the big warrior altogether, but she feared Gemma's activity might draw Frax's attention—something she wished to avoid. The headache was not natural, she knew, but if she could convince Uri a change in the weather or sensitivity to some plant caused it, she could avoid a confrontation with the Geffitz leader. She needed more time to discover the reason behind the persistent, growing pain. Or to recover.

Uri studied her a moment longer, his thoughts shielded then he turned away without further comment.

He hadn't taken more than three steps before she shielded, the tightly leashed control over her pain breaking. She chewed the doxentler vigorously, swallowing the sour juice hungrily for relief.

*"He is right, you know."* Gemma's sending was gentle.

Kaphri caressed the dragon's tail looped about her throat. *"I know something is wrong, but what can I do about it? If they think something else is going on with me, they might kill me."* She sighed. *"All I wanted was a chance to live without anger and hostility all around me. Now I'm a prisoner and pawn, pursued by something that wants to steal everything that I am and destroy me. Manipulation is everywhere around me, Gemma. I will either overcome or succumb to it."* She felt a slight tightening of Gemma's coil: the little dragon did not like her assessment, but she did not disagree.

Despite what she told Uri, Kaphri recognized the aching pain for what it was. It was deep in her head, in that cold place the reversed symbol had isolated. On the first day past the barrier, she mistook it for something harmless, thinking it might be the result of tension or fear. But each day since it had grown stronger, like a dark pit enlarging in her mind. It did not pull her away any more, not since she washed away the bloody symbol, but the cold place was growing. So far, the doxentler leaves she persuaded Uri to give her had controlled it, but the effective time between chewing them was growing shorter. How long before they failed her? A chill of fear ran through her. What would she do then? What was happening to her mind?

The leaves were doing their work now, however. As the pain began to fade, she hastened to gather a few more branches of firewood before returning to camp.

For five days they had trudged through the depths of a forest, beneath silent, towering trees. At their second camp after finding the crystal, Frax gave her a curt order to stand the first watch. She took it gladly, accepting it as a sign that after her recent protests he was beginning to consider her a comrade rather than a prisoner. It remained hers thereafter. Never mind that, as early in the evening as it was, at least one Geffitz was awake, if only silent and pensive with thought.

Meanwhile, they'd seen no sign of pursuit from the black tower and nothing in this new land threatened them. They dared to speak openly, and Tobin ranged further abroad every day. Instead of relaxing, however, the warriors' uneasiness had grown. It was not the same feeling as the crossing in Omurda. There, the Geffitzi had been in a near-constant state of silent alertness, but they had also known where they were going and held a clear purpose. Now, nothing was clear except that they were running before a great danger, to an unknown destination, for an unknown purpose.

And there were other things to consider. After they started walking again on the first day, she caught the end of a mental debate between Uri and Frax as to whether the deadly disease Araxis had unleashed upon their people might still be a threat to them in the south. They had no way of knowing unless one of them sickened. They could only wait and hope that in twenty years the threat had passed.

And a rivalry had developed between Tobin and Velacy Aedec that, like her headaches, was growing steadily worse.

Although Frax had swiftly silenced their verbal sparring, they constantly exchanged glowers, muttered comments, and made snorts of derision. Tobin's skill at hunting, for which he apparently had some reputation, immediately came under challenge. It devolved into a contest between the two warriors, each seeking to bring back the most, then the largest, things they could find, until Kaphri feared that one of them would attempt to bring down one of the herd creatures the Geffitzi called "horses". Although she only viewed the creatures from a distance, they stirred an admiration in her. She would not like to see one killed for the sake of the warriors' egos.

By the time she caught up to Uri at the campsite, Tobin had returned and was lowering some large, furry creature from his shoulder. Dropping the firewood, Kaphri looked at the dead thing doubtfully and finally expressed her concern to Uri. He roared with laughter and called Tobin over to relay her comment to him.

The scout looked at her in appall. "You don't even eat meat. How can you think of eating a horse?"

For a moment, Kaphri was speechless. She started to protest, then stopped. It would be pointless to try to explain. But when she looked between them she caught what appeared to be the disappearing traces of a quickly-erased grin from the scout's face.

"Still," Tobin continued in a surprisingly wistful tone, "It would be good to catch some horses. If we rode, we could move faster."

Uri shook his head. "It would take too long to condition them for riding."

"These nags of the western plateau are hardly fit to carry riders. What we need are some steeds from the Escori Basin." They all turned as Velacy sauntered up to join their group. The younger Aedec looked directly at Tobin. "But then, if one is not use to such a spirited animal, it would be a sad waste of superior horseflesh."

Tobin snorted. "Best stay with something you know, like fins and scales, Aedec. You fishwives of Rhynog wouldn't know a good horse if it bit your—"

"Scales?" Velacy bristled, his eyes glinting. "I speak of breeding and training horses, Cadarn, not of breeding with demons."

"Oh-h-h." Kaphri heard Uri breathe out. She felt a brush of amusement from the big Geffitz as his fingers found her arm. He took a step backwards, drawing her with him. Even Seuliac, working with the fire, glanced up with uncharacteristic haste at the comment.

Tobin and Velacy glared at each other.

"Tell me; what color is your blood, Cadarn? Red like a true Gef-fitz? Or is it black like the soulless pits of hell you'd claim?" Velacy's tone dropped dangerously.

Raising his hands before him, Tobin beckoned with a waggle of his fingers. "Come see, Aedec." A chill ran over Kaphri at the light of bloody anticipation in his eyes.

A sense of deadly tension hung in the air.

At that moment, Frax appeared across the small clearing. He'd been bathing in a nearby stream and didn't even look in their direction as he walked, his hands working his heavy red-brown hair into the long, loose braid that he always wore.

The anger in the air evaporated as Tobin and Velacy suddenly found other things to occupy their attention. They walked away in opposite directions, leaving Uri and Kaphri standing alone.

"*What was that about?*" she asked. The two had obviously been on the verge of coming to blows or worse.

"*Just an innocent exchange on different breeds of horses,*" Uri glanced down at her with a grin.

She mentally frowned in confusion as he walked off.

That night, Tobin and Velacy each did an extra turn at guard duty while the rest of them slept through the night and Uri spent a long time talking quietly with a visibly irritated Frax.

So they passed through the cool, dim, damp regions of a green forest cathedral, to the sixth morning.

Tobin returned from his scouting excursion at mid-morning, his excitement barely contained. He had made his way to the western edge of the forest and out into a scrubby clearing to discover a stone wall. It was the first sign of civilization they had come across. The news stirred Velacy's excitement, also, but the other three reacted with more reserve. Foremost, Kaphri sensed heightened uneasiness. Their people had not walked this land in twenty years and for these warriors it was only a tale or faint memory. It left them unsure of their own reaction.

"There may be a hold close by," Frax observed cautiously.

"*Tools. Packs.*" Uri shot him a quick glance. "Some of the things we lost at the barrier?" Frax nodded agreement. "Then let's go." Much to Kaphri's dismay, they struck out at a slightly southwestern angle, following an impatient Tobin.

The mid-afternoon sun blazed warmly on green fields as they came to the edge of the woods. After the chilled spring damp of forest shadows, its heat was near-bliss. Kaphri and Gemma edged out into the sunlight, soaking it up while the Geffitzi conferred.

Frax was reluctant to move into the open. He didn't like the idea of leaving the sheltering protection of the trees to leave a trail of bent grass that a winged creature could detect from the air. After some discussion, he decided Tobin could explore further into the fields while they moved south along the edge of the woods in the same general direction.

It was with some surprise, a short time later, that Frax, Uri, Velacy, and Seuliac came to a sudden halt. Cutting across the way in front of them was the distinct, wide track of a leaf-filled roadbed. It appeared to wind its way from the fields in the west, climbing upward to disappear into the shadows of the hilly woods to their left.

Uri jumped off the low bank and raked at the leaves with his boot. The stone he exposed beneath glinted wet and dark. "Paved," he observed with a significant look at Frax.

Frax nodded. "Wide, paved ways are most common around the holdhalls."

Kaphri felt a new tension, a mixture of dread and tightly suppressed excitement, rising in her companions. The Geffitz leader turned to Tobin, who had followed the road back up through the fields to re-join them. "What did you see?"

"Scrubby fields and a line of trees along a river to the west.

The land climbs steeply upward to the east of us, but you can't see it right here because of the trees. To the south the land rises in cliffs." His sending carried the image of huge, gray cliffs thrusting up through the green of forest that clustered below and clung to their tops.

The map they had studied days before was suddenly in all their minds. There was an abrupt, dizzying shift of the image that left Kaphri nauseous as the others swarmed over it simultaneously, making swift adjustments.

"Windmer Hold?" They gasped. Before she could comprehend what was happening, the remaining three warriors scrambled down to join Uri and Tobin in the roadbed.

They all took off at a half-run up the road into the forest.

*"Don't dawdle,"* someone snapped back at her.

Boots slipping on wet leaves and slick stones, she hurried after them.

The road sloped upward, then leveled and curved to the right behind a dense clump of trees. The warriors disappeared. By the time she came around the turn, they had followed the road across a brushy clearing and were standing before a huge wooden gate set between two tall stone towers. Away on each side of the towers, grown right up around their bases, stretched a high, thick wall of green hedge. The dense, dark growth was well over twice Uri's height and glinted, even from a distance, with silvery, finger-long thorns. Above the heavy double gate was a stone battlement. A metal plate hung at its center. On it was the image of a graceful stone tower, encircled in a wreath of leaves and thorns similar to the vicious-looking hedge. Two swords at the bottom of the wreath crossed blades over the tower's base. Below that hung another placard with lettering similar to what she had seen on the map.

The gate was ponderously swinging open under the combined effort of the five warriors when she caught up with them.

Together they passed through the outer gate of Windmer Hold.

The trees inside the hedge were as big as the ones outside, but fewer in number. The filtered sunlight allowed a park-like green sward that stretched away in all directions. Flowering shrubs in full spring bloom were a tumble of frothy color on the slopes, but bold saplings, rough undergrowth, and patches of weeds intruded in the long neglect to mar the beauty.

"The High Merrows," Uri took a long, deep breath. From his mind, Kaphri caught the image that the merrows had something to do with the hedge wall they had just passed through.

"Mer," Frax sent to her when he caught her sense of puzzlement. *"The hedge is a nasty plant called mer. One scratch can set up an infection that could take a finger before it can be checked."*

She looked at him in shock. Why would anyone grow such a vicious plant? More to the point, why would they cultivate it into such an immense barrier?

Frax frowned. *"For defense against attack. Windmer, Windhedge. High Merrows, High Hedges. Low Merrows, Low Hedges."*

He turned to follow Tobin, who was already moving off down the road again.

The wooded slope continued upward, but the road they followed turned sharply right and south along a ridge, staying level through the forest until it led them to a sheer drop. A breath-taking view of the countryside stretched away for miles in front and below. A narrower road, more nearly a path, branched away into the forest along the cliff top to their right. Uri said it probably led to a tower he referred to as the West Merrow Watch, hidden by the trees, that stood guard over the countryside below.

West Hedge Watch, she told herself. Sure enough, when she looked down she could see the curve of a green slope and the dark line of the huge, tough hedge slicing the land.

Their road continued to the left, curving gently down and away into the trees, cutting into the hillside so that there was a band of earth and stone to their left and a wall of young trees and bushes between them and the open air on their right.

Before long Kaphri could feel and smell the damp of water and rocks.

Uri shot Frax a glance. "If the bridge is up we won't get past."

Frax shrugged. "It's a long walk around, but there's always the South Gate."

Uri nodded. Kaphri saw him open and close his fists anxiously.

The road opened ahead of them into a broad, stone-inlaid half-circle that stopped at the edge of a ravine. They paused well back in the shadows of the trees to study it. Even from that distance, they could hear the crash and roar of water falling far below. Across the empty space of the ravine, sheer stone rose to the road level once again. Perched there, a lone tower stared down on the open, unsheltered space in front of them.

"Gate's down." Uri breathed softly, almost like a prayer of thanks. From where they stood, Kaphri could see a heavy slab of metal that extended across the gap of the ravine to the dark, yawning opening of the tower.

"*Wait.*" Frax turned to her. "*Priestess?*"

He didn't need to tell her what he wanted.

She sensed out. "*Nothing,*" she told him. The tower was coldly silent and empty.

What if there was something in there? What would her companions have done? She shivered.

Tobin gave her a calculating, doubtful look, but remained silent.

Velacy, however, made no effort to hide his suspicion of what had just transpired. "*How does she know there's nothing there?*" he challenged.

The Geffitz leader gave him a quick, humorless smile as he

stepped out into the sunlight of the half-circle. *"She has better tele-pathic skills than we do and she can work through stone."*

He started toward the tower.

*"What? You trust her? She..."*

*"...has as much to lose as we do."* Frax finished the younger warrior's statement. *"Now, move out."*

Seuliac hung back a step, giving her a long, speculative stare before he followed.

The metal bridge drummed with the footsteps of Geffitz boots as they moved across it, but the sound was barely audible above the noise of the stream below them.

There were no handrails on the bridge and Kaphri stayed in the center, content to only imagine the deep sides of the ravine and the white water that tumbled below. As they neared the tower, however, Uri stopped in front of her, and pointed southward as he nudged Frax.

Her unguarded reaction caused her to follow his gesture. She stiffened with dismay.

Only yards away, to the right, the ravine cleaved the cliff in a monstrous, wide gash that opened on a stunning vista of the land far below them. The bridge held her suspended in the air with the ravine falling away deeply before her. At the bottom of the chasm, frothy, white water tumbled, plunging out of sight into sheer emptiness.

It was then that Kaphri realized the crevasse was much wider than she thought. She'd carefully avoided looking at the tower in any detail. Now she saw that the structure stood on a column of rock that thrust up from the center of a gorge, with sheer drops on all sides. The sensation of standing alone at the edge of a great precipice jolted her for a second time in her young life.

*"What's the matter?"* Tobin stopped beside her, his smile mocking as he took in her pale face. *"Don't you sense open spaces, too?"*

The taunt snapped back her composure, but she didn't pull away when he grasped her upper arm and assisted her the last few steps into the tower.

The place was empty, its broad center passage dim and dark. They moved through the shadowy interior quickly; then they were on another metal bridge and hurriedly across. Tobin kept a firm grip on her until they gained the cobbled roadway, where he released her without comment. She nodded quick, embarrassed gratitude, but he had already turned away, moving into the lead as they continued onward.

The road sloped downward again, the bank along the left side growing steeper until it turned into a gray stone cliff that towered above them. A stone wall lined the right side of the road. It, too, gradually rose higher above their heads, penning them between. Uri told them the outer wall was actually a thick battlement and pointed out slots in the stonework where he said archers could fire arrows at an enemy on the roadway. He said it also allowed the hold guards to attack from the top of the wall, to inflict terrible damage on invaders in the road below. Kaphri looked at the stone around them uneasily, her fear and awe growing.

Finally, the road widened again, broadening into a large square courtyard surrounded by high walls. The road they followed exited on its far side, but they stopped at its center. The stonework was sheer, with bands of archer-slots high above. To their left stood a massive double gate, the real tower from the image on the wreath-circled symbol rising majestically above it. It was duplicated in miniature on a plaque that hung over the gate.

"Windmer Hold," Uri murmured.

"Not the place an attacking army would choose to break into a hold," Frax said with admiration as he took in the broad, protected way. "If anyone ever managed to get this far they would never survive to bring down the gates."

Kaphri's curiosity got the better of her. "*I thought the Geffitzi lived in peace.*"

"*This is an ancient hold,*" Frax told her while Uri approach the gate. "*Before the Geffitzi established the Circle of Lords and the Inner Circle of Elders to keep peace among the clans, there was constant battling and bloodshed. And,*" he did not look at the two Aedec warriors, who stood together a short distance away, though she knew where his thoughts lay, "*there is always the possibility of renewed aggression.*"

"*The Geffitzi are a warrior race, proud and ready to fight—and to take what they claim as their own.*" With a mockingly vicious expression, Tobin raked her over with his eyes from head to foot.

Kaphri felt her cheeks color.

"*That's enough, Tobin,*" Frax gave him a warning glare. The younger Geffitz returned his look with an innocent expression.

Behind her, Velacy made a sound of disgust.

That tension was forgotten when they turned their attention to the entrance before them. They could see that the main gate was not barred from the inside, but, despite their efforts, they could only get it open a narrow crack. Irritated, Frax ordered Kaphri through the opening to add her meager efforts from the opposite side. She slid between the metal doors into a cold, dark tunnel. Although she didn't sense any threat in the blackness, a creeping uneasiness made her expect the cold touch of something horrible on her flesh at any second. It drove her to push as hard as she could, and, with the Geffitzi straining on the other side, they were at last able to widen the gap enough for them to squeeze through.

The darkness inside was total when they moved beyond the thin beam of sunlight filtering through the opening they'd made. They passed through an internal gate, luckily standing open, before they came to the inner hold gate. Much to their relief it open with a light shove and Kaphri and the five warriors stepped out into the late afternoon sunlight of Windmer Hold.

They stared about in shared silence, each immersed in his own personal reaction.

# 35

## Decisions

They stood at the edge of a flat plane, enclosed inside a circle of sheer stone cliffs. A lush, tree-dappled lawn stretched before them with a small lake at its center. Her eyes followed the length of glistening water to the wall on the far side, where a massive square gap was cut into the stone to give a view of the darkening sky in the east.

A paved road branched away to each side of the green, circling the inside of the ring and leading to the halls of Windmer Hold set against the northern side of the cliffs. She stared in awe at the great, many-windowed stone buildings, with their elaborately carved, arched doorways and ivy-covered balconies. Finely worked columns lifted porches and galleries, while huge pots, once meticulously tended, overran with greenery. Vines draped heavily over verandas.

If Kaphri ever thought the Geffitzi a primitive people, she was fast re-evaluating her opinion. Even in its current state of abandonment, the place was the obvious work of master-builders and a people who appreciated beauty. It rivaled any of the images she had ever seen from the Ly Kai.

The realization stirred a terrible sadness in her.

The lake shimmered in the late afternoon sun. On its far end, framed in the vast stone gap, she picked out the details of a stone-columned shelter intimately nestled among unkempt clumps of flowering shrubs. She felt a sudden urge to walk there, to sit and take in this awesome structure, but the Geffitzi were already moving along the road toward what was obviously the main holdhall. She looked at the silent, dark windows, almost seeing faces watching her. What were their expressions? Sad? Accusing? She did not want to know.

"*Gemma, what could Araxis want that would ever justify what he's done to the people of this world?*" she asked the golden dragon on her shoulder as she hurried after the others.

"*This will not be easy for these warriors, Kaphri,*" Gemma replied. "*This hold, being in the north of the land, was able to evacuate more effectively than the ones further south, where the plague began, but this will be the first time they see what is left in its wake. The touch of death is still heavy here. You should remember this took place before you were born.*"

"*Priestess, keep up!*" Frax's command cut across her thoughts.

With rising reluctance, she climbed the last three steps and crossed the stone gallery to where Frax impatiently waited beside a richly worked wooden door. The others were already inside, standing in the dim light.

"*It smells of death in here,*" Tobin complained, his lips curling with distaste.

"*There will be the smell of death anywhere you walk in this land,*" Frax told him.

Uri nodded agreement, but Tobin's expression remained wary as they started forward again. Frax motioned her past then followed her inside.

The grand hallway was dimly lit by the huge brace of windows that towered behind them. The space ran deeper into the hold between a sweep of double stairs that curved up gracefully on each side into the shadows of a second level. A thick layer of dust, the accumulation of years, covered the elaborate pattern of stone tiles on the floor. Dust motes, stirred by the warriors' passage, winked in shafts of fading sunlight.

Uri led them across to a pair of massive, intricately worked wooden doors on the left wall.

"The Great Hall of Windmer," he said reverently. Reaching out, he turned a heavy brass handle and the doors swung silently outward.

Again, sunlight fell through a massive bank of windows on the outer wall to illuminate a huge room. Rows of tables and chairs that could accommodate hundreds ran its center-length in dust-covered silence. A table on a raised dais sat across the far end. A massive hearth yawned beyond it. Tapestries depicting scenes of battle, interspersed with arrays of weapons displayed on wooden panels, covered the walls. Above the hearth hung a detailed tapestry of silver, grays and greens on a sky-blue background—the tower, wreath and crossed swords—clearly the symbols of Windmer. Banners, their colors still brilliant despite the cobwebs and dust, hung in shadows from the heavily beamed ceiling far above.

As the Geffitzi moved into the vast silence, Kaphri stopped. This was a moment in which she was not welcome. She watched them walk the length of the room to the great chair that sat at the center of the head table. With Uri going first, each took a turn going down on one knee with his head bowed. Although their backs were to her, she saw them perform some quick gesture with their weapon hands. Each, in turn, spoke something aloud, the sound short and harsh in the silence.

*"What are they doing, Gemma?"*

"*Giving warrior's homage to the lord of this hold,*" Gemma replied.

"But...is he dead?" she asked.

"*No. Lord Drayven is in the north.*"

Somehow that made her feel even more uneasy.

After each warrior, including the Aedecs, preformed the ritual, they stood in a moment of silence. Then Frax looked about. "*The daylight is fading fast. We'll shelter here for the night, but we must leave at first light. Uri, take Velacy and find what you can in the storerooms, if anything remains unspoiled by time. Tobin, you and Seuliac check out the village down the road. Don't leave any signs we've been here. And, let's secure what we can against entry from the outside in case the Balandra do get down here.*" His eyes locked with hers across the room. Even over the distance, Kaphri could see the fire of determination burning in them. "*Lord Drayven will sit in that chair again, I vow it.*"

A tingle of fear ran over her, but years of careful schooling made her lift her chin and meet his gaze evenly.

Seuliac glanced from the Geffitz leader to her, but, as usual, no expression revealed his thoughts when he brushed past her and left the room. Steps echoing in the twenty years of silence, Frax followed them out of the holdhall. He pulled the doors to behind him, and strode through the thickening shadows to the closest stair. Since no one issued instructions for her, she reluctantly moved to follow him.

"*Don't touch anything,*" he warned.

She ran her fingers across Gemma's tail where it twined about her throat and did not reply.

There was no light in the upper hall. They moved forward blindly until Frax found a door into what appeared to be a sleep chamber. She waited in the passage while he rummaged through furniture in the dark room. Finally, with a grunt of satisfaction, he emerged with some canna nuts, an intricately carved disk, and a delicate net. He crouched in the corridor and cracked one of the spheres with a small tool. The nuts were old, but the sap still gave off a weak light when

he smeared it on the disk. With several twirls of the net, the sap il-
luminated the width of the hallway enough for them to move on.

The blue light fell on what appeared to be a pile of rags on the
floor a short distance ahead of them. Frax in the lead, they moved
forward cautiously to inspect it. He bent down for a closer look and
Kaphri saw him stiffen. On the floor lay the skeletal remains of what
must have been a Geffitzi female and a young child. A bundle of
clothing lay nearby, as if death had stricken them while they were in
flight.

Kaphri had witnessed death many times in Kryie Karth, as one
after another of the Ly Kai returned to their Birthstar. The passing
on of the spirit, at least by illness, was just another fact of life to
her. Nothing, however, had prepared her for this firsthand view of
Araxis' handiwork—the hard proof of the Geffitzi warriors' anger
and accusations. It left her shaken to the quick.

Frax did not look at her. He straightened, murmured something
aloud, made a gesture over the bodies with his hand, and continued
forward.

There were many bodies after that, left where they had fallen
while the ones who still lived rushed to escape the same fate. They
were male and female by their clothing, young and old alike. Some
died in bed, some in flight, others, while engaged in some task. At
first her spirit cried within her at the sight of them, but even the
tiniest bit of grief for each one would have drained her to walking death. There were so many. So many that she grew numb at
their numbers and could only walk past or step over them. Useless, for them, the apologies that ran endlessly through her head
while Frax walked, stiff-backed, and silent—and, she realized
abruptly—shielded.

They went through level after level of the central holdhall,
through silent death. Frax took nothing else from the rooms and
left most doors unopened as he moved steadily upward. She knew

he was searching for something, but he gave her nothing of his thoughts. There was only the rising tension and anger she saw in the set of his shoulders. As they climbed a stair to the fourth level, however, his mood seemed to alter slightly, as if he sensed he might be nearing his goal. He lost a little of the woodenness that had come over him, regaining a purpose beyond merely passing through these halls of death.

The fourth-level hallway was much more ornate than the ones below it. The first door Frax stopped before was double and beautifully carved with a motif of plants and flowers. Carefully he turned the heavy metal handle and pushed it open.

The chamber was much larger than the room from which he had removed the canna nuts. He stepped inside, crossed to a low table covered with papers, and began to search through them.

In the thinning light of a pair of large windows across the space, Kaphri could make out the shapes of furniture. Reluctant to remain in the darkness of the hallway alone, now that she was aware of the dead around them, she followed him in.

She had seen beautiful things before, but the beauty she knew, that the Ly Kai had woven about them, was only illusion. Here there was real softness in the woven cloth rug beneath her boots and an unmistakable elegance in the flowing woodcarvings beneath her fingers. She wished the draperies allowed in more light so she could see the colors and textures better.

Centered against a dark wall stood an immense bed, its coverings eerily white in the gloom. She took another step forward, intrigued with the shadowy hint of so many fine things. When Frax continued his search without making any objection, she moved forward to touch the cloth of the bed's hangings and coverlet. They dimpled beneath her fingers, their weave smooth, like the robe from the Ly Kai Homeworld she had worn in a time that now seemed ages past.

Frax uttered a short-tempered oath, and she snatched her hand away.

Perhaps it might be better to simply look.

On the wall above a huge stone hearth, hung a portrait of a seated Geffitz male with a female Geffitz standing at his side. Kaphri moved closer to study them. Their clothing was amazingly elaborate and elegant, but it was the faces that drew her attention. They were older than her companions, their features lined with the wrinkles and cares inevitable of age, but there was also an unmistakable sense of wisdom and patience upon them.

Such an aura of fierce pride radiated from them! The male seemed to emanate the strong sense of power and will she was growing particularly accustomed to encountering in Frax. But the lady! Uri's image of Ladrienca had been suffused with emotions Kaphri found awkward and embarrassing, so she had only snatched a brief look and then discarded it even more quickly. This was an opportunity to study a Geffitzi female in close detail. The woman was smaller and finer-boned than the male, making Kaphri wonder how she coped with the characteristics she saw in him. She searched the female's face. In it, she found firmness and resolution, but, also, a touch of humor and gentleness that, surprisingly, did not take away anything of her refinement and presence.

Frax glanced up from the clutter of parchments on the desk to see her staring at the picture. *"A painting of the Lord Drayven Caspani and the Lady Adiel,"* he sent shortly. *"She was my aunt."*

Was? Kaphri felt a chill run through her at the word. Gemma had said Lord Drayven survived in the north.

*"Was,"* he repeated, as if aware of her thoughts. *"My mother's younger sister. She died of the plague during the journey north."* He stood for a moment in silence, then swept the parchments off the table with his hand. *"Damn your Araxis! Damn you, Kaphri! Just who the hell do you people think you are, invading a world? Killing! Destroying! Curse*

*you and your damn precious power that you can't even use to save yourself."*

Kaphri stiffened before the onslaught of his rage while Gemma shifted on her shoulder, digging tiny claws into flesh as she untwined and raised her head to stare at him.

*"What happens when he comes after you, Kaphri? What happens? I'll tell you! You will die and we'll go through all of this again. That's what'll happen. And we'll have helped him by clinging to the hope for something better!"* He slammed a fist down on the table, sending a booming echo through the silence.

Her outer thoughts went totally blank, weeks of conditioning preventing her from shielding. But none of the terror, none of the pain that his angry words inflicted, slipped out. No expression crossed her face to betray her. There was only the coldness she had learned in Kryie Karth to keep all the pain away. She looked at him, then turned, crossing the room to the doorway and stepping into the darkness on the other side, where she collapsed against the wall. But the thought of him following her brought her defiantly upright again: he would not see her pain.

It took a moment longer in the darkness for her to realize she had not passed through the double doors back into the hall. She sensed out and touched the walls of a small, circular room with a narrow stairway spiraling upward. She had no idea where it would take her, except that it would lead away from the Geffitz leader, and that was all that mattered. She would not go back into the room behind her.

She took the steps at a near-run, two at a time.

They wound upward for perhaps forty feet before ending at a wooden door. Hands trembling with the feelings she fought to suppress, Kaphri pushed it open to stumble out into the night air.

She found herself standing on the heights of Windmer Hold under a night sky ablaze with stars. Arylla was easy to spot, its light glittering coldly and brilliantly. But she had no desire to see any star from the Ly Kai Hierarch.

The sting of Frax's words grew more acute by the moment.

He spoke the truth: she was useless. When Araxis came he would steal her body and drive her into the deepest recesses of her brain where she would die—and she could not stop him.

To make things worse, the pain from the cursed headache was rising again, further highlighting her inability to defend herself. She suddenly wanted to be far away from the starry heights. Away from the glaring reminder of her failure.

But she dared not return the way she'd just come.

Her desperate gaze fell on another structure, similar to the one she had just stepped from. It would lead back down into the hold somewhere. Feeling as if her heart would burst from the terrible ache inside her, she ran over and slipped through, into the darkness beyond.

As the door snapped shut behind her, she heard a flutter of sound and realized, too late, that she was not alone.

"*Die! You will die! Curse you, die! Curse you, Kaphri, die!*" The words beat at her mind. This was not a stairway down into the hold. She had stumbled into some type of structure and there was something inside it with her!

"*Die! Die! Curse you, die!*" Her agonized thoughts screamed back at her.

A thunderous, rushing sound engulfed her and the air swirled as things battered and slashed at her. A terrible stench rose around her and something raked her cheek with its claws. She threw up an arm to cover her face and bare head while she frantically groped for the door. But she had lost all sense of direction.

Gemma hissed and crouched lower on her shoulders. Terrified, Kaphri began to scream.

"*Die! You will die!*" The words beat at her for an eternity before she heard a sharp oath. A hand grappled in the blackness, closed about her arm, and dragged her back out into the night air. She literally climbed the Geffitz that had seized her, forcing him to catch her arms tightly as she still fought to get away from the things in the darkness. Finally, she quit struggling and collapsed in a quivering mass to bury her face against the rough cloth of his tabard.

It took a bit longer for her to realize the warrior was trying to get through to her. Still quaking in terror, she lowered her mindshield.

*"Now that's better, Willow. Come on. It's okay now."*

Uri! With a mental sob, she clung to him even more desperately.

His arms tightened about her, giving her a comforting squeeze. *"Hey, Willow, it's okay. They are only birds."*

*"But, Uri, they kept screaming and screaming..."*

*"What the hell's going on here?"*

Kaphri went rigid at the all too familiar anger in the sending.

Uri looked over her head at Frax. *"She stumbled into a greny hutch and they attacked her. I've never seen anything like it. They were screaming and tearing at everything. She had to be in some kind of mental state for them to react like that. This little one isn't Tesla, Frax. What the hell did you do?"*

*"Not the right thing, apparently,"* Frax snapped back. *"Since you seem to have the situation so well in hand, you can take her back to the hold-hall."* Turning on a heel, he stalked off, pausing for a moment at the door leading down to the bedchamber to glare back. *"Now."*

Uri let Frax leave before he gently pried her away to look down at her. *"Better?"*

She nodded shakily.

*"You stumbled into a greny hutch, Willow. They're birds that are capable of duplicating a short mental sending. We use them as messengers. I wouldn't have guessed any would still roost in the cote after all these years, though they are rather stupid birds with strong behavior patterns."* He smiled at her. *"You stirred them up pretty badly."*

She nodded again but did not reply. Uri must have caught some of the content in the grenies' mental shrieks. He was offering her a chance to put her upset into words. She could not take his offer.

"*Well*." His hands fell away from her shoulders as the silence drew out between them. "*It's ended now. Are you ready to go below, or do you want to stay up here a while longer?*" His gaze swept the star-studded sky above them. "*Which is this star of yours? Arylla, isn't it? You've never pointed it out.*"

Kaphri shook her head. "*I don't want to talk about anything that relates to the Ly Kai tonight, Uri. But, I do thank you.*" Feeling suddenly awkward with the question she burned to ask, she drew a shaky sigh and stepped away from him, .

He peered down at her as if sensing the change in her mood. "*Ready to go below, then?*"

When she nodded, he took her arm in his hand and lightly guided her in the direction that would take them to the lower levels.

She stopped, swallowing hard in hesitation. Mention of a single word had pushed aside all of her earlier pain and terror. She'd heard it mentioned before and she needed to know. "*Uri?*"

He paused, waiting.

"*Who is Tesla?*"

He stared down at her, surprise etching his features. Then he burst into laughter, the sound echoing off the walls around Windmer Hold.

"*Oh, Kep,*" he said when he finally caught his breath.

# 36

# Moving Forward

Tesla, warrior-general of the Illya, dressed—barely—in ceremonial furs and feathers, sun-browned, firm-fleshed and proud, walked among battle-hardened Geffitzi and Illian warriors as an equal. She was a bold leader: aggressive, flamboyant, sleek. Defiant. In the use of a bladed weapon, none of the males around her would dare to challenge her.

Uri's image of her was admiring and respectful, but nothing more. He knew her well enough through her attachment to his friend, Frax Kitahn, Commander of the Edge, the personal guard to the Holderlord of Cadarn. Kaphri found the word "exotic", Tobin's word for a mateable female of another race, not quite what she would choose to describe the warrioress.

Shielded, she studied the image Uri had given her.

On the other side of the room the warriors were having a noisy argument about something. It was not two opposing factions, or even three. This time they were all in disagreement. She sighed, wondering if the usual silent tension was more preferable.

By the time Uri and she had arrived back in the central hall the others had also returned. There was general agreement the main hold was not the place to spend the night, The Geffitzi were uncomfortable with the idea of sleeping inside with so much death around them.

Their uneasiness toward the spirits of the dead puzzled her enough to raise a question about the logic in such an idea. Tobin pointed out Araxis was still about, and his body was certainly gone. She did not try to explain to him that Araxis had not actually died, but the more she thought on it, the more she understood their feelings.

They withdrew to the guardhouse at the gate tower, where Uri located a discreetly placed narrow stairway that descended through the thick tower wall. This opened onto a rock-lined subterranean passage that led under the road to the outer wall, and up into a large guardroom, which they promptly judged a suitable refuge. Tobin disappeared through a heavy wooden door in the far wall, to return a short time later to report that he'd secured everything off the passageway beyond. Satisfied with the arrangements, they settled in the guardroom for the night.

The stress brought on by their surroundings was more difficult to dispel. Tobin and Seuliac had searched the town outside the hold walls to find the same death Uri and Velacy found inside other parts of Windmer. Kaphri knew the warriors had believed they were prepared for the sight of the disease-devastated hold. She knew now that as young children Uri, Frax and Tobin had made the flight north from Windmer while victims fell around them. But nothing from their elders' stories or their own memories compared with harsh reality. Shocked and confused, it put their connection to her into question again. No apology from her was adequate. But, as Gemma warned her earlier, she was not yet born when it had taken place.

That did not make it easier for any of them.

They settled down to eat, sharing some fresh spring berries and strange, crisp reddish stalks Uri found in the hold's overgrown early-spring garden. Tobin eagerly volunteered to go up on the hold-heights and bring back some of the grenies to roast, but Frax rejected the idea, saying if any Balandra lurked about, they would smell the smoke.

So, the grenies stayed safe for the night, and gloom settled over the company.

Their mood improved, however, when Uri and Velacy began pulling small, sealed jars from a pack. Several of the containers held a thing the warriors called cheese. Scooping out a yellow glob with a metal spoon Uri thoughtfully provided, Tobin observed with distaste that it was too sharp. Kaphri noticed, however, that he ate it just as fast as the other warriors. She sampled it cautiously and was pleasantly surprised at the sour, salty taste.

"*You like it?*" Uri was watching her. He smiled. "*I have something even better.*" He pulled another jar from the pack and carefully pried off a thick wax seal. While the other's exclaimed in delight at the contents, he took her spoon, scooped out a glistening glob of bright red substance, and handed it back to her. "*You eat the plant life without ill effect. Try this.*"

"*It looks like blood,*" she said hesitantly.

"*It's better.*" Tobin shot her a mocking glance. The others chuckled as they happily dug into the jar.

Kaphri touched her tongue to the gel warily. Her eyes widened. "*This is...*"

"*Sweet,*" Uri filled in the word for her. "*Have you ever tasted anything like it?*"

"*Never. What is it?*"

"*Fruit jelly. Made from the tamsin plum.*"

"*It must be a wonderful fruit.*" Kaphri recalled his description of his beloved Ladrienca.

Uri laughed. "*It is. But I wish we had the other half of this treat. Then you'd be really amazed. Our hold kitchens make a sourdough bread that we spread this jelly on. Kep! It is a taste you would never forget.*"

"*The reputation of Windmer's famous bread and tamsin jam has traveled even to Rhynog,*" Seuliac spoke up.

Uri nodded acknowledgement of the compliment, his expression pleased. "*Enjoy it while you can; without a pack animal, the jars are too heavy to carry away in any quantity.*"

"*I'll carry one of the tamsin jars, Uri,*" Kaphri volunteered. "*A little taste, sometime when the day has been difficult, will be worth a little inconvenience.*"

Their mouths full, the others murmured agreement,.

Uri smiled and took her spoon to dip her another scoop. "*Very well. We can divide the rest of the jars among our packs, but you will have the honor of carrying the only other jar of jam I found. This one obviously won't survive the night!*"

The sweet quickly finished, Frax called their attention back to the more mundane results of the day. Tobin and Seuliac had located leather packs and a selection of small tools in the village, but they had no luck with foodstuffs. Besides the jars, spoons, and a cooking pot, Uri and Velacy brought a small sack of grain Uri said they could cook during the day when the fire was not so visible. But in twenty years, the elements or vermin had spoiled everything else.

The balance of their bounty consisted of weapons, flints, whetstones and some old blankets Tobin discovered while rummaging through cabinets in the outer area of the battlement wall. Although the blankets smelled musty, they were in good condition. Kaphri claimed one and retreated to a corner of the guardroom to mull over Frax's angry words—and Tesla—while the warriors withdrew to a wooden table in the opposite corner to study the maps from the Holderlord's chambers.

Despite their secure surroundings, she found it impossible to fall asleep. Her head ached and the argument across the room was getting louder, mentally and vocally. Tugging the blanket tighter, Kaphri put aside her own thoughts to listen.

The warriors had decided to send several of the greny north, in an attempt to get a message to their people. There was no doubt in their minds the birds would find their way to their destination. The question was, what message should they carry?

Should it be that they were "alive', or 'alive and in the south'? Would the second stir too much confusion and an ungrounded hope that might lure more of their people into the grasp of the Balandra? If 'in the south', should they explain how that had happened? Did they really want to mention Kaphri's presence? If they did, would it send a wrong impression and risk disaster if Araxis appeared to them in Ving's form? And, should they warn about the ancient power stirring beneath the tower at the edge of Omurda? The debate was growing more cluttered, unwieldy and rather spirited.

*"It doesn't matter,"* Kaphri broke in wearily. She had tried to remain silent, thinking they would eventually see the obvious flaw in their plan, especially if she could see it, inexperienced as she was. But apparently not. *"They will not get through the barrier."*

The mental flurry stopped as five pairs of gray eyes locked on her.

*"How do you know that?"* Tobin challenged irritably.

*"Because there are no animals in the woods on the far side of the barrier. The Balandra have slain, eaten, or driven everything away."*

Tobin frowned for a moment, then his expression lightened with agreement. *"She's right. Everything on this side moves freely, as if it never met with a reason for fear. I never saw any living thing around the Maugrock."*

*"So animals can't pass through either. Well, that ends that."* Uri sat

back and raised his eyebrows, sending a sense of approval to her. From the shadows past him, Frax merely gave her a narrow glare. She felt a slight flush at his silent appraisal, but she did not need a sending from the Commander of the Edge to tell her she had done well with her observation.

Their debate ended, the Geffitzi returned their attention more quietly to the maps, while she curled up on the stone floor with Gemma. The dragon fell asleep, but the girl lay awake a long time. The headache, after all the distractions of the past hours, filled her awareness, and she dared not ask Uri for more leaves while in such close proximity to the others. It might draw questions from Frax, and he was already in a foul mood toward her. She pillowed her head on her arms and tried to ignore the pain. When that proved impossible, she focused on the events of the day for distraction.

Of all the things she'd experienced, Frax's angry outburst bothered her the most. She could almost understand the reason for his upset. Almost, but not quite. The other warriors had not reacted so fiercely. The screams of the grenies, mocking parodies of his words, echoed horribly in her head, bringing a new surge of anger and resentment to her. He was wrong. She would not die. She would not become a puppet for Araxis. And she would not allow anyone, including the Geffitz leader, to use her.

She frowned. Somehow, her hand had found the crystal on its chain beneath her shirt. Realizing that she held it, her fear and suspicion riveted on it. What, exactly, was the thing? Why had it come to her and what did it want from her?

How could she be sure it wasn't the source of the excruciating pain in her head? The pain had started after they fell through the barrier, after the crystal had come into her possession.

And wearing it was not her choice! Frax had put it on her. Mutinous thoughts centering on the Geffitz commander, she slipped the chain over her head and dropped it into her pack.

Drawing secret satisfaction from her rebellious act, she finally fell asleep.

She woke with a gasp, jerking upright in the dim glow of canna to look about wildly. Three of the warriors stretched out on the floor several feet away, their breathing soft and steady. Another's presence was somewhere beyond the door.

Across the room, Frax glanced up from the map he was still pondering. *"What?"* The strange anger and stiffness that had come over him in the hold was still with him.

*"I was..."* she shook her head in confusion, the dream gone. But her heart still pounded, and her hands trembled as she raised them to press her temples. What had she dreamed? Perhaps something about him or the greny...? Just the attempt at recall drove a twist of fear deep into her.

She shook her head again, at a loss for words.

*"It was just a dream,"* he sent as he turned his attention back to his map. *"It's passed. Go back to sleep."*

He was so very wrong.

* * *

They left the hold early the next morning, retracing their steps up the road and following it out through brushy fields. It led them to a broad stone bridge, where they crossed the river they'd seen in the distance the previous day and headed across rolling hills in a slightly southwestern angle. They stayed close to whatever trees offered cover, but nothing appeared in the sky that was large enough to be Balandran. Their direction kept the nagging sensation of the geas to a low, constant discomfort to Kaphri. The days were sunny and warmer now, and the way was easy, but tension hung over them like a dark cloud that grew steadily denser.

As they prepared to leave Windmer Hold, a change had settled over her companions. They grew even more stressed. Grimmer. More purposeful. As soon as they had awakened, they went through the armory in the outer guard wall, gathering long bows and quivers full of arrows, archer's gauntlets, spears and knives, and other assorted, unrecognizable, deadly looking items. Shirts disappeared into packs, replaced by lined leather jerkins over which they wore their tabards: red and green for Uri, Tobin, and Frax: a white cross with fleured ends on a gray background which, until then, they had hidden under gray jackets, for the Aedecs.

"*For the four winds,*" Seuliac explained when he noted her curiosity as he stripped away his outer jacket in the guardroom. He paused as if he might say more, then turned away to stuff the jacket into his pack.

Kaphri looked over to find Frax watching them.

The silence that followed filled a good portion of the rest of their day.

On the first night out, while the others slept and Kaphri sat first watch, Uri cropped the sun-streaked brown hair on the top of Tobin's head to what, to her, would be the length of her longest finger. That done, the young scout produced some short, green weed stalks that he must have gathered during the day. From a distance, she watched in silent intrigue while the two Geffitzi crushed the stems and worked the sap into Tobin's fresh-cut hair to make it stand upright in a spiky bristle. Uri silently divided the thick, longer length of darker mane into multiple braids, working in an assortment of beads and soft leather strips. A dark red headband with the leaf-and-sunburst symbol centered on his forehead was the final touch.

As far as she was aware, no exchange ever took place between the two during the whole process; they just both seemed to be of like mind in their task.

After finishing with Tobin, they directed their energies to Uri. For the most part, they left his sandy hair untouched at shoulder length while they worked beads into a cluster of tight, thin braids on each side of his face. She winced when they slipped three thin gold rings into the lobe of his left ear, but the big warrior did not flinch. Afterward came another, different, headband. The symbol of Windmer was on Uri's brow, the blue of the sky threading through his dark blonde mane.

Shortly after they began their work on Uri, Velacy woke. When he first saw what the other two were doing, he looked shocked. Then an expression of disdain crept to take its place. He did not go back to sleep, however, and Kaphri could see that, the longer he watched them, the more difficult it became for him to hide his growing interest, until he gradually leaned forward, his eyes taking light. By the time Uri bound the blue headband of Windmer around his forehead Velacy was on his feet.

He and Tobin exchanged a long look. The Kitahni warrior gave a slight jerk of his head for Velacy to come forward.

Uri and Tobin did not seem as familiar with what the younger Aedec warrior wanted. There was a short, quiet flurry of activity, both physically and mentally, before they set to work on him. They spent a long time pulling his dark locks back from his forehead and weaving them into a tight braid pattern against his scalp. At the back of his head they gathered the hair into a mass of narrow braids, wound around with another, into a thick tail. When they finished, they stood up and surveyed each other. A sense of hard satisfaction emanated from them as they silently reached out to clasp fists, the muscles in their bent arms bulging.

Releasing his grip, Uri glanced about, his mind finding Kaphri. *"You better get some sleep, Willow. You've sat through nearly two watches."*

It was true. As caught up in what they were doing as they were, time had slipped swiftly past, unnoticed.

*"Well?"* Tobin's attention fastened on her with a sense of challenge as she walked into the circle of the fire. Standing there in the flickering light, the overall effect of the three warriors was thoroughly barbaric and wild.

*"You look..."* She faltered, at a loss for words.

Tobin smiled, satisfied.

*"What in the hell..."*

All four of them jumped, startled like younglings caught in a forbidden act. They turned to find Frax standing across the fire, his face etched with fury. Anxiously Kaphri glanced up at the warriors around her, but they were all returning their leader's gaze without expression. There was a long silence.

"This is not a game, and these are not the old days," Frax finally snapped.

"Our situation has changed, Frax. You said so yourself." The lack of characteristic defiance in Tobin's tone surprised Kaphri. The scout's gaze went to the red-orange of her braid that still hung from Frax's belt before he looked up again to meet the other's eyes. "We are at war, and this is an honorable part of our past."

Frax's hand went to the braid, his expression hard, but he, too, seemed aware of the absence of challenge in his scout's attitude. He studied them all for a moment longer, then nodded curtly. "All *right. But absolutely no colors on the hair.*"

Tobin nodded quick agreement as the other two turned away with thinly veiled relief, but Frax's gaze had moved past them to fall on her and his mouth tightened. *"And since the three of you are in the mood, before any of you turn in, shave her head. That red streak is starting to stand out like a beacon again."*

Kaphri gave a gasp of shocked protest. The narrow thatch of her hair was barely a half a fingertip in length and was just beginning to thicken.

*"Maybe we could just cover or darken it, Frax..."* Uri ventured when he sensed her dismay.

*"Shave it."* The snarled command brooked no argument. Frax moved off to take his turn at watch.

Tobin stared after him, then turned to look at Uri with a questioning expression.

Uri shrugged. *"Come here, Willow."*

# 37

## Bad Magic

Despite his bold, defiant front, Tobin's uneasiness at approaching the marsh they called the Palenquemas grew stronger with each passing day, spreading to Velacy and Kaphri as well. Seuliac remained silent, observing everything with a detached aloofness, as if nothing they did involved him directly, while Frax stalked along in the ill-tempered silence he had assumed at Windmer. Of them all, Uri appeared the least affected. In fact, there were flitting moments when Kaphri suspected he found something in Frax's foul temper amusing.

Although it irritated her, the Geffitz leader's reassertion of control was only a small part of her troubles. The rising difficulty of moving westward against the geas quickly eclipsed her secret triumph of having the aching, black pit of her headaches disappear after she removed the crystal. The compulsion worried at the edges of her mind, constantly. Given her freedom, she would have turned sharply eastward and south, the image of the plateau in the mountains frequently coming, unbidden, to her now. As Geffitzi prisoner—or companion—however, she moved a different direction. She walked in silence, tension steadily tightening within her.

And the dream she had in Windmer returned.

On the first night out, after the anger of her head-shaving finally let her drift off, she awoke, gasping in terror, the elusive vision gone before she caught any of the details.

"*What's wrong, Willow?*" The starlit sky silhouetted Uri's form from where she lay.

"*Nothing,*" she sent swiftly. "*Just a dream.*" But she stayed awake a long time after, feeling the cold grip of fear as she wrestled to recall some detail of what had just terrorized her.

She puzzled over it all day, more than once earning a hard glare from Frax as she blundered absent-mindedly through some brush or stumbled into a hole.

"Pay attention to what you're doing before you break an ankle," he snapped. He spoke aloud, in Geffitzi. She didn't realize she understood as she nodded quickly and tried to push the dreams from her mind.

That night it came again, and she lay awake until morning, afraid to return to sleep.

"*Gemma, something is wrong,*" she admitted to her companion, and to herself, the next afternoon while they walked along.

"*The dreams?*"

So, Gemma was aware of them, even though this was the first time Kaphri mentioned them to her. She should not be surprised: Gemma always knew everything about her.

"*Do you see them, Gemma? I can't recall anything except a terror that lingers afterward. What are they?*"

"*A veil of darkness hangs over them that I cannot penetrate,*" Gemma told her. The dragon's deep concern would have been disquieting if Kaphri hadn't sensed the strong reassurance overlaying it. Whatever they were, Gemma seemed confident in Kaphri's ability to deal with them. *"They steal softly upon you and then leave witllout a trace, just as you perceive."*

*"I'm frightened, Gemma. I'm beginning to fear sleep again."* She'd tried avoiding sleep once before. It had not worked out well. *"I would suspect the crystal of bringing these dreams, but I took it off back at Windmer."*

*"Do you think that was wise?"*

After devoting nearly two whole days and nights to considering her action? *"My headaches have eased since I took it off, and I didn't have any nightmares before the crystal."*

*"You did not begin to have nightmares for many days after donning the crystal."*

*"Perhaps. But perhaps the thing took time to insinuate into my sleep. No, Gemma, I don't trust it. I will not wear it."*

The discussion did little to ease her mind.

***

*"Hey, are you alright?"*

Kaphri looked at Tobin blankly.

*"Are you alright?"* he repeated, his expression full of uneasy irritation.

*"Yes."* She stared at the small metal cup that he held out.

*"Have you heard anything I've said?"*

Wishing she could lie, she shook her head. *"No."*

Frax snarled as he pitched the water from his own cup into the grass. *"Tobin, take the first watch tonight."*

That was her watch!

*"No!"* Her protest drew a dangerous glare. She eased her tone. *"I can take my watch."* Sitting guard gave her a reason to delay sleep.

*"We're on the edge of the Palenquemas, Priestess. I don't want to die in my sleep while your mind wanders off to pick flowers,"* Frax said.

She flushed hotly but maintained her ground. *"I can take my watch. Please."*

*"Then get your focus back on the things at hand."*

Rising to her feet, she picked a spot a short distance away from the others, to familiarize herself with the surrounding area.

Their camp sat on the crest of a hill overlooking a large plane. A line of dark growth in the west marked what the warriors said was the outer edge of the Palenquemas. As they had made camp in the late afternoon sun, the swamp had stretched away in the distance, its details soft and smudged beneath a blue haze. Now the place glowed with a near-luminescence as moonlit fog crept over it. The land around and below the hill remained clear and bright, however.

In the last several days, the trees and grasses of the south had greened heavily.

She drew a deep breath. *"Everything smells so sweet and fresh."*

The warriors looked over at her with odd expressions.

*"It's spring,"* Tobin sent. With a doubtful shake of his head, he rose and walked off to stare out across the swampland. He stayed there, unmoving, while the others prepared to settle in for the night.

Spring or whatever, the world held a newness Kaphri had never experienced before and she found it exciting in spite of her fears. Even the threat of the Wyxan swamp did not dampen it completely.

She got through an uneventful watch with a mix of determination and apprehension. She woke Uri, wrapped in her blanket, and settled to the ground to look up at the stars.

Despite the disruption to her sleep the past three nights, fear of the dreams burned too strongly to let her rest. She searched out Arylla, hanging bright above her, and studied the star while thinking on the few things she knew about it. The brilliant white blaze that hung high in this sky was strange to her, though in another place it would have dominated her whole life. How did things go so far away from what they should be? How could a child, highborn of the Ly Kai, become so severed from the things of that people?

But that child had been lost many years ago.

After a long time staring at the sky, Kaphri murmured a short prayer, the first she had ever offered to her Birthstar. Gemma lay on her belly, aware of the thoughts running through her mind, but offering no comment. After a while, reluctant as the girl was, nature won out and she fell asleep.

In the early hours of the morning, she awoke screaming.

*"Kep! Be quiet!"* A hand clamped over her mouth to stifle her cries. Still in the grip of dream-horror, she began to fight wildly.

An arm locked about her ribs to stop her struggles. *"Damn it, Priestess. Wake up!"* Frax's harsh sending finally penetrated the terror that enveloped her and she stopped struggling.

*"What the hell?"* The other four warriors stumbled to their feet, weapons in hands, to stare at the two of them wrestling on the ground, their limbs entangled.

Frax released her with an oath, and she scooted away.

*"A dream. That is all!"* she explained. She snatched her blanket and wrapped it around her shoulders defensively. *"It was nothing but a dream."*

*"That's what you said two nights ago,"* Uri said as he sank back down onto his blanket.

Frax was halfway to his feet. He stopped. *"That's what you said at the hold, too. And last night? Was there a dream last night, too?"*

She nodded with miserable reluctance.

*"Kep, now what?"* Straightening, Frax massaged his temples in irritation. The movement froze as he and Uri exchanged looks. *"The amulet!"* they exclaimed simultaneously.

Before she could react, Frax seized her arm and ran his fingers around beneath her collar, searching for the chain.

*"Stop!"* She struggled awkwardly, the blanket hampering her efforts to pull out of his grasp.

"*Where is the damned thing, Kaphri?*" he snarled when his search failed to turn it up. "*What did you do with the cursed thing?*"

"*I took it off back at Windmer,*" she said. "*It gave me headaches. Maybe it causes the dreams, too.*" She jerked her arm free.

"*You're wrong.*"

Her attention shifted to Uri, her defiance fading to uncertainty at his troubled expression.

"*What did you do with it? You didn't leave it behind?*" His tone was urgent and, for the first time, she realized his sending was tight with suppressed anger, something she had never felt in the big Geffitz before.

Frax had shaken her out of her dream-terror with his rough handling: now the fear began to rekindle inside of her. If her action upset good-natured Uri, then she must have made a serious error in judgment. "*It's over there. I put it as far away from me as possible.*" She gestured to where the pack lay in the grass across the fire from her.

Uri snatched the bag up with an expression of relief and poured its contents on the ground as he pawed through it.

"*This is bad, very bad,*" he mentally mumbled.

Watching his near-frantic movements, her uneasiness grew.

"*What are the dreams?*" Frax demanded.

Wishing mightily to avoid an inevitable tongue-lashing, she kept her eyes on Uri as she answered. "*I don't know. The memory is gone as soon as I wake up.*"

"*Bad magic,*" Tobin observed.

"*Bad magic, helped along by stupidity.*"

That stung! Frax had no idea what she was experiencing.

Before she formed a response, however, Uri found the crystal. He thrust it at her. "*Put it back on.*"

As her fingers touched Uri's the world exploded in a white-hot blaze.

*"Oh, Kep!"* One of the warriors gasped in pained confusion as she was snatched away.

***

A sharp tug inside her brain plunged her into a terrible, familiar darkness—the darkness that had formed in her head when the Balandra painted her starsign, reversed, in her blood at the Maugrock. She writhed in a silent scream of horror, caught in the deathless cold. Then she dropped back into the familiar world.

The warriors! She reached out, only to find she was alone. The warm, sloping hillside was replaced by a colder, darker one.

As she hung in the air above it without a physical form, terror flashed inside of her. Hredroth, was she dead? Had Frax finally lost patience and slain her to protect his world? Had Araxis attacked and stolen her body before she even had a chance to act in self-defense, leaving her in this disembodied state?

Her lungs swelled when she gasped for air, which meant she retained a link to her body. That brought a rush of relief. She was not dead, Despite the absence of a body, she had sight and she could feel the damp in the cold air around her.

It felt unpleasantly familiar...

This was an extension of her dream!

She stared in horror at the slope below her, seeing the scars in the dirt and broken brush. This was the place where the Geffitzi and she had fallen through the barrier.

The barrier. The massive presence struck her, the same way it had the first day she'd found it. Panic tightened inside her. All she felt was the power of Arylla coursing before her, but the coiling, evil force from the black temple had to be somewhere close by. The memory of it sent a terror equal to her fear of Araxis rushing through her.

But now she saw something even more huge and frightening on

the slope. Hundreds of dark-winged Balandra covered the mountainside. They stood silent and unmoving. Waiting.

Waiting for what? She scanned the dark mob, even though she knew she would not pick up their thoughts. Then she found something that drove a jolt of horror through her. In the midst of the gray warriors huddled a small group of thin, ragged figures.

The Twenty-three!

What were they doing in this place? She had left them in the far north, living in fear but unwilling to leave the sanctuary they claimed in the tower of Kryie Karth. She had tried to warn them that evil had found them! They should be terrified, standing here among these creatures; but she did not have to touch the Ly Kai men to sense the familiar anger and hostility emanating from them.

Why had Araxis brought them here? What had he told them? What was her evil uncle plotting?

A figure stepped away from the clustered Ly Kai. She watched Kali weave his way down the slope through the Balandra, his eyes locked on her, even in her bodiless state. He stopped a few feet from the wall of power and raised a hand to trace a pale green sign in the air.

A sudden wrench brought her to eye level with him, with only the barrier to separate them.

Hredroth! What had he just done? She tried to move back, away from him, but she was wedged into place.

The man glared across the space, his eyes burning with cold hatred. She was only a mental essence, invisible to sight, but he knew she was there.

"Take us to our Homeworld," he said loudly in his harsh, rusty voice.

Take them to... That explained how Araxis lured them here. He must have told them as Ving that she could return them to the Homeworld he'd stolen from them all.

And they believed him...

If he thought she would break the barrier, it was a promise he could not keep.

*"I cannot open this—"*

"Liar! You have crossed. As ever, you think we're fools, but you're wrong. When you were a small child, Rath suggested we weave links to bind you to the Council's will. Much as we despised him, we did listen. And now you are here at our bidding." Kali's tone became a purr of triumph. "We are the Ly Kai Council. High One or not, you cannot refuse us and you cannot escape our will. We demand that you take us to the Homeworld."

The Ly Kai men thought they could force her to act, and it appeared they did have some power over her—they had drawn her to this place. But she knew Araxis would never let the surviving Ly Kai return to their home: they were witnesses to all the evil things he'd done on this world. He had lured thousands of adoring, unsuspecting people here, then murdered them when they refused to worship him as a god. Beyond their rejection, they had maimed him, destroying his physical form. He would never forgive them.

Now he was back, stealing the bodies of the unwary to resurrect his plan. He'd stolen the form of Rath and destroyed it; she realized now she was not to blame for the man's death. Araxis had pushed the hapless man's body beyond the limits of its starpower and killed him.

And now he possessed Ving's form with which to speak his lies and manipulate the last survivors.

He would use the Twenty-three and destroy them in his effort to capture her because she was Arylla-born, like himself. With her stolen form, he would reclaim his lost power and begin his evil plots anew.

Whatever the survivors had done, lying to her and hating her the past sixteen years, she could not leave them to his cruel intentions.

They had never listened to her before, but she had to try. *"Listen to me. There is danger—"*

"You are the danger. Ving came to you, pleading for your help. You let your murderous allies attack him and you left him for dead."

They thought Ving... She choked back protest, knowing nothing she said would convince them of his deceit.

Where was Araxis? At this level on the slope, it was impossible for her to see anything but gray bodies. *"How did you get here? Are you prisoners...?"*

Kali's words were scorching. "Ving found us allies. They will protect us against the bloody, murdering barbarians that you consort with."

The Ly Kai had no idea what they claimed as allies. *"Those creatures are killing the people of this world!"*

"They protect us. That is all that matters."

And there was the kernel of truth. Some of the Ly Kai were as ruthless as the Geffitzi claimed and they would gladly sacrifice her if they thought it would get them back to the Homeworld.

The Twenty-three had no inkling of the trap they had walked into. All Araxis wanted was to destroy her and take her form. He would let the Balandra kill them as soon as he achieved that.

*"You're in deadly danger but it's not from me."* The same words she used to warn them in Kryie Karth. *"Araxis is—"*

"Do not try to plant your poison in our minds."

*"Little fool."* Kaphri flinched as the sending dropped into her head. *"They know what I am. They just refuse to admit it to themselves. You are the price they are willing to pay to get off this world."*

Araxis, in the same disembodied form as she, lurked somewhere nearby; she fought panic at the realization. This strange, ethereal state must be how he lived when he was unable to secure a physical shape. This would be all she could hope for if he overpowered her here and stole her body.

*"Where is Ving? Why aren't you here, in his form, doing your own dirty work?"*

*"Your filthy allies—"* The scorch of his fury dizzied her. *"You will do what my followers demand!"*

Bitterness twisted inside Kaphri at his use of 'followers' for the Twenty-three. So many Ly Kai had died to deny that term.

Now, however, she suspected he was on the opposite side of the invisible wall neither of them could breach. Otherwise, he would not need the Twenty-three to do what he could not.

Her heart, somewhere, raced. *"You know I can't open this barrier. Only you, as its creator, can do that."*

A cold mental chuckle tickled her mind. *"There are times when we must reach beyond the things we know."*

Fear squeezed her. *"This is between you and me. Let the others go back to Kryie Karth."* They wouldn't appreciate the gesture, but it was better than the fate Araxis planned for them.

*"Your concern is touching, but, no; I require their combined power."*

*"You do not intend to let them go home."*

*"They will not believe that if you tell them. You are the monster trying to trick them. Besides, I won't kill them. You will, if you resist doing what I want. So, let us make this simple: open a way through the flow of Arylla's Power now or the Ly Kai will force you to do it."*

Such evil simplicity. Did he really believe she had broken through on her own?

A rush of dizzying realization rolled over her. Araxis did not know about the crystal and blood that had crusted her clothing. Another question, this one with more horrific implication: did he know about the force that lurked inside the barrier?

That didn't matter. Nothing would stop him. *"If I do what you want, will you return them to the Homeworld and leave this world in peace?"* She had no idea how to open the barrier, but perhaps she might negotiate a settlement at the cost of only one life lost...

"Do you refuse us?" Kali, not privy to their exchange, had grown impatient with her seeming silence.

"*Little fool, I don't have to negotiate with you.*" Araxis shifted his attention away from her.

"*Recalcitrant child!*" Ving's mental warning blasted them all. "*She refuses to help us! Make her obey the will of this Council.*"

Before Kaphri could react, the combined power of the twenty-three remaining Ly Kai men seized her and slammed her forward against the barrier. The contact sent a blaze of starpower through her bodiless form.

Stunned, she fought to pull away.

Whatever binding they used, however, was strong. With her unable to move, starpower poured in, burning along her nerves. If she did not stop it...

"*Open the way. We command you.*" The pressure of their combined will increased, drawing her deeper into the wall of power.

Meanwhile, Arylla was reacting to her contact, white light spreading upward and outward along the surface. In the same way it behaved on the heights of Kryie Karth at her first encounter, the star's strength burned in chaotic fury, its heat rising, eroding the places where she contacted it. The fire would consume her if she did not take control.

But, as Araxis warned, the others would fight her, and some of them would die the way Rath died in the hallway at Kryie Karth, their physical capacity exceeded by their effort. Much as she despised them, she could not bear the thought of causing their deaths. Araxis knew that and he was using it against her. Which left her two choices: take control of her birth power and open a way through, or dissolve into it and die.

A tiny burst of light flared inside her head, a gleam in the cold dark place, then another. Arylla's uncontrolled starpower was beginning to affect her.

White light sheeted around her, blinding her mentally and physically. The places where power touched her were growing hotter.

Taking what Arylla offered on the heights of Kryie Karth had been natural, right up to the moment Rath intruded and brought everything down in a fiery blaze of chaos. Here, she was already in the middle of an assault, with the Ly Kai hampering her attempt to defend. She needed to get back to that place, that point where Arylla recognized and flowed through her rather than burned her away.

She fumbled, trying to catch onto something she could control.

The white light dimmed in the area where she directed her efforts.

She could affect the barrier.

If she didn't do this right, she would die, along with the surviving Ly Kai. But she was not Araxis, and the barrier was not her working. Her only option was to control the massive power feeding it. Perhaps, if she weakened its flow in a specific space...

No doubt; no fear. She must be the entity, born of Arylla, living here and now. She focused her mind and reformed the thing that she was and began to withdraw from the force that threatened to burn her away.

Slowly she reclaimed back the things Arylla had taken from her. Power sparked and slowed, discovering new channels for its flow. Then the force was rushing again, this time flowing through her instead of against her.

In the process, she became the thing the Ly Kai had feared for sixteen years and now insisted that she become. She claimed the power of her Birthstar.

She had no time to feel the joy of claiming Arylla, however. The power might belong to her, but this vast creation did not, and she could not change that. She could only affect the source that powered it. Reaching into the space beside her, she pushed outward with her mind, willing the flow of Arylla to channel elsewhere. The power thinned and separated.

She heard a shout and dark shadows rushed her and swirled past.

Araxis laugh coldly inside her head. "*Stupid child, you cannot deny me.*"

Kaphri gritted metaphysical teeth, the need to concentrate too intense to form a reply, while the shadows—Balandra stealing their way into the south—flowed past. Arylla pressed hard, its resistance to the break she created rising. Inexperienced as she was, she could not maintain control over the power indefinitely the way Araxis seemed to do with the barrier.

Up the slope, the will that held her prisoner was weakening. The world began to resolve around her again.

Why were the Ly Kai still standing on the hillside? If they didn't hurry, her control would collapse and the barrier would close. "*Move!*" she gave a mental scream.

But now she saw the Balandra that encircled the men. They were not letting them pass! The Ly Kai, exhausted by the massive use of their Power were too weak to fight through them. Their hold on her slipped even more when one made a feeble effort to push past.

"Ving," Kali screamed. "Tell them to let us through!"

The last of the moving Balandra were rushing through the opening in the barrier and Kaphri saw Ving, carried by an entourage of gray warriors, cross into the south. He looked back at the remaining Balandra encircling the Twenty-three and said in clear Ly Kai, for all of them to hear him, "Kill them all now, while they are weak, and do as you will with their flesh."

A wicked, barbed spear pierced Kali, thrusting out of his chest. He staggered a step, expression shocked, and then collapsed in front of her.

"*No!*" Despite everything they had or had not done, the men did not deserve to die here.

The horror of what had just happened was too much. Her control over Arylla slipped and the star's power surged over her. Tiny stars flamed and burned in the cold darkness inside her head.

Her mental essence gave a twist. Araxis was trying to sever her connection with her body! Before she could react, a blaze of purple fury rushed over her. The force that lurked in the barrier slammed her hard.

The crystal blazed with an explosion of powerful forces meeting. It flung Kaphri out of Arylla, out of the barrier and back into the cold blackness. A faint sense of another essence snatching desperately to follow her, flickered then disappeared.

She searched out to find her physical form, blindly groping in black ice.

Araxis! Terror seized her. He could not have her form. The crystal had flared. It must be somewhere...

Nothing.

But it was at her fingertips, her mind screamed. She could feel it. She could...feel it? Fighting panic, she searched out again; seeking her physical self to confirm what she knew was the truth. There. Very faintly. There was warmth where her flesh touched Uri's, and the bare weight of the chain, the coolness from that thin strip of woven metal lying on her skin.

The coolness began to grow as she sought it. Became like the touch of ice as she concentrated. Ice. No. Like fire. Heat rose now, extending inexorably through her fingers, running up her arm, her shoulder, sinking into her body like a flame.

A monstrous outrage, more terrible than anything she'd ever experienced before, ripped at her. Kaphri twisted, dodging as Araxis lunged and fell away.

She found herself staring at the chain, Uri's flesh still touching hers as he passed it to her. Her fingers closed spasmodically about the delicate strand.

"What the hell was that?" All five Geffitzi stared at her in appall.

She had no time for a reply. Snatching the chain, she dropped it over her head.

As it fell on her breast, she thought she saw a tiny burst of light flare within the depths of the crystal.

\*\*\*

She huddled on the blanket, eyes wide and unfocused, the crystal clasped in numb fingers.

Frax knelt beside her. *"Priestess,"* his sending was firm. *"We are all in danger. You have to tell us what's going on."*

Her eyelids fluttered, then closed. She sagged into a small heap as tears began to course down her cheeks. *"Araxis. He used the others to pull me back to the barrier."* It was the barest of mental whispers. *"They forced me to open a way for the Balandra to pass into the south."*

Shock and outrage ran through the warriors. *"You let them through? Now we have Balandra and Ly Kai—"*

*"No! He killed them. He—ah!"*

Swearing at the intense stab of pain that ripped through their heads, the Geffitzi warriors shielded and Gemma silently withdrew from mental contact.

For Kaphri, there was no escape. It was the price the Ly Kai people paid for telepathy, to experience the severing of the mental links they had shared with the dying. The Balandra were killing the remaining Ly Kai men and all she could do was sit helplessly, leagues away, and feel them die one by one.

It was not the same terrible pain as Hyfas' death. With him, her role as student forced her into telepathic contact every day for years. But the men on the mountainside were all she'd known for sixteen years. Her father was on that slope. She could not distinguish his death from the others their attachment was so thin. Araxis had stolen that tie away from her when she was two years old, when he abandoned his Ly Kai followers on this world.

Now she truly understood the meaning of the word that Hyfas hissed in accusation on his deathbed. In the end, Araxis had murdered them all.

Choking back a sob and gripping the crystal hard in her fist, she pulled her knees up to her chest and curled into a tight knot.

"*Well, Kitahn,*" she heard Seuliac observe through the haze of her misery. "*You wondered if she would know when he made his move to come through the barrier.*"

# 38

## The Palenquemas

*"The question is, can that thing protect her if he tries to snatch her again?"* Frax paused in his pacing to look at Uri.

The warriors, in mental contact with her when Araxis whisked her away, had been unwilling participants in a portion of her ordeal. They'd experienced the sudden sensation of Arylla's blaze, then a long moment of blankness, as if frozen in time. Seconds later the crystal had blazed with light and released them to stare in shock as she snatched the chain and collapsed in horrified tears.

Uri shrugged unhappily. *"If she keeps it on, maybe."*

If she kept the amulet on! Kaphri's fingers closed tighter about the crystal. She did not intend to take it off again. Ever! *"It was the dreams,"* she said. *"I think his attempts to reach me while I wore it gave me the headaches. Taking the crystal off left me unprotected."* She did not add that the headaches were centered inside the cold pit the Balandra had created when they reversed her star sign in blood on her forehead.

*"We've got more than one problem here, you know."* Tobin paused in tying his bedroll to glare at the rest of them.

*"He's added players to the game."* The warlord's quiet observation drew their attention. He regarded Frax keenly.

*"Yes."* Frax nodded curt agreement. *"The Wyxa won't ignore this."*

*"Will they reach beyond their lands to investigate?"*

*"With the Wyxa? My gut reaction is to say yes."* He looked at Kaphri. *"Priestess, does the Evil One know where you are?"*

*"I don't think so."* Her mind touched Gemma's for comfort. The little dragon had remained a silent pool of calm throughout the whole incident.

*"Then he may try another attack, to locate you."*

*"We might be hit from two sides if we're not careful."* Uri said gravely.

*"So, what do we do?"* Velacy demanded.

*"We move away from this spot as far and fast as we can."* Frax's reply was tight. *"But, regardless of what just happened here, our purpose still remains the same."*

That said, the others turned, preparing to break camp, only to discover Tobin lacing the last bedroll to a pack. Except for trampled grass and the blanket wrapping Kaphri, all signs of their stay, including the fire, were gone.

He glowered back at them.

A flicker of smile lifted Frax's mouth. *"All right. Let's move out."*

They were back to the long-legged, ground-covering pace that pushed her to a half-run, but fear fed Kaphri's energy enough for her to keep up as they made their way swiftly and silently through the dark.

Uri withdrew into thought, while Tobin, already vociferously unhappy with their proximity to the Palenquemas, seethed with ill-contained outrage. He had just undergone a brush with a power he hated and, although he did not say it, Kaphri knew he was ready to rid himself of both her and the crystal. He lapsed into an angry silence after the burst of energy that fired him to break down their camp around them. The Aedec warriors' temperaments were less familiar to her, but she suspected that, despite their experiences at the barrier, Seuliac and Velacy had not believed the threat real, thinking it some devious plot the other three had dreamed up, until the moment they'd experienced it firsthand. Now Velacy was greatly agitated, venting his tension in short, hot bursts of questions, while Seuliac's silence merely deepened, if that were possible.

Then there was Frax. Perhaps his previous encounter with Araxis left him cooler in the face of the attack. Although he claimed he had not expected it, Kaphri was sure he had considered the possibility. Beyond his initial shakeup, the only effect the experience seemed to have on him was to harden his resolve, so that, as the remainder of the night wore on he mercilessly pushed them forward. Surprisingly, Kaphri found comfort in his inflexible, driven attitude. There was a strange sort of relief in having someone else take control of the situation with firm reason when such hot fear seethed inside of her.

The deathpains were gone. She had no idea when they stopped; the horror and agony had put her into a state of near stupor. She only knew that after they stopped, the Twenty-three were gone.

The cold ache inside her head re-emerged. She thought it might have grown larger. She didn't care enough to examine it.

As the hours passed, she settled into the grip of the nightmare, aware of her companions but unable to think clearly, coming back to the immediate present only when something forced her attention. Even Gemma's soothing presence fell short of easing her as she moved through the darkness.

"... *shock,*" she overheard Uri murmur once to Frax as they stared at her.

She could not stir herself to respond.

*** 

*"Do you realize what could have happened tonight, Uri?"* Frax's send-

ing was tight, for the Caspani warrior only. *"Something could have followed that link back to her body."*

*"Are we sure it didn't?"*

*"You felt it. What do you think?"*

*"It felt pretty much like the hysterical, terrified female back in the greny hutch."*

*"I tried to get to her during the attack, Uri. I wanted to kill her, but my body was locked in place. That terrifies me."*

*"I, and probably Tobin, tried, too. I can only guess the crystal paralyzed us all to protect her, but that's risky speculation."*

*"This is all a risk. Can we really trust the Guardian? It said she might be our only hope of getting our lands back. We might lose everything if we act rashly, but I still wonder every conscious moment if we're putting our whole world in peril for a ridiculous hope. I don't know. I just don't know."*

*"We're closer to achieving something today than we were sixty days ago, Frax, with more information, and we're no more at risk."*

"True." Frax sighed. "If we destroy her, we have nothing and Araxis remains a threat, though a lesser one. We should continue to watch her closely, and be prepared to act. If we can," he added as a bitter afterthought.

"Should we tell the Aedecs the real situation, just in case?"

"No. I trust them less than I trust her: she, at least, believes she can't lie in mindspeak. If there's a way that can be done, you can bet the Aedecs will have found it."

"And the Kitahns?" Uri flashed his cousin a grin.

"Oh, we found a way ages ago." Frax smiled back wearily.

***

When Frax called a stop for rest, Kaphri let her pack slide off her shoulders and dropped limply to the ground beside it. She wasn't sleepy, but she laid on the damp ground and tried to force emptiness into her mind as the others settled in the darkness around her with soft moans and curses, .

Gemma curled into a tight ball on her chest.

As Kaphri's mind began to drift away, the little dragon lifted its head.

*** 

It had been years—ten, specifically—since Gemma had shifted. That time she had moved to sun-baked boulders on a lakeshore to await the arrival of a young girl child.

The directive binding her to her task was simple: protect our world. The ones who placed the charge on her had not foreseen the consequences of such a broad command. Now they began to perceive their oversight, the unintended flexibility and expansion of their order, and they were not pleased. They demanded an accounting.

The events put in motion would not stop with their displeasure, however.

The child was in good hands. Relying on chance, the little dragon let her mind go blank as she shifted.

There was a sensation of physical blur. A cool touch of humid air. A consciousness stirred around her.

"Hello, Little Sister," it said. "Something has stirred in the north. Tell us what you know."

"It has returned."

"You are in peril."

"Yes."

"Come to us, then."

***

Kaphri woke lying on her back, staring into seething grayness. An eerie, muffled silence hung around her and cold dampness beaded her skin.

Memory jolted her—memory of waking, half-conscious, drugged and unable to move in the middle of a fog-shrouded lake. She jerked to a sitting position, drew a deep breath, and fought to calm her racing heart. It was fog, yes, but fog over land.

Something was lying heavily across her legs. A cold, creeping sense of foreboding stole over her as she sent out a cautious mental probe.

Frax?

Leaning forward, she reached out to nudge him awake.

More than once while sitting her turn at guard she'd seen the Geffitz leader roused from sleep by the slightest change in the night air around them, he slept so lightly and warily. Now, vigorously shaking his shoulder drew no response.

Fighting panic, she paused to think. Uri or Tobin. Perhaps one of them...

When she reached out, she touched Tobin's mental presence, also heavy in sleep, somewhere in the grayness. Uri and the Aedecs were nowhere around.

Neither was Gemma.

Kaphri looked at the drifting whiteness that enveloped them. She must do something, and shaking Frax obviously wasn't going to awaken him. She hardened herself to the only option she knew was left open to her.

Mindspeaking a sleeper to wake them was discomforting. Touching a dream was like touching a fever-induced sending: it was very personal and confusing, similar to invading the inner mind. Kaphri had never dared address the Geffitz leader mentally without his awareness and consent. After his harsh warning in Omurda, she feared what his initial reaction might be, but she couldn't see any other way to rouse him.

She pushed into Frax's mind.

To her immediate relief, there were no dreams. Instead, his slumber seemed strangely heavy and sticky. Her intrusion barely drew a flicker of response. It was slow. Much too slow for his normally swift Geffitzi reaction.

Desperate, she pushed harder.

When it finally came, the reaction was as shockingly swift as she'd feared. Before she could react, she was enveloped in startled awareness, seized and held firmly as he recognized her presence.

"*Kep!*" He sat up with an outraged mental snarl, his hands reaching out to grasp her physical form. "*Priestess, I warned you...!*"

Kaphri did the only thing that she thought might bring him to clear thinking; she blasted him with a sense of imminent danger.

"*Oh, hell!*"

As his mental grip slipped, she fled out of his head.

"*Something is wrong with Tobin, and I can't find Uri!*"

"Where?" With a reaction more in line with what she expected, Frax leapt to his feet, dragging her up with him. Hand locked on her arm, he pulled her along as he located Tobin's still form a few steps away in the drifting fog.

"*Stay put.*" He squatted down beside the sleeping scout. "*Not one step without me!*"

He didn't have to repeat the order. Shivering in the cold, drifting dampness, she hovered as close as possible without touching him while he tried to wake Tobin. He quickly discovered, as she had, that shaking was not enough. He drew a breath and shot the scout a slightly milder sense of danger than she had given him.

Tobin jolted awake, sitting up with a wild expression that didn't change when he saw the grayness about them. "*Kep, Frax, what the...?*"

Kaphri's mouth went suddenly dry. "*Where are we?*"

Frax looked up impatiently. "*Kep, Priestess, what do you—?*" His question broke off as he followed the gesture of her hand toward the ground.

They had settled to rest on the dried leaves of a thin wood; now they stared through wisps of fog ands stood on a thick mat of dry, broken reeds.

Frax's only visible reaction was a slight tightening of his mouth, but Tobin surged to his feet in one movement while voicing a stream of oaths. The words fell heavy and muffled in the close air.

"*The Wyxa have moved us.*" Frax stood to look around at the grayness that hung close about them. "*It looks as if the disturbance tonight got their attention, after all.*" There didn't seem any doubt in his mind about who had done this, and she didn't sense anything that hinted of Araxis or the dark force from the barrier in the surrounding air.

"*Priestess,*" Frax turned to her, "*Do you sense anything—anything at all—close by? Be thorough in your search.*"

As far as she reached, there was only flat emptiness. Not even a tree or tall reed broke the plain.

It was an eerie feeling to have fog press in so solidly about them that they could barely see each other, and yet not sense anything.

Skin creeping with uneasiness, she inched closer to the warriors.

"*Perhaps the others escaped,*" she said.

"No." Frax shook his head. "*I don't think so.*"

"*The Wyxa.*" Tobin grew even more agitated. "*They worked some sorcery to bring us here.*"

Frax and Tobin's sleep had definitely been under the influence of something. "*What should we do?*"

"*Find Uri and get out of here. The Wyxa mean us no good, Frax,*" Tobin snapped.

Frax swore softly. "*Tobin is right. Wyxa and the Geffitzi share no friendship. What are they plotting, separating us like this?*"

"*Do they want her?*" Tobin jerked his head in Kaphri's direction.

"*If they wanted her, we'd all be standing under a tree at the edge of the Palenquemas right now, scratching our heads and wondering where she'd gone. No. They want something else.*"

"*This.*" A chill of instinct ran through her. With mixed feelings, she found the chain and drew it from her shirt while the warriors watched.

Frax's expression was thoughtful. "*If they wanted that, why didn't they just take it? Why pull us in?*"

"*Maybe they mean to kill us. The bugs don't like our people, Frax. Kep, I knew something like this was going to happen.*" Tobin looked at the fog surrounding them.

"*They could've slain us and left our bodies at the edge of the swamp, Tobin. As things are, no one would ever know what happened to us.*"

"*Except Araxis and the Balandra,*" Kaphri murmured, half to herself.

"*Using us as bait to lure them?*" Frax gave mental frown while Tobin swore. "*Possible. My guess is the Wyxa were in the process of moving us somewhere when you woke. They might not be able to handle us all at one time. That would put the others either ahead or behind us in their plan.*"

"*That doesn't mean they don't intend to dispose of us,*" Tobin persisted.

"*No,*" Frax agreed. "*You're right. But we're awake now, and that complicates whatever they planned. Priestess, you said you can't locate the others?*"

She swept out as far as she could reach again before answering. "*No.*"

"*I don't believe they're anywhere close by, and we can't risk getting separated in this fog. If the Wyxa haven't harmed us there's no reason to think they'll harm them.*" A frown darkened his expression. "*It may be only a matter of time before they retake us, but I don't intend to make it easy for them. Let's move out of here. Stay close together.*"

Which direction should they take in the grayness? "*Is it daylight?*" Kaphri asked. "*At Kryie Karth the fogs usually went away with the day.*" But this did not appear to be a natural fog. Should they wait for it to go away? They needed to see something in order to pick which direction they should go. They certainly didn't want to wander deeper into the marsh.

Frax cursed aloud. "Good question."

"*Well, what about you?*" Tobin turned to Kaphri. "*You're supposed to be driven by that cursed geas of yours. What direction is it pulling you?*"

She blinked in surprise at the question, then turned her attention inward, searching for the thing she'd been trying so desperately to avoid lately. Both the geas and the cold, black pit in her mind were gone.

She should feel relief at the change. Instead, she felt fear.

Guessing at the answer from her silence, Tobin swore. "*Filthy bugs.*"

A low, deep keening sound broke the gray silence. It rose steadily in pitch before it peaked and slowly faded.

"*Kep!*" Tobin whipped around toward the sound. "*Now what?*"

The sorrowful, haunting call came again. In spite of the fear it stirred inside her, Kaphri sensed out, hoping it might tell her something about their surroundings.

Nothing. Not even a flicker of its source. She started another sweep over the area.

Something large had come into range. Despite the speed of its approach, it moved cautiously and stealthily. It was a movement she had seen before. It was stalking them.

Pressing closer to Frax, she pointed a trembling finger. "*Out there, and coming at us fast.*" Perhaps Tobin was right and the Wyxa did have ill intentions.

Frax hissed in dismay as he shifted beside her. "*It's a kitsk.*"

They both felt the quiver of fear and anticipation that ran through Tobin.

"*It has fed and is only curious, Tobin. Let's move before it gets any closer.*" Frax's sending held a note of urgency. Clasping Kaphri's arm, he took a step to move away, out of the creature's direct path. Tobin, however, did not follow. "*Tobin!*"

"It'll track us," the scout told him.

*"It'll lose interest in us long before it needs to feed again. You know that! This isn't the time to seek warrior-trophies. If you stand there, it will read your action as a challenge to its territory. Move. That's an order!"*

Kaphri felt a surge of movement and a dark shape loomed out of the swirling whiteness to their left. Tobin, however, had already drawn his blade and was plunging forward as she caught a glimpse of a great, gray, shaggy body and hairy arms that ended in shiny black claws longer than her fingers.

"Tobin, no!" Before Frax's shout finished, a roar of animal rage rent the air. There was a cold, hard sense of triumph from Tobin. First blood! As the fog swirled to enfold him, he crouched and moved forward.

Frax dropped her arm and started back toward the scout as a horrible, thunderous roar of rage split the air again. There was a sense of triumph from Tobin, then a blast of red pain.

His mental presence abruptly disappeared.

*"Run!"* Frax grasped her arm again. He pulled her away from where the scout had disappeared, as the kitsk, deprived of its original prey, turned toward them. Kaphri stumbled along frantically, dried reeds rolling and splintering under her boots as she struggled to keep up with the warrior.

"But Tobin..." she protested, trying to comprehend what had just taken place.

*"Shield your mind and don't open again until I tell you to."* The underlying fear in his sending frightened her even more.

Seconds later the crushed and flattened reeds came to an abrupt end as they sloshed into water. Frax slowed, as if trying to decide what to do next. Then he pushed past her, towing her along as he waded through the shallow water. They kept going as the water deepened halfway up her thighs before dropping to ankle-deep once more. A shape loomed beside her and Kaphri shied away from it, frantic, until she realized it was only a reed. They pushed their way through a forest of the plants nearly as dense as grass and higher than Frax's head until they broke through into waist-high grass.

Kaphri quickly learned to keep her hands above the blades as the sharp edges slashed and clipped her exposed flesh in nasty, stinging nicks. Arms held high, they ran until they plunged into reeds and water again, going waist-deep before crossing to another area of grass. At last, Frax slowed the pace.

Gasping for air, she stumbled to a walk.

"You can lower your mindshields now." The sound of his voice was startling in the silence.

"*Tobin.*" She sent. "*What about Tobin?*"

"The Wyxa took him." Frax continued to push forward through the swamp grass.

"*But that thing hurt him.*" She sensed out, but there was no living presence around them. "*We can't...*"

A sudden, horrific curl of rage and frustration ran through the warrior in front of her. He spun about, his face etched in fury. "*I said the Wyxa took him. What do you think I can do? Kep, he's my brother, Priestess! How do you think I feel? First Uri, now Tobin. Our packs are gone again. Our weapons are gone. We're lost. Damn!*"

The announcement that they were lost did not surprise her as much as the revelation of his kinship to the younger warrior. She made a quick effort to gather her composure. "*What are we going to do?*"

He looked away, his mindset hard and angry. The fog was thinning and, hopefully, the kitsk had lost interest in a prolonged chase.

"*I think we've lost the Wyxa,*" he replied slowly at last. "*As long as we don't disturb anything that might draw their attention with its distress they won't be able to locate us again for a while. We can find our way out of this cursed place, but I still need to see the sky or something before I can tell which direction we should go.*"

For the first time, Kaphri noticed the fog was thinning and she could see a small space of the grass around them. It fired a twinge of hope and more questions. *"If the Wyxa took the others, how can we help them?"*

"We can't. Not now, at least." Frax was pushing his way through the grass again, pulling her behind him. *"If our only hope of bringing down the barrier is to go south, that's where our efforts must lie."*

*"But Uri and Tobin and the others..."*

*"Will be all right."*

*"We can't simply abandon them."*

Frax stopped, turning angrily again. *"Despite what Tobin says, the Wyxa don't kill the Children of Kep. They subject us to a thing they call Ankar Mekt, a devastating but survivable mental joining, and they will eventually let them go. They will survive."*

When she moved to protest again, he grasped her shoulders and gave her a hard shake. *"Listen up, Priestess. Haven't you caught on to any of this yet? I said they don't kill Geffitzi. You, on the other hand, are a different situation. Up until tonight, it was just us against the Evil One and his servants. Now another, extremely powerful player has joined the game, and its interests are not the same as ours. The Wyxa don't care about Araxis or the barrier. They never have. Their only interest will be to secure our world against the return of the force creeping around below the tower. You heard what Uri said about the first reckoning of the Wyxa—what they did to the Balandra. What do you think they'll do to you once they find out how you fit into Araxis' plans, especially if he's made an alliance with that force in the Black Temple? I don't think you want to know.*

*"Am I scaring you, Priestess? Am I?"* He gave her another shake, and she nodded her head numbly. *"Good. Because it's the only way you're going to get out of this. Now lock that fear away. Tightly. Because the Wyxa guard their lands against invasion by sensing distress in the creatures that live here. Walk lightly. Disturb nothing unless I tell you. Walk carefully around any creature that you encounter. It's the only way we'll get out of here."*

His attention suddenly riveted more sharply on her. "*Where in the hell is that cursed serpent of yours?*"

Gemma? Gemma was...

Kaphri could only shake her head.

# 39

## The Long Walk Back

"*Salt.*" Frax spat out the water he'd cautiously sipped from his cupped hand. Flicking away the liquid, he stood up to look around. His mental state was defiant, but Kaphri saw his broad shoulders sag ever so slightly. "*We're very far from where we camped last night.*"

As if he could feel her puzzlement, he glanced at her with a frown, then his expression lightened with realization. "*The water. You can't drink it; it's salt water.*" When she still did not understand, he heaved a sigh of exasperation and explained the briny nature of the Great Water.

The Great Water. A vague image of Tobin's map flashed in her mind. They were standing on the opposite side of the Palenquemas?

Leaving her to ponder this new, unpleasant turn of events, Frax withdrew from the bank of the channel to stare out across the grassy marsh that stretched around them.

She followed his line of sight toward the east. She could not tell whether the darkening blue line of the horizon was a change in the landscape or merely remnants of fog.

They had only caught their first glimpse of the sun a short while ago. The day had grown lighter around them despite the dense fog, letting them know they had awakened just before daybreak. Then a slight breeze rose and within moments the fog dissolved to reveal the current landscape of grass, mixed with channels of water that stretched to the western horizon.

And they noticed the growing discomfort of thirst.

They were still thirsty. But now they knew where they were.

How could they be so far west and the geas not react? Kaphri searched and found only emptiness where there should be a raging drive. Had these Wyxa blocked it by accident or design? Were they that powerful? Were they the force behind the geas? She would not discover the answer standing here.

The sky was a clear, cloudless dark blue over the silvery green flatness of the marshland and the sun had begun to penetrate her damp clothes with welcome warmth. Kaphri stretched her arms, grateful for the sun's heat. Her movement drew the warrior's attention.

Squinting, he looked up at the bright ball. "*You'll wish that away soon enough, Priestess. There's no water here fit to drink, and it may be awhile before we find any.*" He gave a snort of disgust. "*No food, no water. Lost. Most of our party captured...*" He shook his head.

"*What now?*"

"*We go east. Back. Start looking for food and water. Try to stay alive. Unless,*" he glanced at her, "*you have a better idea?*"

"*We should find the others.*"

"*I told you, they'll be all right. We keep going.*"

"*But—*"

He shook his head. "*Trust me; you're the one in danger here, not us. If you listen to me and do what I tell you, we'll get out of here. We can talk about the rest of it later. First, we have to survive. Let's go.*"

She soon discovered he was right about the sun. In the heavy humidity of the swamp, her clothes rapidly became uncomfortable. Frax shed his tabard without a thought, pulling it over his head and tying it about his waist, the scatter of auburn hair on his broad chest glinting copper with sweat in the sunlight. Relief was not so easy for her, however. The heavy geffitz shirt, damp with sweat and saltwater, clung to her thickly and caused her skin to itch. Once, she might have innocently pulled off her shirt without a thought, but her first encounter with this warrior still burned fresh in her memory. And Frax firmly refused to cut off what remained of her tattered sleeves when she asked, saying she would need the protection after dark. He unsympathetically advised her to push them up and make the best of it. Before long, she was hot, thirsty, hungry, filthy, and totally miserable. She could only look at him doubtfully while fanning gnats away from her face, when he said they were lucky it was spring and not summer, when the heat and insects would make the place unbearable.

But the Geffitz stalked on, and she plodded along behind him in determined silence. For once, they had a shared purpose. She had no idea who these Wyxa were, or what they wanted, but they were not going to stop her, not after she had come this far.

Frax showed her how to crack the seed heads of grass to get at the kernels inside, but he cautioned her strongly against accidentally swallowing the tough husks, so the risk of the effort was almost not worth the reward. He insisted, however, in spite of her reluctance, that she make the effort.

They had a stronger disagreement when he discovered the unprotected nest of a marsh bird.

Kaphri stared at him, dumbfounded, when he handed her one of the eggs. "*What am I supposed to do with this?*"

"*Eat it. This time of year they are fresh-laid.*" He carefully tapped holes in the ends of the one he held and sucked the inside out.

She paled. "*No.*"

He caught her hand before she could throw hers away. "*Don't be a fool. In case you haven't noticed, food is not hanging from the trees in this place. You take what you can find, and you can't be picky. Not if you hope to get out of here alive.*"

"*I will walk out alive,*" she gritted at him. They glared at each other over the egg.

"*Then you'll eat this,*" he told her. Still clenching her wrist, he managed to balance the egg and tap holes in the ends before he placed it back in her palm and released her wrist. His mental set told her she would be foolish to defy him. With a shudder, she followed his example of moments before.

Gagging, she flung the empty shell away. "*Only this once,*" she managed to send through shuddering revulsion.

He gave an exasperated sigh. "*We take only a little, when we can take it without disturbing anything. But we must take when we can. I told you, the Wyxa arduously watch over this land and its residents. The smallest sign of distress beyond what is normal in any of its creatures could bring them down on us.*"

Bent nearly double as she fought nausea, Kaphri wondered if the Wyxa might sense her distress, too, but the unsympathetic Geffitz turned away and struck off through the grass again. Resentfully, she stumbled after him.

When they came to another forest of reeds, and he handed her some tender plant shoots he uprooted from beneath the waterline, however, she took them gratefully, glad for what they were. They shared them in silence.

With all the water around them, it seemed a cruel trick of nature to Kaphri that none of it was drinkable. The sky was growing dark before they finally came upon a channel with a noticeable current flowing back in the direction from which they had come. After a cautious sip, Frax pronounced it drinkable.

Wearily, she settled beside the stream and drank her fill, then dipped handfuls to her face, reveling in the cool, clean feel as it ran off her skin. Oh, to be free, if only for this moment, of the mud and salt and heat of this place.

She opened her eyes to find the Geffitz watching her, his thoughts shielded.

As their eyes met, Frax smiled wryly and shook his head. *"If you were not here, what would a High Priestess of the Ly Kai be doing right now?"*

She tightened in instant wariness though her expression did not change. *"I am no longer a High Priestess of the Ly Kai."* The horror of the previous night, forgotten in the heat and misery of the day, stirred in her again. There were no more Ly Kai.

*"Indulge me."*

Wondering at his sudden curiosity, Kaphri took the time to splash another handful of water on her face, and to compose her thoughts. She wiped the water away with her hands. *"At this time of the day? Leading prayers, studying, reciting passages of the laws, houses' lineage, that sort of thing."*

*"A spare, bleak existence?"*

For the first time in many days she almost laughed, though it came from a bitter humor. *"Here, yes. But there is nothing about the Ly Kai Homeworld that is spare."* A shade of thoughtfulness passed over her. *"My impression is that they lived a life of easy, genteel luxury."* She gave him a few of the images she had gleaned from the Ly Kai men over the years: vast, opulent, richly furnished rooms: breathtaking, towering halls: windows of glorious, multicolor light, gardens, pools, graceful fountains.

*"Do you long for that?"*

This time she did laugh aloud. *"Me? Those are stolen images, Geffitz Lord. Crumbs fallen from another's table. Life in the tower of Kryie Karth was a struggle just to survive. No. I long for enough food to fill my belly, a safe place to sleep, and to be out of this place. Those would be luxuries."*

He did not smile. *"When this is done, when you have defeated the Evil One and removed the barrier, will you go there, to your Homeworld?"*

*"It is not my Homeworld,"* she snapped.

At his upraised eyebrows, she flushed and looked down.

*"That bad,"* he said quietly.

That bad. The bitter vehemence in her response to his question surprised her. It also left her thoughtful. She had never considered what she would do when this all ended. She knew now the power of Arylla was hers, pure and clean, if she could ever find a way to walk the Paths of Power and remove the childhood blocks. But the lure of returning to the Homeworld that Araxis had tried to bait her with in the Maugrock had not even penetrated her thoughts until now. Something inside her hardened at the thought: that place held nothing for her.

*"No. I don't think so. It's not mine."*

*"What will you do?"* he persisted, watching her intently.

Of course, he would want to know. This world belonged to him, not her.

The conversation was becoming acutely painful all of a sudden. She looked away, out across the marshland. *"I don't know. All I want is to live as I choose, without the pressure or influence of others."*

*"Yes. Well, sometimes that can seem too much to ask for."* He sounded rueful.

His tone drew her reluctant interest back into their conversation. As long as they were pursuing the subject, let it flow both ways. She looked at him, catching his eyes evenly. *"And you, Lord Geffitz? What of you? What would the Commander of the Edge of Cadarn be doing right now if you were not tramping through the middle of an enemy's lands?"*

Frax paused with a note of surprise. He studied her for a moment, then smiled without humor. *"Tramping through another enemy's lands,"* he said.

He made light of the answer, but she knew there was a grain of truth in it. When he saw she waited for further elaboration, he relented with a slight grimace. "Doing boring things for my older brother and Holderlord, Riftkin Kitahn, if he could locate me. Observing younger warriors at weapons training, leading patrols and battle exercises, watching out for Cadarn's best interests: in short, civilized things."

"Weapons training is civilized?"

"It's necessary." His reply turned sharp, bordering on the edge of anger. "Do you think the inhabitants of the north simply moved over and welcomed us into their lands years ago, Priestess? We've fought many bitter battles and many more people have died beyond the ones the Evil One killed with his cursed disease. But we've won space to live, and an uneasy peace holds with the Illians. The Hrsst," he shrugged eloquently. "Who knows? We talk, but it's difficult to know what they are thinking even at the best of times. We patrol the lands we claim against them constantly. And the Illya, their nature is so unpredictable..." he studied something in the distance. She could see a tiny muscle working along his jaw.

Unpredictable, just like the Geffitzi, she thought to herself.

Frax stared off into the distance. She could read the deep mistrust in the tense lines of his body and could guess at the doubt in his thoughts. Had he said too much already? Could she use what he said against his people? Why would she want to know about them, anyway? The same things ran through her mind, too. She waited while his doubts warred within him.

At last, he heaved a sigh. *"What do you want me to say?"* He sent and spoke the question at the same time, as if he had to put the things inside him into sound, then he dropped back into telepathy. *"The last twenty years have not been easy for us either, Priestess. We all work from sunup to sundown, just like you, struggling to grow enough food* for everyone to eat and to ensure everyone is protected and has a roof over their heads.

"When I look at it right now, after what you just showed me, I guess your people and mine aren't that different. We were forced to leave a lot behind, too. You saw Windmer. It's a wonderful place; I don't think you can deny that." She shook her head. "You can't rebuild in twenty years what took hundreds of years to create." He frowned. "Two peoples' lives in up-heaval for the last twenty years, all because of the ambitions of one man ...

"Did you know he appeared to us on one of our highest holidays? No, of course you couldn't. Every year after harvest, we celebrate Kep's blessings at the fall equinox. Back then, everyone traditionally gathered at the city of Triana, a place that was central to most of the holds. It was a tremendous event. Everyone brought their families to the harvest fair: the Holderlords would gather to conduct personal business in a relaxed atmosphere outside the formality of the Circles, while the farmers and tradesmen negotiated their business.

"With so many people gathered, the ceremony was held outside the city around an immense, ancient altar. Every family traditionally brought a bit of their harvest to place on it. There, on the third day of festivities, in the presence of everyone, the Elders of the Inner Circle would conduct a prayer of thanks to the Goddess.

"Right at the height of festivities, while our priests were leading the prayers of thanks to the Kep Mother, he suddenly appeared in the air right over the altar. At first, everyone thought he was a messenger of Kep, but he dashed that illusion when he announced he was taking all the lands of the south and that everyone must leave. He said if they didn't, he would destroy them with a horrific plague. Then he just disappeared.

"My people were stunned. He had appeared and disappeared so quickly—and he obviously had no connection to Kep. But they put him out of their minds as they returned to their homes. What else could they do? The last days before winter passed busily with little thought given to the incident. Then the sickness and deaths began. It happened slowly at first, so *it was difficult to tell if it was just the usual sickness that came with colder weather and preyed on the weak and old, or something worse. A child here, a man or woman there: but they always died. Quickly. Whenever it struck, it always acted quickly; people would complain that they felt strange, but usually not enough to stop the business of the day, then, within a short time they simply fell in their tracks."* Frax's sending drifted off to silence.

They sat there for a long time, unmoving, while a breeze rippled the grass and the sun beat down on them. Kaphri's mouth felt dry from the horror of his recollections, but she could not bring herself to lift a hand of water.

*"Do you want to hear the rest?"* It was a soft question in her head.

She nodded reluctantly. She had to know.

*"I remember the night Riftkin arrived at Windmer. He was so young—barely fourteen years old—but even at that age he led the people with the same skill as our father. I was six. I remember standing there on the portico of the main hall, the torchlight flickering around us."* She caught a flash of an image—it was the same portico she'd walked across to enter the holdhall—and her heart gave a twist of pain. But the image vanished again just as fast, and she bit back anything she would say as he continued. *"I remember my breath steaming in the cold night air, but the fire from the torches the house guards held felt hot on my face. I clutched my mother's hand while feeling the terrible tensions around me. Tensions I was too young to understand. So many people gathered before us on the green by the lake, shadows of so many people. but a weary, hushed silence hung over them all as Riftkin stepped forward to address my uncle, Lord Drayven and my mother. My father had sent my mother, Tobin and myself north a month earlier, to be with her sister, Drayven's wife and Uri's aunt. Tobin was a mere babe in arms, but I know that as he clung to her that night he felt it too.*

*"Although the sickness was in Windmer, it was not yet as bad as in the southern caers. Our healers had tried everything, but they were fighting a losing battle against it. More women and children were falling daily. Strong*

*men went out to their chores only to die in the fields and stables. It was a terrible admission of defeat that my father sent his heir north with what remained of our people.*

"*But, defiant to the end, he stayed behind with his best men, making plans to go up against the Evil One as he embraced Riftkin and sent him away.*

"*Riftkin was a pale, slim child in the flame light. But, as he urged the Holderlord of Windmer to gather his people and flee northward, he spoke with the strength he would be called on to exhibit again and again from that night forward. Lord Drayven's face was like stone, carved and cold as he stood there and listened. And the silence that followed Riftkin's words was like the silence of a grave as the people of the hedgehold awaited their Lord's decision.*

"He spoke one word: yes. He says it was the most painful word he ever spoke in his life.

"I remember the silence behind us in the hall, and how it erupted in shrieks of sorrow and relief as the people of Windmer flew into action, snatching up only what was immediately at hand, crying out names of children, husbands or wives as they prepared to leave the place. People were falling in death even as they ran. It was a horrible night, one I long to forget. It comes to me often in my dreams, as it does to every Geffitz that fled the South." Frax's eyes were haunted as he stared off across the plane, lost in the horrors of that night.

"*It was well for us that Patra Metaim, Theyr Regant and the Nighe' family already had the holds of Pen Gehrig, Fir Darryg and Eryni established in the north, or we would have been hard put to organize at all after the scourge. And things would have gone better if cursed Rhynog had not stubbornly refused to join with Cadarn or anyone that stood with us. The Aedecs took off to the northeast, drawing off whatever houses they could muster in alliance, weakening us all further. Our only consolation has been that their way has proven just as difficult and bloody as ours over the years.*" Deep anger and bitterness seeped into his sending. "*But at* least they still participate in the Circles and hold with the laws, keeping a peaceful front with us and confining their intrigues mostly to themselves."

Kaphri realized for the first time that the viciousness and petty rivalry that dominated Kryie Karth was not exclusive to the Ly Kai: anger at the same types of things permeated Frax's sendings.

"Is there that much hatred between your families?" she asked.

Frax snorted as he settled back in the grass across the stream from her. Once he'd made the decision, he seemed strangely glad to talk.

"Since the beginning of Geffitzi memory. Even before the reign of the Priests of Darkness at the Black Tower, the house of Kitahn and the house of Aedec warred. It's how the great caers of the south came to exist in the first place." The girl caught the image of giant walled fortresses, sitting high and alone, secure and deadly in their obvious purpose. "Cadarn and Rhynog were the first Caers built. Caer Glastig and Caer Azay Rhiad came later, as the Children of Kep moved out over her lands. Their lords became embroiled in the feuding between Cadarn and Rhynog, and from intrigues of their own devising. Caer Bryne and Rhydu came to exist against the others and, by desperate need, during the times of the Dark Reign. Ours is a long and bloody history, Priestess," he looked at her earnestly, "Unlike some, I will not claim everything my ancestors did was honorable and worthy, but most of it was necessary. And out of it came warriors whose feats of bravery, daring, and honor send our blood racing with their telling." A trace of memory briefly softened the hard, proud features.

"Rhydu and Bryne no longer stand, leveled, along with Caer Cadarn, by the great quaking of the world during the cataclysm that ended the Dark Reign. But Cadarn came back even stronger. It became the first and the last of the great Caers built, as new families, gaining strength and claiming lands, built the smaller holds to defend their lands. Windmer was one of the first of those, and, of all the strongholds in the south—even Cadarn—it is the only one that can make the claim it has never fallen to its enemies.

*The Caspanis are a family with a reputation for shrewdness and great military prowess; they have been invaluable allies of the Kitahns since the earliest times."*

# 40

## Truths

"*You still war with each other?*" Thoughts of these strongholds, left empty in the south, and what might happen if their lords returned to them, sent a shaft of alarm through her.

Frax shook his head and this time a smile lingered, stirred by some thought. "*Not openly with armies, at least, for many years. You see, the constant warring between the Kitahns and the Aedecs eventually began to make greater demands on the smaller houses than they were willing to shoulder in their alliances. They grew restive against the feuding families. They finally assembled in secret and devised a plot to bring the endless bickering and bloodshed to an end.*

"*It was a bold plan and would have been disastrous if any one of them had wavered the tiniest bit in their resolve. Targ Caspani and Meial Rhydec, under the pretenses of hunting parties at their respective holds, succeeded in abducting the heads of the embattled houses. They carried them off to a chapel in the Shada, the stronghold of a family who occupied their time with the pursuit of knowledge—a family with a reputation for careful neutrality in all matters relating to the great houses.*

"The companies of the lords were hot on the heels of the abductors the whole way. The Holderlords whisked the lords inside while their companies, one arriving at the west gate and one at the north, were brought up short by the massive outer walls of the fortress. When the commanders of each army got word of the other's presence the confusion deepened. Their forces, although captained by the family warlords, were only escorts to guest parties in friendly holds and not outfitted for a battle of any scale. The warlords could only send word back to their caers for their armies, and settle in at their gate to await their arrival. Meanwhile, within the chapel, since named First Peace, they seated Brein Kitahn and Stolemee Aedec side by side, much to their chagrin, and the other holders put their grievances before them. A plan was further proposed to give all the current lords equal voice in an open assembly, with a certain percentage majority required on any issue to rule a decision. A code of behavior applicable to all the Geffitzi people would be drawn up, and two ruling bodies: the Lords', or Outer, Circle, made up of the Holderlords, and an independent, impartial group, the Inner Circle, made up of wise and learned elders who owed liege to no house regardless of their bloodline, who would oversee the impartial administration of the laws.

"The minor holders presented a solid front and Brein and Stolemee were confronted with the unpleasant fact that, united, the others could set a formidable force against them if they refused. And neither dared refuse if the other agreed, seeing that would set the whole land and their ancient enemy against them. Barely containing their fury, they acquiesced.

"That ended the wars between Cadarn and Rhynog, though peace is hardly the word to apply, either. Brein would not receive his ally, Targ Caspani, for more than a year after, until Brein's son, Geyr, aggrieved at the rift between such good friends, arranged for the Lord of Windmer's admission to a celebration at Caer Cadarn. There Targ confronted Brein, boldly taking him to task for his obstinacy. He whisked him away once again, this time to a library in Cadarn, where he proceeded to point out other areas besides war, in which Brein could best Stolemee to the benefit of the caer's coffers rather than as a drain upon them. All within the new laws.

"Since that day the Lords of Kitahn have taken every opportunity to best Rhynog that has presented itself to them. And for two hundred years, peace of a sort has reigned over the south, with battles won and lost in commerce, social events and government instead of on the battlefield. The defenses of Caer Cadarn and Rhynog, along with the other holds, are continuously maintained and refined, however. To do less would be a betrayal of our ancestry.

"But, there are always unforeseen challenges to be met. The Lords of Cadarn never cease to study war. Which is why Riftkin, at such a young age, is a powerful force in the Lords' Circle. The red and green of Cadarn is charged with overseeing the defenses of our people in exile."

Frax paused, any amusement at the story of his ancestors' tumultuous history fading in the face of the attack the Geffitzi had not been able to meet. For the first time, there was no accusation in his eyes when he looked at her. Instead, she saw deep sadness. *"It is not an honorable enemy who attacks and does not allow its opponent the slightest hope of fighting back. That is foulness even beyond the Aedecs."*

He got to his feet. *"Enough rest. Avoid getting your clothes wet. When the sun goes down you will get cold. You don't have enough flesh left on your bones to get you through the night without a fire, and a fire's not possible out here. The light can be seen too easily. Kep, the night is going to be cold."*

They resumed their journey, each wrapped in their own thoughts.

The sky behind them was running from crimson, to mauve, to rich, dark blue when Frax allowed them to stop again. They were in the middle of a grass-covered field and the predicted chill of the evening air was beginning to close about them, causing their breath to steam. Frax drew a knife from his boot and weighed it thoughtfully in his hand before he passed it over to her.

"Cut as much grass as you can, and pile it for a bed. And, for Kep's sake, don't cut off your hand."

She took the blade with a glare, and set about the task.

The grass was easy to cut at its tender base. Before long, they had flattened a circle and had a fair mound of grass at its center. Wearily Kaphri dropped at the edge of the pile and held out his blade to him.

He studied her for a long moment before he mindspoke. "Keep it. We're at a point now where we don't know what will happen next. Just be careful."

"I've carried it before without injuring myself," she snapped tiredly. The moment she sent it, she wished she hadn't.

He stiffened, reminded of her escape at the barrier. "Yes. So you have." Shielding, he stretched out in the grass, and they silently watched the rich colors of the sky fade to darkness and the swamp settle into velvet blackness around them.

As the first star gleamed brilliantly above them, Kaphri blinked in sudden realization. This was the first time since being in the south that she had actually had the opportunity to see nightfall. Before, there had always been a canopy of tree limbs overhead or the distraction of tasks as they made camp. She tilted her head to look up.

"The Even' star," Frax's observation held a note of curiosity. "That is...?"

A tiny jolt of dismay ran through her when she realized he was watching her. "Arylla," she answered softly.

"Ah." He exhaled heavily. "So, our Star of Promise fuels the wall of our exile. That is a cruel irony. It's well we didn't know that these past years."

She looked around in surprise as Frax moved up to settle beside her. He picked up a twig of grass and absently rolled it between his fingers, the seed head fluttering as he frowned. "You say you get your power from them. Are these things we name stars Gods to you?"

"Gods? Not really. They're just suns with worlds around them, like this one."

*"Like our sun? All of them?"*

*"Not all, but many of them."*

*"You know this for truth?"*

She shrugged. *"The Ly Kai have always known this."*

*"How do you draw power from them?"*

*"The sun shines and plants grow. Perhaps that's how."*

*"Then shouldn't you be able to use them all?"*

*"It doesn't work that way. I don't know why. There are certain Stars that move across the Ly Kai sky in a specific pattern. Those are the stars of the Hierarch, from which we draw power. Each one of them passes through a certain point in the sky where it seems to hold influence over the Homeworld for a period of time. Children born while a certain star is at its zenith are able to draw power from that star. It is their Birthstar. It influences their ability to do certain things. Anyone can draw on a star below his or her own position in the Hierarch, but attempting to use anything of power higher than one's own is dangerous. You might do it for a short time, but if you persist, it will kill you. It burns you up. The weaker stars hold influence over the sky for many days, the stronger for shorter times, which means there are many more Ly Kai born to the stars of the lower levels of the Hierarch."*

*"And Arylla?"*

*"Araxis and Alexar were the first to be born to it in two thousand years."*

***

Two thousand years. And then three births in rapid succession. Too strange to be an accident. A chill ran through him. If they had re-discovered some ancient secret, how many more births had there been since?

No point in pursuing that right now, however. It would only be speculation and there was other, more useful information to be gathered at this moment. *"Why so few, if those of Arylla are so powerful?"*

She shrugged. *"The days of its influence are extremely few."* A slight sense of bitterness ran through her sending. *"I know very little about it. Even its—my—symbol is new to me; there was certainly no information about Arylla in the tower for me to study."*

"Don't you think that strange, considering?" Frax asked. "If it's so important, doesn't it seem there should be more information. Scholars devote their lives to the pursuit of such knowledge. And Priests." He added.

*"Perhaps there's information somewhere. But the abandoned Ly Kai feared Arylla, and me. They would not put such information in my hands."*

"Yet, at one point they were enthusiastic enough to follow Araxis here."

*"Yes. They never denied that."* Kaphri frowned mentally. *"They just claim—claimed— he became evil and betrayed them after they came here."*

"Huh. If only they knew... Did they blame the influence of my world for making him change?"

*"No. Only Arylla."*

"I wonder if there are books in this city that you speak of."

He felt a flicker of surprise from the girl. *"That's a thought. Maybe they call to me."*

"I've never heard of a book laying a geas on anyone. Though, maybe something, or someone, wants you to see those books. Was anyone left behind in the city?" He frowned when Kaphri shook her head. "So sure?"

*"Everyone fled northward in fear of his retribution."*

And that bothered him. "Why flee northward, away from the gate and any hope of rescue, even if they thought it destroyed?" he asked her.

*"They feared Araxis' vengeance after they rejected him. And they had turned their backs on all the Ly Kai arguments against following him here. And Alexar did not re-open the gate after Araxis broke it."*

"Only those born of Arylla have the power to open a gate?"

*"To open or to repair. From what little I gathered, the Ly Kai never held hope of rescue."*

Even with a child born of Arylla in their midst, that they could have used to repair the gate home? They had feared the power that much. Why? *"Still,"* he said, *"to flee the area and strike out into the unknown. It doesn't make sense."*

The girl shrugged again without reply and Frax stared up at the star his people named the Even' Star. They believed if one greeted the star when it first appeared in the night sky, it would bring them luck. Maybe if someone had seen it on a specific night twenty-odd years ago... Sadly, things weren't that simple. *"Is this the same night sky as the Ly Kai world?"*

*"No. It's different here. I can still find most of the Hierarch, but the stars are scattered and two are missing."*

*"Are they as strong here?"*

*"I don't know,"* she confessed. *"I can't compare them."*

*** 

In the silence that followed, more stars appeared overhead and Kaphri found herself searching them, seeking out those of the Hierarch she knew. They were scattered widely across the darkness, but she still recognized them. A chill ran over her when she realized what she was doing. Those stars had claimed back every one of the Ly Kai that lived in Kryie Karth except two. She bit her lip against the unexpected sadness that crept through her. She had not liked the others, but they had not deserved to die, and certainly not in the manner they had, at Araxis' hand. Turning her head, she stared out across the flatness of the swamp until she realized her breath created a heavy curtain now when she exhaled. Frax had been right: with the setting of the sun, the temperature had dropped dramatically. She shivered as a slow stream of white vapor rose from the ground of the swampland. Even the breath of the marsh was chilled.

Together they watched the eerie columns of ragged vapor drift in the starlight.

*"It is said,"* Frax began after a long silence, *"that those wisps are spirits of Wyxa who have moved beyond this world to another, purely mental,*

*plain of existence. Their spirit forms return each night to act as guardians over this land."*

She looked at him. *"Is it true? Where do they go?"*

The Geffitz shrugged, surprised at her interest: he had always considered it just a child's tale. *"I don't know."* He reached up and rumpled his hair vigorously, the heavy, dark strands glinting between his fingers in the starlight. She caught a strong sense of weary resignation from him. *"And right now I don't care. We have another long day tomorrow. You'd better get some sleep."*

Kaphri did not argue as she moved to curl up in the middle of the mound. Frax shoved more of the grass over her, then he settled back at its edge to take first watch. She was sure the nagging fear of the dreams, or fear of the Wyxa, or worry about their missing companions would keep her awake. But nothing overpowered the needs of her weary body. She plummeted into sleep.

\*\*\*

Once again, Kaphri woke to the closeness of fog.

For a long, confused moment, she stared at the sun-browned, muscular forearm lying inches from her face before she felt the weight across her ribcage and the heat of a body against hers.

She tensed, her heart racing. Had the Wyxa attacked them again? She sent out a quick tendril of searching and touched the warrior sleeping behind her.

Sleeping?

Behind her, Frax muttered something indistinguishable and his arm tightened around her, drawing her up against his body. He breathed a contented sigh, his warm breath brushing the skin of her neck. It sent an unexpected flame of pleasure shooting through her. Her senses, clean from sleep, filled with the scent of him. It was a pleasant smell, slightly musky, and for a moment, heavily male. For the first time, Kaphri became aware of the hard muscles beneath taut leather pressing her back and legs.

Everything inside of her twisted sharply with awareness. It was a painfully delicious, confusing sensation, and it terrified her. Choking back panic, she tried to lift his arm so she could slide out from underneath.

She froze at the soft draw of breath behind her.

*"Priestess? Is something wrong?"* His breath fanned the side of her bare head, heightening the awareness that held her in its tingling grip.

*"No. I was just getting up."*

*"Up?"* His sending was drowsy and mildly amused. *"It's still dark. Be still and go back to sleep."*

To her rising horror, his arm tightened, pulling her closer to him. He nuzzled the side of her neck then pressed his cheek against the smooth skin of her head and fell back into sleep.

Sleep? Panic held her rigid. Sleep was not what her body wanted. She might be untouched and ignorant of the details, but everything in her was screaming for his attention. She could not stay next to him this way. A shiver ran over her.

Frax was instantly awake, every muscle in him tensing. She tried to stop breathing in the silence that followed.

*"Priestess?"* The word carried a different tone now. Aware, questioning. And gentle. Too gentle.

*"Let me go!"* It burst from her. Panic, fear, pleading.

It was too late. Before she could move, he shifted, sliding his arm forward so his weight rested on his elbow and he was above her, his body flattening her to the ground. His attention tightly focused as he stared down at her. *"Priestess?"* Again. It was one word, but the question behind it... The languid promise...

*"Please. Please let me go."*

His hand gently cupped her cheek, the sensation of the rough skin of his fingers on her flesh becoming the focus of her whole world for a dizzying moment. She closed her eyes, terrified at the thought of what might follow. Waiting.

Inside a long silence.

She opened her eyes slowly. Frax stared down at her with an amused expression. *"Are you all right?"*

All right? He set her on fire, and then he asked if she was all right? He—

A sudden chill doused the heat in her. He had done nothing. *"Let me up, please."*

He rolled off her without comment.

Shaken, she sat up.

As the grass fell away, the cold air hit her back with a shock that nearly sent her nestling back down again, but she dared not. She turned her head away, her cheeks burning with a mixture of excitement and embarrassment she prayed Frax could not see.

He drew a slow, deep breath as he pushed to a sitting position behind her. *"What was it? Another dream? We're not moved again?"*

Kaphri shook her head, unwilling to send a reply in her current agitated mental state. Instead, she reached out to touch the ground. Her hand met the cut stubble of grass. Frax was also checking around him. As they moved further apart, she caught herself regretting the further loss of warmth and another blush of hot embarrassment ran over her. The cold was enough to make anyone wish for something to break it, she told herself defensively. A shiver ran over her to confirm it.

Frax heaved a sigh of relief behind her as he settled back down into the spot where he'd been sleeping. *"Are you sure you're all right?"*

*"Yes."* She had taken advantage of their activity to move to the edge of the grass mound, where she sat rigidly now. *"Did you try to wake me to sit watch?"*

*"No. The more I thought about it, the more pointless it seemed. We both desperately need the rest. For tonight, I think, we'll be all right."* She

heard the grass rustle as he burrowed deeper into its sweet-smelling warmth. *"We can't find our way in this fog. You may as well settle down and go back to sleep."*

When she didn't move, a sensation of concern came from him again. *"What's the matter...?"* Then sudden comprehension replaced the sense of question in his sending. *"Ah."*

Her cheeks flamed. *"I have never slept with—"*

*"And you still haven't."* He cut her off, irritation running through his sending. *"Kep, Kaphri, it's called shared body heat. It's a means of survival. I don't have to resort to attacking little half-starved innocents to satisfy my needs."*

The conversation was moving in an uncomfortable direction. *"The Ly Kai did not touch,"* she snapped defensively. *"I do not feel comfortable being touched."* That was not totally true, especially of late.

There was a long moment of disbelief, then Frax burst into strong, heartfelt laughter. *"I've dragged or carried you, willing or unwilling, nearly half the way to this point."* He gasped when he finally caught his breath. *"How much touching must you endure before you become accustomed to it?"*

She looked at him, discomfited by the truth in his words. *"That does not mean I liked it."* She pointedly laid down at the edge of the mound with her back to him.

He gave a throaty chuckle as he settled deeper into the grass at the center. *"Ah, Priestess, sometimes I almost allow myself to forget you're female, but you really, really are, aren't you?"*

Inexplicably irritated at his comment, she curled into a ball and nestled in what sparse grass she had around her while wishing mightily for one of the warrior's long, dark cloaks to curl up in. Even Gemma's small presence would have helped. But the cloaks were gone, lost at the edge of this swamp. And Gemma? Who knew?

Kaphri's heart gave a twist of loneliness and apprehension at the thought of the little dragon.

Her heart racing, her body chilled, and angry, she could not return to sleep. She lay awake in the silence, watching the fog grow lighter around her and listening resentfully to the soft, regular breathing of the warrior sleeping behind her.

# 41

## Painful Revelations

Innocent.

She was as sweetly innocent a female as he'd ever encountered, which was surprising, since she'd been the only female in a place with—what?—twenty-five? Twenty-six men? And she was not the worst-looking little thing, dirt and all, he'd ever seen.

They must have hated her a lot.

Last night had been a bit of cruel diversion. He would be the first to admit he was not above that sort of thing, but it had been too irresistible not to tease her. He wasn't laughing, however. His actions were more than a game. It had been necessary for him to re-establish certain boundaries that were eroding between them in the past day-and-a-half.

Because of the cursed swamp. The endless heat and hunger. The shared misery had enticed them to talk. To share information. They talked too much, gotten too comfortable. He was careless and stupid to get so relaxed with the enemy.

Let her think she'd been in danger of things going further. She hadn't been, but let her think so. Now she was on edge again, sensitive to the threat he presented.

A certain necessary distance had been re-established.

That necessary distance blurred again over the next few days as their struggles became an endless stretch of heat, water, mud, weariness, insects, hunger, fog and cold in the slog through the swamp his people called the Palenquemas.

The girl knew nothing of survival techniques. He had to show her how to smear her flesh with mud to discourage the stinging, biting insects that tormented them day and night. At first astonished and repulsed, she quickly grew to appreciate the relief it offered. The crusted dirt might dry and cause their skin to itch, but it was considerably more tolerable than the burning, itching welts of the bites. The leeches that attached to them when they waded the numerous, watery forests of freshwater reeds became her particular horror, however. Just the thought of the things, after he explained what they were, sent her into paroxysms of shudders. Although she did not voice it, he could see her utter appall, and after each passage, he patiently and thoroughly searched her over, removing any he found, before he checked himself. Then they would both swallow one of the bitter orange berries that abound in the place, 'to prevent any sickness' he would say, before they moved on.

Eventually she ate whatever he handed her without argument, trusting to his judgment, clung to his back without protest to cross deep waters, and curled up with him, both of them grateful for the warmth against the freezing late-spring nights. During that time, there was no sign the Wyxa were aware of their presence.

On the fourth day, the blue haze of the east became a cypress swamp that made their movements even more difficult as they struggled with treacherous footing, impassable places they had to backtrack around, and an increased need to watch out for the denizens of the place. Their passage was merciless and grueling, and by mid-afternoon things became an endless, torturous blur through which Kaphri could barely stumble. Frax watched her lethargy with a rising concern. The heat, humidity, parasites, hunger, and filthy water, singly, were dangerous. In combination, they could be deadly.

It jolted him when he noticed how thin and frail she had become. For the first time the Commander of the Edge realized the swamp might kill her. If she gave in to silent despair, it would definitely see her end.

***

*"Milady."*

Kaphri looked up to see the Geffitz warrior smiling at her as he held a branch back to clear her way. He motioned for her to pass with a broad, elegant gesture that could have only originated from actual, courtly etiquette. The sight of such ridiculous gallantry, the gleam of even, white teeth in a mud-encrusted face, caused her to pause.

He had to be every bit as miserable and desperate as she, yet he was taking the time to cajole her out of her despondence. Kaphri's dark eyes flashed a gratitude deeper than simple thanks as she stepped past him. Behind her Frax heaved a silent sigh of relief.

Within the next ten steps, the easier mood shattered.

*"Priestess, stand still and keep your thoughts calm."* Frax's abrupt warning whispered in her mind.

Kaphri froze in mid-step. *"Danger? What?"*

*"A kitsk, ahead of us."* The Geffitz, in the lead again, paused. His sending was carefully expressionless to discourage any startled reaction from her.

Hunting? A chill ran down her spine as she recalled the long black claws that slashed at Tobin through the fog. Her eyes searched the heavy undergrowth in front of them feverishly, but the greenery was too dense for her to find it. Giving up on that approach, she cautiously reached out and found the animal moving slowly across their path perhaps forty paces ahead.

She dared a brief touch of its mind. The burning desire to satiate a gnawing hunger caused her to gasp. *"What should we do?"*

*"Pray to the Goddess it scares up something in the next few steps,"* Frax answered grimly. *"If not, we're in big trouble. If it scents us, it will attack. Even if we slip past, it will probably find our trail before we can get far enough away to be safe. Once a hungry kitsk gets a scent, the creature will not abandon the hunt until it feeds."*

Pointless to run, then.

Kaphri glanced around. All the trees were large-girthed and tall, their lowest branches too high overhead.

*"Damn."* Frax had obviously eliminated that possibility, too. *"If that thing attacks, there may not even be time for the Wyxa to pull us out."* He was careful to keep his sendings calm, and she struggled to follow his example.

Strong fear or distress—he said those might bring the Wyxa right to them, to snatch them away, the way they had taken Tobin. But they had not taken the scout until the kitsk injured him. The kitsk or the Wyxa? Poor choices and certain disaster, either.

She finally sighted the great, shaggy hulk of the thing through the dense leaves.

*"There must be another way."* She studied the mat of dark fur. Down on all fours, snuffling in the dirt, it didn't look as if it could move quickly, but she knew better. She had felt the speed of an attacking kitsk.

*"How? And none of those pain blasts of yours unless I tell you to. That might be our only, last hope."*

*"No."* That would certainly bring the Wyxa.

The kitsk stopped moving. Kaphri felt the color drain from her face as it rose on its hind legs. The thing would tower well over

Frax's head. The glint of black, knife-like claws hanging loosely at its sides sent her stomach queasy.

Crouching in the brush, they held their breath until it lowered back to the ground and began to shamble forward again.

She wrestled with the problem: how could they get rid of the creature without distressing it?

"Whatever you do, don't move," Frax cautioned. "If it sees us, we're done. My grandfather always insisted the Wyxa used the kitsks to guard their lands, watching for disturbances along the paths of their movements to tell them when something was amiss. One thing for sure, the warriors of Cadarn never could resist going up against the cursed things at any opportunity."

And the Wyxa had snatched Tobin so fast in the earlier attack. What to do? They were dead if the kitsk discovered their trail or saw them; they exposed themselves to the Wyxa if they acted to prevent it discovering them.

"Sleep."

"Can you do that?"

"Perhaps. I've been forced to do much worse." She did not sever the sending, letting the Geffitz felt the sticky, smothering weight of the Lake God's mind as she shuddered at the vivid recall.

"Then do it now, Priestess, before it's too late."

She reached out again, seeking the kitsk's mind. The creature was searching for food on the cool, wet ground, its hunger like a burning ember that was beginning to flare into a consuming flame. She moved cautiously, seeking an opening in its thoughts through which to invade. She doubted it would understand what her intrusion was, but she might startle it into a reaction the Wyxa would detect as something awry.

Wariness seized the animal and Kaphri nearly fled out of its mind before she caught herself. Had the creature become aware of them, crouching in the shadows? Was it, at this moment, charging her helpless form?

No. The kitsk was standing immobile, watching the play of sunlight on some nearby leaves.

She forced herself to relax. Control. She must maintain control. She waited.

After what seemed a lifetime, the kitsk decided its alarm was unfounded and turned its attention back to the quest for food, giving her the opening she sought. Before the creature noticed, she slipped into its thought-stream.

"*It was nothing,*" she sent through its mind. "*A leaf shaken by a breeze.*" This was a good place. A safe place. A pause here would be most restful.

The kitsk shook its head, resisting the urge she pressed upon it. Kaphri held firm, not lightening her touch, but waiting until the resistance stopped being an active force before she could continue.

"*Sleep would be good. It was cool and dark here. This would be a safe place to hide from the heat of the day. Sleep.*"

The focus in the creature's mind was changing, the flame of hunger dimmed by a creeping muzzy sensation. Sleep. Much too sleepy to hunt. Cool darkness was welcome. The kitsk half-heartedly searched about a moment or two longer, checking its surroundings, then settled to the ground.

Sleep. Sleep would be good. As the urge took hold, she began to edge out of its thoughts, wrapping a portion of the drowsiness about her so her withdrawal would not stir it to alertness again. She lingered at the edges of its mind to be sure it fell into a sleep state before slipping out.

"*Priestess?*" Frax's arm shot out to catch her about the waist before she collapsed. A sound now would be disastrous.

A few deep breaths drove the cobwebs of drowsiness back

enough for her to find steady feet. When she pushed away, Frax's grip lightened, but he did not let go.

"*All right?*" When she nodded, he released her.

Kaphri straightened, discreetly trying to flex as many of her muscles as possible to force the last vestiges of induced sleepiness away.

"*I'm impressed. Can you do that with any creature?*"

"*You mean a Geffitz?*" He knew she could.

He sighed. "*I guess I owe you thanks. Let's get out of here.*"

Shortly afterward they found a stream of running water in the seemingly endless swamp and waded upstream for a long stretch to eliminate the threat of pursuit from the hungry kitsk when it woke.

\*\*\*

"*Are you sure this is wise?*" Kaphri stared at the roaring fire in the middle of the small, elevated island in the cypress grove.

"*Lightning strikes cause fires in here all the time,*" he'd explained.

As night settled, she understood the real reason for the blaze. Eyes caught the firelight and glowed out of the darkness at them from every direction. She watched them uneasily, not interested in discovering what they were or what motivated them. She feared touching on the hunger of another plains cat, or its swamp brother.

After a while, Frax glanced up from where he sat across the flames, sharpening one of his blades. He grinned wickedly as he took in her tense posture.

With the kick of a booted foot, he shoved a large branch deeper into the flames, making them burn more brightly. "*On nights like this,*" he said, "*Geffitzi sit around the fire and tell scary stories that would curdle one's blood.*"

She frowned at him. "*Scary stories?*" She caught a mental image of eeriness and spirits of the dead. What kind of entertainment would that make? The thought of Araxis flitted through her mind, and she shuddered.

"Don't the Ly Kai people have any frightening stories they tell for amusement, just to make their skin crawl?" He switched to speaking aloud, reinforced by mindspeech, and his voice dropped eerily lower in pitch.

"No."

He frowned. *"Any stories?"*

"No."

*"Not very imaginative, are they?"* He slid the knife back into its sheath and picked up a long stick to poke at the flames. *"We have many stories. Many of my people out in the countryside do not read written words, making the telling important. Stories pass down from elder to child. Some tales teach our history. Some teach a lesson or a fact that is important to remember."* He frowned thoughtfully. *"We have lore-masters—people who learn and record the stories and travel about from hold to hold, sharing them. When Uri was young, he took the first training to do that. That's how he comes up with some of the strange stuff he knows. He really likes that sort of thing. But he can't pursue it now."* A shower of sparks flew skyward as Frax thrust the stick hard into the depths of the fire. *"When the plague came, the heir to holdership in the Caspani family died and Uri became the next in line, forcing him onto a different path in his life."* He stared across at her, his eyes picking up a brief glow like the animals that hovered in the darkness about them.

Kaphri swallowed hard, unable to tear her gaze from his.

*"There is one story all the Children of Kep learn at their mother's knee. A child may ask if it's true and his parents and grandparents will only shrug and smile. Who can say? No one knows. But other peoples of our world tell similar stories, too, about a small, mysterious creature. Almost god-like, perhaps...?"* He broke off and stared at the fire, chewing his lower lip as if he were coming to some decision. She waited, not daring to breathe. After a moment of tense silence, he seemed to make his choice. His focus came back to her. *"It's called a Guardian."*

A Guardian? She had heard the word before. He used it on the day they took her captive.

A wave of cold dread rushed over her. No. She did not want to hear this. She wanted him to stop. Somehow, she could not bring herself to say it.

*"It's always described as a small golden dragon. Stories have it appearing down through the ages in different places, with different peoples, at different times, but its effect always seems to be the same. Its presence influences the events of our world. A man might have second thoughts about something he's about to do, or he might hesitate in an action only to find out later he narrowly avoided disaster by the merest blink of an eye. A people may view the appearance as a sign, making a choice they would not have otherwise considered. A leader might suddenly reconsider the repercussions of an act he's about to take. It doesn't advise or direct. 'As stone-tongued as a Guardian', is an Illian saying. But its presence is enough to re-direct events."* He paused as if waiting for her to comment or protest, but she was silent, remembering how the warriors had reacted on seeing Gemma when they captured her in Omurda, Recalling now how Frax called Gemma "Guardian" and the dragon accepted it, and how he had refused to let Tobin slay her. At the time, the horror of falling captive to them and the isolation he imposed on her had pushed any questions about those things out of her mind.

She felt him watching her intently, but she avoided his eyes. A great ache twisted her heart. If Gemma was this Guardian-thing, as he seemed to be saying, was she only seeking to influence her in some way? Could Gemma be using her somehow?

Sudden fury seized her. *"This is just another little mental game to see how I'll react,"* she flared. *"You have never liked Gemma."*

*"Like? 'Like' doesn't enter into the matter with a conniving, manipulating serpent. 'Like' is not a part of its purpose."*

*"You lie."*

*"Do I?"* The question was hard. Realistic. Her fury withered in the face of it.

Kaphri realized she was twisting her fingers in agitation. She laced them together to stop. Somewhere deep inside of her the answer to a question she had never asked, but that had always been there, was forming: Gemma had a purpose, just as all other things had purpose.

No pain. Prayer-like, the thought ran desperately through her mind. Please do not let me feel this hurt. Please—no pain.

Still, it came. Like a roaring whirlpool, sucking her down its maw.

"*Priestess?*" The warrior's mental prod was gentle.

She looked up, her expression coldly void of the turmoil tearing at her.

"*It had to be done sometime,*" he said softly.

"*Did it?*" She could not keep the icy anger out of her sending. This was not the first time he'd told her something that shattered her world. Did he draw some perverse pleasure from doing that? She stared across the fire at him, hating him for telling her.

She half-expected to see a gleam of harsh amusement in his eyes.

Instead, Frax looked weary. "*You knew already, deep inside. You must have wondered at her interest in you. You were just afraid to give it voice, for fear of what you might discover. Uri might have told you more cleverly, but he's not here and it needed to be done.*"

"*Why? Why did it need to be done?*"

"*Because she's a Guardian, Priestess, and, considering how long she's been with you, the lack of her presence around you right now means as much as her being here would.*"

"*What?*" She stared at him for a moment before comprehension came to her. "*You mean what is she trying not to influence right now? That is ridiculous. The Wyxa took her captive when they took Uri.*"

"*Do you believe that?*"

She wanted to believe it, but something inside her refused. There was a reason Gemma was not with her.

She did not want to examine the pain the thought fired. She drew on cold remoteness, instead. "Hredroth, *if I allow myself to think like that, then everyone on this world wants something from me: the Geffitzi, the Ly Kai, Araxis, the force in the tower! The crystal... Who knows what else? The geas, I dare not even think on. I feel pushed, pulled, driven, and lured by everything around me. I am here for everyone else's purpose but my own.*"

"*Everyone else's purpose—!*" Frax's anger was a sudden mental scorch. "*Kep, Kaphri, if you only knew the depths of the manipulation around us—how we're all being used. You don't get it, do you? We've been as much your prisoners since we captured you in that ravine, as you have been ours. We've protected you, fed you, guided you, clothed you—rescued you. We haven't had a choice. That's what's frustrating. We have no choice. And neither do you!*" He glared out into the darkness. In the firelight she saw the muscle of his jaw line working with anger. "*Look, I'm sorry. I truly am. You don't have to like this, but we're stuck with each other. I can't walk away. And I can't afford sympathy for you, because it's my world at stake. The only way I can look at this is you have to do it because no one else can.*"

"I am not one of your heroes, striding out of one of those legends of yours, Frax Kitahn," she snapped bitterly. "*I am not made of such bold stuff.*"

He gave a bark of harsh laughter. "*Is that how you think? That those people went seeking?*" He turned back to her now, his expression hard, unrelenting. "*Kep, Kaphri, no one in their right mind sets out to be a hero. All the old stories that send our blood racing—they weren't that way for the people involved in them. Ask any of the old warriors: they'll tell you. They were just as scared as anyone, and they weren't happy when the task fell to them. But they did what they had to do, anyway.*

"*This is the same. I don't know if we'll succeed, either, but we at least have to try. And I will swear this to you,*" his face was pale but unyielding in the firelight, *"there is nothing I would ask of you that I would not expect to be by your side, to help you."*

*"I do not want to talk about this anymore. I'm going to sleep."* She shielded before he could say anything and laid down on the hard earth as close to the fire as she dared.

What Frax said was outrageous, she fumed. She fought to ignore the cold sensation deep inside her. Gemma would not... She had never made an effort to influence her. She did not tell her what to do. She was just there for support. She was just... Gemma.

Kaphri's whole being had become one huge ache. Was it possible that what the Geffitz said was true? She wanted to scream denial. She wanted to shove it aside as a lie, but she couldn't do that, either. There was an immense amount of manipulation around her. It had started before her birth. Araxis had dragged the Geffitzi into it.

That did not make Gemma a part of it.

Her thoughts kept circling in her head, pulling her apart with conflicting emotions. No matter which way they went, however, they always came back to one thought; what the Geffitz warrior said rang too true: Gemma had made a huge impact on her life by being with her.

For a long time, she laid there, staring at the fire, mulling the thought. What would she be like without Gemma? Far away, in a lonely tower, with no kindness or happiness, constantly surrounded by resentment and anger, what might she have become without the serpent's companionship. What twisted, bitter creature might the little dragon's mere presence have averted? But what could Gemma possibly expect in return? Any power Kaphri might control was far beyond her reach. Gemma knew that too well. Gemma had never indicated she expected anything from her. She was simply there, offering companionship, giving her strength to do what she needed to do.

And now this world, Gemma's world, was in trouble. She could not think of refusing to help. Gemma had taught her to care too much to turn her back.

Kaphri opened her eyes. Was that it? Could it be that simple? Was her inner character the thing the dragon had taken a hand in forming? She sat up to look across the fire at the Geffitz.

He glanced up moodily.

*"Are we sitting watches tonight?"*

He nodded.

*"I will take the first watch."*

*"Just like that?"* His eyes narrowed in the firelight. *"No cries of betrayal, no bitter recriminations? No accusations, no tears or self-pity?"*

Her chin came up in defiance. *"I know what I know, and no matter what you say, no matter what name you put on her, Gemma would never do me harm. I trust her. And even if what you say is true, it could have been worse."*

*"Much worse,"* he agreed softly. She couldn't interpret the expression in his eyes. It vanished as he abruptly shifted back to the issue immediately at hand. *"Keep the fire going. And whatever you do, don't stir up any of the creatures out there. If something feels like it's getting out of hand, wake me."* Without any further comment, he settled swiftly to sleep.

***

Despite Kaphri's acceptance of what Frax told her, a certain degree of tension had risen between them once more. A silence settled over them that neither had the energy or will to break as, each immersed in their own thoughts, they pushed on.

Their fifth day in the Palenquemas was a miserable, endless stretch of heat, hunger, and mud as they finally made their way to the other side of the cypress swamp. By the sixth day, they were happy to find themselves back in a marsh area, although the plant life was more bizarre and difficult to make their way through. There were broad stretches of low-growing vicious brambles they had to work their way around, and scattered, thick-stemmed, grayish weeds with fuzzy leaves that burned the flesh like a firebrand when they brushed them. Strange black, leafless trees thrust up across the flatness, their limbs bare except for occasional ragged, trailing tangles of dull moss. There was no green of spring on the land. It was a place of tired grays, despite the blue sky that hung hotly above them.

Sunset took on a sullen orange color that made Frax mutter uneasily about an approaching storm, and, as the sky darkened, a low wind began to rattle the marsh grass and caused the eerie trees to creak ponderously when an occasional strong gust hit them. The wind took up a sad moan over the distance to underscore their isolation. Lightning flickered on the horizon in all directions.

As darkness thickened around them, the eerie trees appeared to take on a strange blue glow. At first Kaphri thought her imagination played with her, but as the night grew darker the light increased.

"Graffoi," Frax said when he noticed her uneasy glances. "Witch-fire trees. They only grow in the deepest, most ancient parts of the Palenquemas. We are nearing the heart of Wyxan territory."

"*Should we approach so close to them?*"

He shrugged. "*It's the last place they'd think to look for us.*"

"*The others...?*" Gemma?

He shook his head. "*I told you, the Wyxa will release them eventually. We keep going; otherwise this is all a waste of our efforts.*"

It would be futile to argue with him. She only hoped he was right and Gemma would find her once they escaped this place.

Looking at the graffoi trees Kaphri sighed. Their blue glow painfully reminded her of the blue light of Freya. It stirred an emptiness that would not leave her as the night deepened around them. She shivered as she huddled in the grass.

\*\*\*

She woke to the deep rumble of thunder and cold splats of rain on her skin. The wind had risen sharply, sweeping across the marsh with an angry howl, bending the grass and driving the raindrops in gusts before it. A blaze of lightning lit the area, followed by an ear-numbing crash of thunder. Pellets of ice pounded down for a moment then turned into a gushing downpour.

Frax! Where was the Geffitz? Kaphri started to her feet in terror.

A hand closed about her arm, pulling her back to the ground. *"Stay down. The lightning..."*

As if in response, there was another blinding flash and roar. A graffoi tree in the distance sent a shower of sparks into the air. She scurried backwards to come up against him.

They huddled together, the rain driving so hard and cold it was sometimes difficult to catch her breath. She'd been in storms before, but nothing like this. All the forces of nature were unleashing their fury on this desolate, miserable piece of land. Each searing blaze of the sky caused her to twitch in terror.

The Wyxa must surely detect her distress. Fight as she might, she could not stop the panic rising inside her.

*"Talk to me, Kaphri. Tell me what it was like to grow up in the tower of the north."* The words fell into her mind, firm and clear, breaking through her fear and confusion.

Gratefully, she snatched the diversion. Burying her face against his tabard, she picked a point in time that later she did not recall and poured out her memories while the storm raged about them.

# 42

# Sigalithe'

Gemma's absence gnawed at Kaphri. Much as she mistrusted it, she sensed Frax's question was valid. What was her little companion trying, or not trying, to influence? But, she also wondered if Gemma was trying to influence anything at all. What if something else had happened to her?

The dragon had gone missing at the edge of the Palenquemas. Perhaps she sensed what was happening and escaped. If so, why had she failed to warn Kaphri and the warriors? Was that a part of the 'not influencing' Frax spoke of, or had she left them in order to avoid contact with the Wyxa? To Kaphri's recollection, Gemma had never reacted in any way to the thought of the swamp dwellers. But, she reminded herself, Gemma was silent and non-reacting to most things until Kaphri encountered them directly or asked about them. No doubt, that fit into Frax's argument of her mysterious role. Maybe the Wyxa had not been aware of Gemma's presence when they spirited the rest of them into the swamp.

*"I doubt that,"* he said. *"The serpent is Eldren, too."*

She'd heard them use the term before. *"What is Eldren?"*

*"Kep's First Children. They are very ancient. The Geffitzi are Kep's Second and most beloved Children."*

*"What does that mean, Second Children?"*

*"Eldren history extends further back than our own."*

*"How much further?"*

He gave her an annoyed look. *"Too far back for us to know. They do not share their story with us. How long have your people claimed oneness with your stars?"*

Too far back for her to know.

*"Well, then."* Frax shrugged emphatically and turned his attention back to his task.

Kaphri's eyes swept their surroundings, wishing for Gemma to appear, winging toward her with perfect timing like she had on the mountainside in Omurda. All she saw were trees, rocks, and dirt.

She had to admit Frax was right in his assessment: the tiny dragon would be there if she could. Which did not rule out 'could not'. Granted, Gemma might have chosen—for whatever diabolic reason Frax might conjecture—not to be there, but what if she couldn't get to her? What if the Wyxa had some protection in place Gemma couldn't breach?

Perhaps she waited for her at the edge of the swamp.

*"How much further, do you think?"* The quicker they got out of this place the sooner she could reunite with the little dragon.

Blankness came from Frax's mind without being a direct reply. It reminded Kaphri of Gemma's frequent responses to her questions. Sighing, she squelched her feelings of abandonment. No need to increase her misery by dwelling on her missing companion.

Leaning back against a huge swamp tree, she dug halfheartedly in the leaves and dirt with her knife while she watched the Geffitz. He lay on his belly, balanced precariously across the broad trunk of a fallen tree that hung out over a large pool of water.

They had come upon the pool, within its sheltering circle of trees, during the late afternoon rain. The strange formation stuck out in odd contrast to the flat, grassy marsh around it, as if some monstrous animal had wallowed itself a stony bed down into the ground. Boulders pushed up from the earth, shoring dirt in a circular bank that sloped steeply down on the inside to a pool deep at its center. Huge trees ringed the perimeter, their massive roots draping over the boulders like creeping vines, running down the banks to the surface of the water. Attesting to the place's age, several of the trees had fallen and lay rotting among the brush that struggled in the shadows and damp. Kaphri did not like its heavy, closed feel: it was too different from the dreary marsh surrounding it. On her own, she would have given it a wide berth, but the sight of fish in the depths of the pool had overjoyed Frax.

He lifted a sharpened stick and prepared to strike at the glints of silver darting in the dark water. They had not discussed eating fish yet. Hungry as she was, she still hoped his efforts would not succeed. It would save them both a great deal of argument.

Seeing the muscles in his shoulder bunch, she clenched her teeth and suppressed an urge to frighten the swift darts away as she turned her attention back to digging for roots.

\*\*\*

Frax glanced up with a startled expression that deepened into a puzzled frown when he saw the girl idly picking at the ground with the knife. She'd been thinking of scaring the fish away, but changed her mind. How did he know that? Had they grown so familiar that she was that predictable?

No. The thought-sense of it felt much clearer than just a suspicion of her feelings.

An accidental sending? Not likely. She was a far better telepath than he.

Maybe heat and hunger were beginning to affect him. He turned back to the water just as a pale swell of movement in the depths sent the fish darting in all directions.

And that had not been the girl's doing. He felt sure of it. Something else worked against him now.

He got to his feet with a rueful sigh. *"Another time I would've had them."*

\*\*\*

Kaphri masked her relief. She did not doubt the truth of his observation.

Still, they hadn't eaten for the better part of a day, and they were both weak. Water might stave off their hunger a bit, but it did not give strength.

*"I have done no better. Just a tree root."* She dejectedly poked at the thick, pale root with the point of her knife, then blinked in surprised.

She could have sworn the thing twitched.

With a shrug, Frax started back up the broad length of fallen trunk toward her. He stumbled as he stepped off the log and looked down with a puzzled frown.

Before he could move, a long white tentacle shot up out of the earth, snapping about his waist and catching his arms close to his body. Another one lashed up out of the water to coil around his thighs, seizing him securely.

A surge of horror ran through him. *"Kep, Priestess, get up! Move!"*

*"What is that?"* She scrambled to her feet at the first sight of the things, but paused, unsure what to do as she balanced on the steep bank above him. The warrior was struggling. She could see his muscles strain against the strange white bonds that held him, and more were springing up from the very mud of the bank.

*"Sigalithe'! Bloodvine!"* He blasted. *"Get away!"*

Bloodvine? She paled as the ghastly white, thick cords knotted about his arms began to take on a pinkish tinge that ran back up their length away from him.

Frax succeeded in freeing an arm enough to draw the blade from his belt. Instantly a white cord lashed up from below to coil about his wrist. Its end slipped on to glide about his thigh, trapping his hand.

For the first time Kaphri felt pure fear run through him.

*"Get away!"*

"No." In his already weakened state, this thing would kill him if she did not help.

*"I said get away."*

Kaphri choked down horror as the pallid coils took on more color.

Through Frax's anger and outrage, she felt the rising sear of his pain. She took a step towards him and stumbled, just as he had done moments before. Looking down, she saw a ghastly coil looping about her ankle.

She still clenched the knife she'd been using to dig in the dirt. Without a second thought, she bent and slashed the tentacle. The severed end fell to the ground, twisting and writhing. She stared at it blankly for a moment before the Geffitz's rising agony penetrated her shock-numbed mind once again. Hopping over it, she plunged down the bank.

He was fighting mightily, his muscles corded and glistening with the sweat, pain, and fury driving him. But the vines were contorting his body in a backward bend that lessened his resistance, while they tightened and squeezed him in their merciless grip. She reached out and sliced the vine that pinned his weapon hand, half-freeing it. The severed end thrashed wildly, slinging a pale, thick fluid tinged with runny strings of red. Blood. Geffitz blood. She attacked the other vine, hacking at it until she completely freed the hand, then she dropped to her knees and sawed at the vines where they came out of the bank to trap his legs.

"*Look to yourself, Priestess,*" he gasped as he became able to slash at the other tendrils binding him. At the same moment, something brushed past her cheek, She recoiled in horror as a vine tried to glide about her throat.

She struck at it. Felt the hardening resistance against her hand when she tried to push it away. In the next breath, the thing went limp, severed from its base.

Frax pulled her to her feet and shoved her up the slippery bank. "*Go, now! Go!*"

They were scrambling in the mud, frantically crawling where they could not stand. She passed the small pit she'd dug into the dirt, recoiling in horror as the pale root inside writhed. The ground cracked and heaved as it struggled to unearth itself. Frax caught the back of her shirt and pulled her onward. Together they reached the top of the slope, stumbling and falling over tree roots and broken branches in their mad retreat. Then they ran.

It seemed to Kaphri as if they ran for leagues before the warrior let her stop, but finally they dropped into the grass to lie limply, every gasping breath a burning agony. Slowly the pain faded and she lay there, letting exhaustion hold her while the terrible pounding of her heart slowed. Her breath ceased its rasping, but the sound continued. After a moment, realization penetrated her senses: it was not the sound of her breathing.

She pushed to a sitting position and looked at the warrior lying beside her. Tiny lacerations ran in long lines across the bare skin of his arms, chest, and ribs where the bloodvine had caught him. Blood oozed over his flesh in bright, thin sheets. His eyes were closed, his breathing ragged.

Quaking with sudden fear, the girl reached for his mind and found it solidly shielded. His whole body, tense and rigid, spoke of intense pain. She shook him. She pressed at his mindshields. Nothing got through to him. And the blood did not clot. It just kept flowing in a slow sheet that began to darken the ground around him.

Kaphri looked around for something to staunch the bleeding, knowing beforehand it was a wasted effort. The stand of trees with the deadly pool stood across the field, far behind them, and endless marsh grass stretched in all other directions. But if she did not do something quickly, Frax would die.

Gemma! She mentally screamed for the little dragon, but received no response. She prayed to Hredroth, desperately begging for some help. Some insight. She even pleaded with the Geffitzi Earth Mother, Kep, begging her to be a merciful Goddess to her own.

Nothing.

"You bitch," she screamed her frustration to the slow wind. How could a god ignore its own followers' needs so callously? But her cry was a foolish, empty gesture. She wasted precious time the Geffitz commander did not have. Trembling, she pressed her fingers to her temples and tried to gather her thoughts.

Arylla? She considered and discarded the possibility. Although a part of her schooling in Kryie Karth included attending the sick with Har and using her power to assist his healing arts, she dared not use it on the warrior. It required free access to his mind and he had already warned her she did not have that. Her recent experience in trying to waken him still burned fresh in her memory. If she attempted to enter his mind and he mistook it as a threat, he might imprison her within and destroy them both.

Bitter with helpless frustration, she tried to stem the flow of blood with her sleeves until she was smeared and wet with red, and still it seeped and the Geffitz's breathing grew more hoarse and shallow.

He was going to die. If only Gemma...

But Gemma was not there: Kaphri's thoughts came together

coldly. Neither was Har nor any other assistance. She must draw on her own limited experience.

Forcing panic aside, Kaphri tried to think.

There were no injuries like this in Kryie Karth, but the planes cat had injured her arm. What had Gemma done? She tore back through her memory.

Leaves. Gemma used leaves to plaster her wound. But there were no leaves in this place. She looked around, her panic rising again. Her eyes fell on something else. Mud. Gemma and Har both used that to cover wounds. It had been raining for days in this place and the ground was thoroughly soaked. She tore at the grass, ignoring how the tough blades sliced her hands as she scooped the sticky soil up and slapped it onto Frax's arms and ribs. Caked on his skin, it might hold the blood to the wounds long enough for it to clot. She tried not to think of how hopeless things would be if it began to rain again.

She prayed fervently for dry skies to any God who would listen.

As she worked, she continued to look about, seeking anything that might serve her desperate purpose. Then her eyes found the dark clump of a small, broad-leafed bush growing low in the grass a short distance away. The leaves were big enough to help stabilized the sticky pack. Hastily pressing another handful of mud across the oozing flesh of Frax's ribs, she scrambled for the plant.

Pulling up the whole plant and taking it with her to strip the leaves seemed the quickest course, but it took several hard jerks to uproot the small clump. Triumphantly, bush in hand, she turned back to the Geffitz.

Her heart froze in horror.

Frax was gone.

She stood, too stunned to move, staring at the blood-soaked ground, then she began to back away.

Wyxa. It must be the Wyxa. Memory of Frax's warnings rushed in as she looked about with a rising panic. Nothing moved in the silent emptiness. But as she turned to run, she felt another mental presence close by. Instinctively her hand went to the crystal as darkness pressed in, sweeping her away.

*** 

She was falling.

No air rushed past, everything was silent; but she knew she was falling. She flailed, her limbs meeting no resistance from the air, and felt herself begin to turn in a long, slow spiral. Gradually the circle tightened and she moved faster and faster until she spun madly. She opened her mouth in a silent scream and fell into oblivion.

*"Who are you?"* The question boomed hollowly down mental passages as Kaphri came back to awareness.

The spinning ceased. She gave a mental moan. Who was this creature, its question echoing so stridently in her head? She made a first attempt to gather her thoughts into some type of order.

And froze.

Many other presences, like thousands of cold, hard points of light, hovered around her. They were focused intently on her, but she could neither see nor feel anything in the green murkiness. It was as if she floated bodiless in a cloud, with everything else stilled to silence.

Memory flooded her. Frax!

*"The Geffitz commander—he is dying! Please, you must help him."* Whoever these creatures were, she needed their help. She snatched out, mentally snaring a nearby awareness in her desperate grasp. It recoiled, startled, then firmly disengaged her hold, easily eluding her frantic attempt to re-capture it.

Dismay and anger rippled out, strengthening as it expanded. Before she could react, a huge mental wave struck her, rolling her beneath its surface and pressing her down. She couldn't breathe! Strange and alien presences poured into her mind, overwhelming her. She fought to resurface, but she was sinking beneath the sheer volume of the mental flood. They pulled at her brain, each of the presences drawing off a tiny bit of her. Memories flashed, every piece an experience vividly relived in a flicker, all swiftly discarded as other bits were snatched in a blinding whirlwind. Turned out. Examined.

Her essence was being ruthlessly scattered on the winds!

Kaphri gave a mental cry of terror.

*"Exercise restraint. This creature is not one with us."* The command came hard. This was a different presence, every bit as imposing as the first, yet somehow less removed: less ruthless and aloof. The sea of minds engulfing her ebbed away like a multitude of tiny lights extinguished as the senders withdrew their invading presences.

Kaphri curled within herself, quaking with horror and dismay.

*"Know, intruder, that your power is nothing here."* The first hard, imperious presence returned. *"You will answer the questions of this Ankar Mekt clearly, and precisely, or the information will be taken from you in the manner you just experienced. Now, who are you? What manner of being are you and what have you to do with the disturbance that occurred on the border of our lands eight nights ago?"*

Ankar Mekt? Then these were the Wyxa.

In that moment, it became frightfully clear to Kaphri why the idea of falling into the grasp of the swamp dwellers struck such fear into Tobin. What they had just done to her mind left her quaking with fear. But there had been something worse in the experience. Something that drove fear even deeper into her. In those few seconds they violated her mind, she'd experienced the coldest, most remote, most penetrating scrutiny she had ever known. A Ly Kai council was an exercise in the rigid control of emotions, but this went a thousand times beyond that in its lack of feeling. She knew now, there was no sympathy anywhere in these creatures for the plight of her or her companions.

Her mind raced with the memory of Frax's warnings. He said they did not care what she wanted, felt, or fled. Now she knew he'd spoken the truth.

Control. She must exercise control. She needed to speak with clear reason if she was going to be of any use to her or the warriors. Fighting down the emotions that burned inside her, she struggled for a response to the Wyxan's question. What could she say to help her and her companions? Or, Hredroth forbid, harm them? These Wyxa seemed as prickly and difficult as Geffitzi in their nature.

Well, the thought ran through her mind, she had observed difficult creatures interacting for weeks and succeeding in making their differences work. She must have learned something from that. How would the Geffitzi warriors handle this?

Only one thought came to mind: challenge. Over the weeks, she'd watched the warriors deploy it effectively in their interactions. Sometimes it worked well, forcing another to divert and channel attention away from their issue to a defensive position that produced a desired exchange. At the worst, it simply failed to change the subject, but it still forced an exchange of views.

*"You attacked us. Why? What do you want? Why have you interrupted our passage? Where are my companions?"*

*"You are presumptuous."* The cold aloofness in the response could have frozen the lake at Kryie Karth. But her ploy worked: they were responding to her directly—at least for the moment.

She squelched the sense of intimidation that ran through her and pressed on. *"Because of what you have done my companion is in desperate need—"*

*"In desperate need? We find that, with your sudden appearance on our border, our whole world is in desperate need. An ancient evil we thought long banished is suddenly trying to invade our land. Who are you, who brings this evil..."*

*"I did not bring evil—"*

"*It seeks you. And the scars of its foul touch glow within you.*"

She recoiled mentally from the accusation. What scars did they mean, glowing inside her?

But that could come later. She couldn't allow them to divert her. "*The Geffitz commander. What have you done with him? He is dying.*"

"*And what are we to make of that? The Children of Kep and one of the strangers from the stars: your peoples do well at destroying themselves. The loss of one more could be of no great matter to this world.*"

The statement was so callous and unfeeling, so unexpected in its implications, that for a moment it left her at a loss for words. She groped for a response while, somewhere, Frax might be bleeding to death.

Was this to be their fate—to die in this godforsaken swamp while the Wyxa watched on?

No. How dare these Wyxa tell her she and the Geffitzi were nothing to this world after its forces had maneuvered them to the brink of death. They had not fought their way this far just to perish in this place at the hands of these creatures!

"*Who are you, to determine such a thing? Release my companions and me. You have caused us enough delay.*"

She succeeded in dodging the darkness they tried to press upon her again. Reacting instinctively, she lashed out, snaring the Wyxan mental aura closest to her in a furious, frantic grip.

Once again, the massive surge of minds burst upon her. This time, however, she was prepared. The aura she had seized could not wrest free. She managed to capture a second presence as the invading wave struck, washing them all three under in a tangle of struggling, churning mental confusion.

The encounter was swift and shallow, cut short by the unexpected presence of the two Wyxa. She re-surfaced to a hot sea of outrage. The two mental essences, their initial shock worn off, easily wrestled free of her and retreated in blazing trails of fury.

All around her settled a cold, angry Wyxan presence. They were more wary now, giving her a wide berth, but she knew they were not finished.

"*Wretched creature, cease your resistance! You will cooperate—*"

She gave them an angry mental sweep—a warning she was prepared to defend herself against another attack—and felt them withdraw slightly further away from her. Then something else drew her attention.

Somewhere outside of her she felt a rising warmth. It was remote yet familiar and it caused her to pause with the briefest flicker of confusion. Gemma? No. The crystal! Her mind flashed back to what she'd been doing when the Wyxa had swept her away. She must still physically hold the thing! And its fire was rising, blazing in response to her need against the threat around her.

Twice before, it had served her. Now it was answering again.

Before she could act, however, a corresponding recognition and shock rippled around her, rising and echoing, voiced by an increasing number of minds.

"*She. She has it. She carries it!*" The whispers of horror and awe were like tiny waves, lapping at the edges of her mind. The fear in the waves rose, building into a thunderous roar. "*She is able to exert some control over it!*"

"*No, you will not use that here!*" There was a sense of absolute finality in the imperious tone now as it boomed out at her.

Feeling the imminent threat in it, Kaphri drew on the crystal.

There was a terrible blaze of outrage around her, and she was falling again. Darkness swallowed her.

# 43

## Wyxa

Uri drifted in dreams, with Ladrienca sleeping beside him. Contentedly he reached out a hand to caress her warm, soft flesh. When his fingers encountered a hard surface instead, he woke.

Yellow? He blinked. He was surrounded by yellow? He blinked again as the initial shock wore off and he realized he was on his back, staring up at a yellow surface above him. The next moment he saw that he was lying in a large, ovular yellow tub of clear green liquid.

He groaned. Windmer didn't share the same fascination for the Palenquemas that their Cadarnian brethren held, but he'd heard enough stories to know he must be soaking in one of the curative baths in which intruders into the swamp sometimes found themselves.

So, the Wyxa had gotten them, after all.

He sat up. A short distance away, more bodies soaked in tubs similar to his. Dark locks, particularly the one with the wisp of white in it, identified the Aedec warriors. Beyond them, he could see sandy brown curls with the braids and leather strips that he had worked into Tobin's hair. There was no sign of Frax or the girl.

He stood up cautiously, unsure of what reaction to expect from his body or from his captors. If any Wyxa observed him, they did not react, and, beyond a slight stiffness of unused muscles, he seemed fine. Stepping over the side of the tub, he gathered his clothing from the neatly folded stack on the floor. There was no need for a towel: the liquid on his flesh dried instantly on contact with air. He dressed quickly, noting the absence of his weapons and boots without surprise, then moved to check on the others.

Seuliac and Velacy appeared to be sleeping quietly in their vats of restorative green fluid, their breathing regular and deep. As he moved past them toward Tobin, however, he frowned. The color of the Kitahni warrior's skin was not right, and he was lying much deeper in the fluid than the other two.

Uri drew a long breath of dismay as he looked into the tub.

Tobin lay up to his chin in brownish, opaque liquid. That could only mean one thing: blood—lots of blood—mixed with the fluid.

The younger Kitahn's flesh was so pallid and cool it was as if Uri handled a corpse when he grasped the shoulders. Heart beating with dread at what he would find, he pulled Tobin higher in the tub to search for wounds. He paled at the sight of three deep, uniform gashes in the muscles across the warrior's left shoulder and breast. The flesh had begun to heal, but he could still see shattered bone through the gaping tears in the tissue. Only one creature Uri knew could do that much damage with what appeared to be a single swipe of claws. A kitsk.

He let Tobin's body slip back down into the fluid, making sure the wound was completely immersed, and glanced about the rest of the area.

A new chill of apprehension ran over him.

Where were Frax and the girl?

A quick inspection revealed the room was deceptively larger than his first impression. The self-illuminated, uniformly yellow walls and floor eliminated any shadows that would give the place a sense of depth. The space was circular, with a massive, columnar structure of the same material running up through its center. There was a door-sized opening in the column. A glance within confirmed what he suspected; there was a basin-shape of clean water on the inner wall and a hole for simple toilet facilities.

He heaved a sigh, his mouth tightening. It appeared the Wyxa were expecting them to stay for a while.

Uri made a second search of the outer wall. There were no seams in the smooth surface that would indicate a doorway. He'd circled back around to the tub from which he'd emerged, when a moan, followed by a sharp exclamation sounded behind him. He turned to see Seuliac sitting up, looking about.

He waited in silence until the raven-haired Warlord's eyes found him.

"Where the hell are we?" The question was low and cautious, spoken aloud when Uri would have rather he mindspoke. But the Aedecs, like many of the clans did not resort to telepathy as their first choice in communication. It was a skill they negatively associated with the Eldren Races. And with the Kitahns.

"The Wyxa have us."

An amazingly elegant expression of distaste flitted across Seuliac's face when fluid streamed from his lifted hands. "What is this stuff?"

Uri felt hard amusement at the disgust in the warlord's voice. "Diffwys. It accelerates healing. The Wyxa seem to have this strange habit of bringing people back to health before they throw them out of their realm." He shrugged at Seuliac's look of disbelief. "I don't know why. Maybe they consider it some type of compensation for their actions in the Great Cataclysm. I guess most intruders they capture are half-starved and ill by the time they get them. The Palen-quemas is a tough place."

"Well, the stuff works." The Aedec warrior turned his hands over, examining the smooth flesh. "All the scrapes and cuts are gone."

"Given enough time it even heals old scar tissue."

The Warlord erupted from the fluid with a sharp oath and Uri suppressed a wash of bitter amusement. Bloody Geffitzi. That had been his first concern, too, when he realized what he was soaking in. They were all too proud of their battle-scars.

"How did we get here?" Seuliac's eyes swept the chamber while he pulled on his clothes.

"I have no memory beyond the point where we stopped to rest. You?"

"The same."

"They must have taken us in our sleep and brought us here."

"Where is here?" The warlord walked over to stare down at Velacy's unconscious form.

"Probably in the heart of the Palenquemas, days from where we stopped.

"He won't wake up until they allow it," Uri added as the Warlord gave the younger Aedec a prod. "They have total control over our situation right now."

"Total control?" Although Seuliac's expression remained un-changed, Uri saw his hand, resting on the side of Velacy's tub, tighten until the knuckles showed white. "How long have we been here? How did they bring us here? And what do they want?"

"The Wyxa have telekinetic skills. They must have mentally pulled us in. And there's no way of knowing how long we've been here unless we ask them. Now we wait until they decide to speak with us." Uri eyed the warlord curiously. "Don't you know anything about the Wyxa?"

"No." The raven-haired Warlord's eyes were cold. "Do you know anything about how to pilot a ship through the Straits of Cascilar?"

"No." Uri felt a flicker of amusement, the point well taken: sea-faring Rhynog was the width of a continent away from this place and had its own esoterically local concerns. Still, the Warlord was from the central foothills of Rhynog and commanded the Caer's ground force; he did not command its navy or pilot its ships.

Uri could not resist the jab. "Do you?"

Seuliac flashed a lean, wolfish grin, as he turned his attention to the walls about them. At the same moment, Velacy made a startled sound of waking, drawing Uri into another explanation of their situation. By the time he'd finished, Seuliac had made a complete round of the chamber with the same results as his own earlier examination.

"What in Kep's name...?"

The Caspani Geffitz turned to find Seuliac bending over Tobin.

"It had to be a kitsk," he replied grimly. "I can't think of anything else that could do that kind of damage. Sliced the muscles of his shoulder open and shattered the bone."

Seuliac looked up with a questioning expression and Uri shook his head. "Any other time he would be severely crippled. Oddly enough, he's lucky the Wyxa have him. Here, with a little time, he'll heal completely."

Velacy moved over to stare down at the Kitahni scout as Seuliac frowned. "When did it happen? Did it come upon him at the edge of the swamp while we rested?"

The younger Aedec glanced at Seuliac, his expression troubled. "But kitsks are territorial. They don't move..."

"Outside the Palenquemas?" Uri nodded. "You're right, Velacy. And that means, somehow, Tobin was in the swamp, not just at its edge." The slight tightening at the corners of Seuliac's mouth gave him a perverse feeling of satisfaction: it was comforting to see their current situation ruffled the exasperating Rhynogian Warlord, too.

"How long have we been here?" Velacy's question drew his attention away from the Warlord.

"Hours? Days? Who knows?"

Like Uri and Seuliac, Velacy began a tour of their cell, seeking a means of escape. Neither of the others attempted to stop him; a good warrior did not consider himself infallible. Meanwhile, the Warlord walked over to Uri.

"So where is the rest of our merry little company, Caspani?" he asked in a low voice.

Uri shook his head. "The Wyxa might have separated the girl from us for obvious reasons of gender. Frax? I don't know. Maybe they got away. Maybe they're lost in the swamp, evading the Wyxa. Or, yes, maybe they're dead."

Seuliac weighed the possibilities for a long moment then shrugged, dismissing his thoughts without sharing them. "What will happen to us now?"

"If it's anything like the past, they should hold us for a while, then release us at the edge of the swamp."

The Warlord's expression went sharply incredulous. "Wait, let me see if I understand this correctly. These creatures rescue their captives from death, nurse them back to health, and then set them down safely outside their borders. What the hell was Tobin Kitahn so worked up about, then?"

"Oh, they have their nasty little deterrent, too." A frown darkened Uri's face. "They have a thing they call the Ankar Mekt to which they subject intruders. It's some sort of group mindmeld. I'm told it feels like having your brain pulled apart, examined, and rammed back into your skull, all while you're awake. All I know is most warriors who experience it don't return to the Palenquemas."

Seuliac's eyes narrowed. "And what about us?"

"We didn't invade their land, so I'm not sure," Uri looked uneasy. "Normally it would not be for me to speak of this, it being another hold's business, but since we are all at risk... Sometimes warriors that undergo the joining seem to suffer brain damage. They wander around in a, uh, state of confusion for the rest of their lives. Others have terrible nightmares. But not all," he hastened to add at the outrage he saw building on the Warlord's face. "And there is some type of defense. A few of Cadarn's trappers have found a way to thwart it. A thing they call the 'trapper's edge'. But, none of the old ones who have mastered it will tell how they did it. All they'll say is if you can't figure it out before the Wyxa take you into Ankar Mekt, you shouldn't be trapping in the swamp. It seems that if you can catch on to the trick, the Wyxa can't take you into their mindmeld. That's how some of the old trappers from Cadarn kept going back into the swamp. The Wyxa consider Geffitzi a great nuisance."

"If they're judging from experience with the Kitahns, that's no surprise," the white-locked Geffitz observed.

The Warlord was furious over the revelation of the danger they were in, but Uri didn't feel any guilt or concern. He had accepted the risk as part of their task, and the Aedecs would have come along with them, regardless of the threat. They could never let anyone say they had refused to go where the Kitahns dared.

Sometimes there was a price for bravado, whether Kitahni, Caspani, or Aedecian.

Velacy came over to join them. "There's no sign of an opening," he said. "It's like we're inside some living thing."

"You're probably right." As the other two stared at Uri in dismay, he explained. "The Wyxa exercise power over living things, especially plants. It's said that they cultivate giant plants, living inside of them and directing their growth to accommodate their needs."

"Even to healing their captives, then doing cleanup after them?" Seuliac asked. He gestured at the chamber behind them.

The tubs in which they'd awakened had disappeared. Only Tobin's remained, spotlighted in a brighter yellow light.

A chill ran down Uri's spine. The structures had disappeared while they stood within two arms' reach of the things. He realized that the room had also changed. The walls were shaded in cool greens and the floor had changed to a speckled brown. Plant colors. He looked back at the yellow light glowing around Tobin and realized it reminded him of sunlight.

"It would seem that, as you say, we must await our hosts' pleasure." The familiar, humorless smile lifted the Warlord's lips as Seuliac grudgingly conceded to himself, and Uri, that their captors did appear to have the upper hand.

At least, for now.

Uri nodded.

\*\*\*

"Caspani, this plant of yours is going to either puke you out or swallow you down for making its throat sore with all that pacing."

Uri paused, pulling out of his distracted thoughts to look at Seuliac. The warlord was sitting on the floor, observing him with a mixture of irritation and thin amusement.

"So, you're awake again, for a little while," Uri came back shortly. "I can't sleep all the time the way you do." It seemed that the other warrior only roused long enough to eat before he was napping again.

The warlord got to his feet in a single fluid motion and gave a long, languid stretch. He moved like a cat, Uri thought irritably. And there was the thing of lightly napping off and on all throughout the day...

Seuliac sauntered over to stand in front of him. "How long have we been here?" he asked softly.

"Two days, if we can rely on the cycles of light and dark that penetrate this cell." Uri's frustration surged. "Two days too long."

"Exactly." The raven-haired Aedec sounded surprisingly reasonable. "And we have no idea how long we'll be here. Until young Kitahn awakens? Beyond that? We don't know. But, if what you've said holds true, we will not die. We'll be freed eventually."

Uri nodded, suddenly weary. So, what was the warlord's point? He saw that Velacy, hearing their voices, had emerged from the area on the backside of the center column and was listening, too.

"We must look to the time when the Wyxa no longer control us." Seuliac waited for Uri to nod agreement again. "The food," his lips twitched in distaste at the mention of the endless supply of fresh, uncooked vegetables that materialized at regular intervals, "seems capable of sustaining our health. So, the rest is up to us. We are Geffitzi warriors waiting the call to battle. I suggest that we maintain the discipline of a siege camp. We exercise vigorously several times a day. We participate in combat matches, genuine contests of skill, tournament rules applied. And mealtimes," he paused as Velacy drifted closer. His eyes flicked across both their faces with a hardness that challenged either of them to object. "Mealtimes, there will be conversation appropriate to a hold table. Civilized discussion. Debate. Anything that will stimulate the mind. We must occupy our time with something besides senseless frustration."

He was right, of course. Worry and pacing were pointless and nonconstructive. Uri secretly suspected that the Warlord had waited for them to get to this point of boredom so they would welcome his suggestion of a military regimen.

It had worked. He heaved a sigh and nodded agreement: it was the intelligent thing to do.

Velacy's silence spoke for him.

So they fell into a routine of warriors, encamped and waiting for battle. Everything they did: practicing, eating, talking—even sleeping—was devoted to the specific task of honing their bodies with whatever methods they had available to them. Hand-to-hand combat, arm wrestling, leg wrestling, even thumb wrestling filled the hours. Mind games, riddles, puzzles from childhood became challenges taken as seriously as any call to combat. They discussed art and music, theories of combat and trade as they ate. And argued, shared bawdy stories and hunting exploits to fill other gaps in their time. Temper and frustration still seethed below the surface, but it did not rule them.

\*\*\*

Two days later, while Uri and Seuliac were engaged in a slightly less than congenial bout of hand-to-hand combat for exercise, Velacy gave a sudden shout.

Another tub of the green diffwys, highlighted in bright light, had suddenly materialized within the main chamber.

"Holy Mother Kep," Uri breathed in horror.

Slow drifting streamers of bright red blood were staining the diffwys brown even as he stared down at the muddy, gaunt, unconscious form of Frax Kitahn.

# 44

## Klandar Bayne

Kaphri opened her eyes with a jerk.

A sense of impending threat seized her. Just as swiftly, it dissolved away, replaced by an overwhelming sensation of calm.

Lights flickered above her, evolving into the shadow play of sunlight shimmering through leaves outside a smooth curve of nearly transparent ceiling. She blinked, trying to snatch at an elusive memory. Calm was not the reaction she should be experiencing right now, waking in this strange place, but it was the only one she could find.

A breeze shook the leaves, setting off another display of light and shadows, and she mentally frowned. Where was she?

The frown deepened as she raised a hand to touch her eyes and thick green fluid streamed from her fingers. Confused, she looked down to find her naked body immersed up to her shoulders in a shallow tub of the pale, glistening stuff. Her attention returned to the firm, healthy flesh of the arm she still held raised before her. It was smooth and curving, not the thin, bony arm that belonged to her.

She looked about in bewilderment.

"*You must not fear the bath. It heals and restores the body. You were in great need when you arrived here.*" The firm mental voice that had ordered restraint upon the Wyxan awareness invaded her head.

Wyxa! The thought sent her rigid, instant fear and antagonism flaring. Her reaction struck a wall of calm that forced the turmoil back down to a quiet level again.

Her rush of horror and fear were also pushed aside as the Wyxan continued. "*To rid your body of the scars that mar it, you must remain in the diffwys longer. The Children of Kep do not choose to have their scar tissue erased, but you are not of their people. We woke you to ask; what is your wish? You may remain in the bath if you desire. You may return to sleep.*"

Sleep? Was this creature insane? She needed to know about Frax and the others. They had to get out of this place and continue their quest. Kaphri's eyes searched the cool green shadows in front of her, the sense of panic she should feel only a vague trace inside her.

She could not find the sender.

Memory of her earlier experience with these creatures made her cautious. "*No. No, I don't think so.*" She continued to cast about in search of the other. Fear flashed in her mind, to dissolve away, but the realization stayed with her: something was modulating her emotional responses back to a steady calm every time she reacted. This creature obviously possessed a greater control over her emotions than she did and protesting would change nothing. It appeared she had no choice but to behave a little more circumspectly during this encounter than the earlier one. Very well, despite the exerted control, this creature did not seem to be threatening, and was acting much less imperiously than the multitudinous gathering.

*"Where am I? How long have I been here? Where is Frax? Where are the other warriors? And what have you done with Gemma?"*

The Wyxan ignored the questions as a long silence stretching out between them. Uneasiness nagged at her despite the gentle aura the thing was attempting to project over her. She still remembered: this was one of the creatures who had spirited her and her companions into the swamp, then wondered if their deaths would be of any consequence.

Her pulse quickened and she reached up, her heart giving a painful wrench: the chain and amulet were gone. *"The crystal! Hredroth, what have you done with it?"* Beyond the quickly dissipated flare of her horror, she still felt a deeper concern the Wyxan could not dull. This being might control her outward emotions, but it could not control what she knew. Despite her earlier suspicions of the crystal, she had begun to accept the idea that it had come to her for a purpose. She still might view it distrustfully, but she did not want to surrender its protection to these creatures.

The thing you call the crystal is in safekeeping. The Children of Kep are in safekeeping. You are in safekeeping. All is well for the moment. All will remain that way with your cooperation."

Did this creature have any idea what it was talking about? Her cooperation was not what should concern the swamp dwellers right now! Did they have any idea what was happening beyond the borders of their land? The stream of questions and their accompanying flares of emotion flamed and died insider her, snuffed out of her mind.

She caught a vague sense of mental confusion from her captor. *"Your questions will be answered soon. I will tell you this to ease your mind: the Geffitz, Frax Kitahn, is recovering from his injuries."*

She sensed the Wyxan preparing to withdraw. *"Wait!"* Green fluid splashed as she surged up in an attempt to stop the creature from leaving.

Too late. The Wyxan was gone.

Its exit instantly freed Kaphri's suppressed emotions. They struck her with the force of a torrent crashing into an empty cup. Fear, outrage, and confusion roared through her head. Now she struggled to force calm, knowing the storm of emotions that ripped through her would not help her solve her problems. She settled back into the tub and stared blindly at the shadows flickering on the wall across from her while she tried to sort through what had just happened.

The creature was right about one thing, she had many questions. But, for the moment, she must appease herself with the knowledge Frax and the others were being cared for. Other answers must wait.

Meanwhile, the wall she was staring at came into focus. She must search for answers on her own. Standing, she stepped over the gracefully scalloped, pale green edge of the tub. As she set her foot on the cool smoothness of the floor, the green gelatin the Wyxan called diffwys fell away from her skin, leaving her flesh dry. She stared down at her body with interest. Like her arm, it glowed with health. Her limbs were still long and slim, but there was a curving firmness to the flesh she had never seen before. She turned her forearm over. The thin line of the knife scar from the Maugrock gleamed against her skin, the ugly welt a smooth, silvery brand across the warmer golden tones of her flesh. So were the claw slash on her shoulder and the spiraled marks about her ankle. A secret rush of relief ran through her at the sight of them. They were badges, as Uri had indicated—marks of lessons hard learned—and something for which the warriors had high respect. She suddenly knew she would not give them up without a great deal of regret.

Another thought sent her hand to her head. She almost collapsed in shock as her fingers tangled in the feathery mat of her hair. The fiery tumble was a finger's length in growth! How long had she been in this place?

And how close had the evil that pursued her drawn during the delay?

Best to dress, and then seek answers. She looked about for her clothing. Her eyes fell on a small pile of neatly folded white material near her feet. She unfolded it to reveal some underclothing, a simple pair of white breeches, and a long-sleeved tunic top that fell to mid-thigh. Closer examination revealed a fabric unlike any she had ever seen. The material seemed to be one smooth, solid sheet, as if grown into its shape. As the cloth draped her body, the cool softness fitted as if made specifically for her. She did not find any footwear, however. After looking about, she shrugged. Perhaps the Wyxa did not recognize the need for shoes. She only hoped they would return her boots before she left this place. She did not savor the thought of walking barefoot in the swamp.

Closing her eyes, she raised her arms above her head and stretched. She might be a confused captive, but she could still allow herself to savor being healthy, clean, and comfortable for the first time in many days.

As she lowered her arms, however, her mind was moving on to other things, going over the details of her first encounter with the Wyxa. They had certainly reacted strongly to the presence of the crystal. She could still feel the burn of shock and outrage that had flared when she reached out for it. They must know something about the thing. How could she persuade them to share the information?

Uneasy with the presence of the crystal or not, the Wyxa had taken it.

And dropped her here, with an emotional buffer around her when they communicated with her.

This other, he said all was well as long as she "cooperated". What, exactly, did cooperation entail? How could she be sure they really held her companions?

The creature said the Geffitz warriors did not choose to have their scars healed. Did that mean they, too, had found themselves in the strange, healing green bath? Her heartbeat quickened. If they were healing the Geffitz commander's horrible wounds, maybe Frax had been in error when he said the Wyxa would be a threat to her. Surely, they would not nurse her back to health just to destroy her. Would they really harm her?

The answer came back a resounding yes. Her experience with the Ankar Mekt had shown her they were capable of doing anything to her without remorse.

Which meant she might be forced to defend herself. She was not surprised when a quick mental check did not raise the slightest flicker of starpower. In the swamp, she'd been aware of the lack of the geas, but she'd never thought about testing her starpower for fear of revealing their presence. What manner of creatures were these beings if they could block the power of Arylla and, yet, had made no effort to stop Araxis?

Certainly not to be considered as potential allies.

Well, her resolve hardened, she'd lived without the power of the stars. And, with the threat of Araxis hanging over her, they would not be a source she would choose to draw on—unless it became a last resort.

How long before she found herself pushed to that last resort? Would Araxis find her here, deprived of all her defenses. Would the Wyxa hold her captive that long? Or would they free her and the others eventually, unharmed, as Frax said was their habit?

And where, oh where, was Gemma? Impatience ran through her. So many questions.

Time to stop speculating and do something. She glanced about for the presence of a captor she could not even see before crossing the small, circular room to examine the wall. The surface was cool and slightly pliant under the pressure of her fingers, its soft, greenish surface letting light and shadow play through in the vague shapes she had seen earlier. A cautious mental probe revealed nothing of the wall's nature, but she felt certain it was living material.

Sudden memory of the bloodvines caused her to snatch her hands away. She stepped back with a shudder. She had to take several deep, controlled breaths before she was able to touch it again, to continue her examination.

Kaphri made a full circle of the chamber before stopping. There was no sign of an opening, not even a seam.

Thoughtfully she turned to face the room.

The tub had vanished. In its place stood a sleep platform, piled extravagantly with pillows and throws of the same material as her clothing. A small, richly formed, dark wood table held a bowl of assorted, unfamiliar fruits. What appeared to be some type of toilet facilities had formed in a tiny niche in the wall opposite her.

A slow, creeping chill slid down her backbone as she stared at the room's new fixtures. Had this change transpired behind her back, silently, as she moved about the outer perimeter of the space, her concentration centered on looking for an opening? Or, had the Wyxa rendered her unaware and she not even realized it? She rubbed her suddenly damp palms against the soft stuff that covered her thighs then jerked her hands away, her earlier pleasure in the touch of the material gone.

This was a cell. More comfortable than the chains and cold darkness of the Maugrock, but no less fixed and confining. She was definitely a prisoner of the Wyxa.

She glanced about the domed room. The air of the chamber was fresh and comfortable and she could almost hear the rustled of the leaves outside. The walls did not appear to be impenetrable. Would they block a sending? Could she mindtouch the warriors? Would the Wyxa interpret a seeking as not "cooperating"?

No matter. She must try.

Cautiously she reached out.

Her probe did not penetrate the wall.

Concentrating harder, she tried again.

Still nothing.

Gaining confidence when the Wyxa did not immediately retaliate by snuffing her consciousness, she tried several areas of the dome, all with the same result. Nothing she sent passed through.

*"For what do you search?"*

She mentally recoiled, startled by the sudden return of the Wyxan presence. It hung in the air beyond her, waiting.

Caution warred with curiosity. Was it wise to respond?

She'd already drawn its attention. *"Who are you?"*

*"I am Klandar Bayne, the Swampfather, leader of the Wyxa who abide on this plain of existence."*

Finally, a real answer. She carefully considered what her next question should be. Would he tell her about her companions or why the Wyxa had spirited them into the Palenquemas?

*"The true-naming."* Klandar Bayne seemed pleased. *"How is it you know the true name of our land.?"*

What was he talking about?

*"The true naming of our home, the Palenquemas."*

Kaphri gave a mental frown. She had not meant to send those thoughts. Not shielding among the Geffitz warriors had made her careless.

She must not let this creature draw her focus off the things that concerned her. *"Where are the rest of you?"* she asked, ignoring his question. Although she only sensed the one presence, memory of the awesome, invasive joining sent a chill creeping down her spine. She did not relish the thought of finding herself immersed within that again.

*"The Ankar Mekt is not currently joined. The members are considering the present situation. For what do you search?"*

"*My companions,*" she answered.

"*They are safe. We have given you our word.*" The creature seemed puzzled, as if it did not understand why she might doubt it.

Safe? Safe from what? She fought to contain her reaction of anger when she realized the mental buffer of the earlier encounter had not re-occurred with the reappearance of this Klandar Bayne. She must exercise caution: the creature seemed to be in a more amenable mood now. Perhaps she could appeal to some sense of reason in it if she contained her reactions and presented a credible argument.

"*We are not safe from you. You attacked us for no reason: you hold us captive for no reason. You delay us in our task. You took the crystal. With each passing moment, the danger from the evil that moves beyond your land increases. What do you call safe?*" She did not try to disguise the apprehension that slipped into her last question.

"*This conversation would be best carried out face to face,*" the Wyxan mused, half to itself.

The light faded. Dizziness and nausea swept over her, then she found herself standing in a much darker, cooler space that stretched into blackness around her. A thin white vapor drifted about her ankles, its currents writhing slowly in the circle of light that fell around her. A faint sound, reminded her of the moaning wind of the swamp.

Teleportation. And the Wyxan had done it while she was in a waking state. Apprehension tightened in her belly. What else were they capable of doing?

Memory of the Ankar Mekt flashed in her mind, sending another ripple of fear through her. Such power, coupled with a cold lack of emotion was a dangerous thing.

She turned to Klandar Bayne.

Tobin's uneasy label of "bug" stole through her mind. It was difficult to pick out details in the shadows of the place, but the thing did look insect-like. But not ugly like some hard beetle; it reminded her more of the delicate dragonflies that buzzed around the swamp.

Her gaze traveled from the huge, dark eyes, down the graceful taper of long snout to flared nostrils and the narrow slit of mouth, then back up and over the narrow curve of the head, with its crest of thick, spiky hairs.

The long, graceful neck tapered to a narrow body that curved out behind. It stood upright on strong, insect-like lower legs, with a pair of long, thin arms that ended in three thin fingers. Its flesh was greenish, lightly speckled, and striped about with darker narrow bands. She thought she saw the glint of gossamer wings at the edge of the dark carapace on its back. There was a strange, undeniable beauty to the creature. It would tower over the Geffitz by at least half a height, but it also seemed graceful and delicate.

Her gaze went back to the dark eyes that studied her. They were so beautifully calm—so deep and restful. Surely, this being must be kind and gentle, not a cold, cruel creature of the Ankar Mekt. But then again, she had discovered long ago with the Ly Kai that physical beauty had nothing to do with a thing's true inner nature.

The Wyxan crouched in the dimness, its great, deep eyes solemnly regarding her.

"*The Starchild.*" Its acknowledgement was soft, yet edged with acute interest. "*By what name are you called, Starchild?*"

Starchild? The name surprised her, yet, on quick reflection, did not seem unreasonable. "*Kaphri.*" Her reply was short and uneasy.

"*Kaphri. Nothing more?*"

"*Just Kaphri.*"

"*And your people?*"

"*I have no people.*" Years of anger and resentment toward the Ly Kai men, mixed with the pain and horror of what Araxis had done to them at the barrier, roiled within her. "*There is only me.*"

"*Ah, I distress you with my questions. My apologies. It is just I have* found one's people are one's roots, the essence of one's being. Surely that is important to defining one's self?"

"One does not choose one's people." Memory of her encounter with the Ly Kai in the council chamber and their heartless revelation of betrayal over her Birthstar brought a surge of bitterness to Kaphri. Define herself in Ly Kai terms? Not likely. If this creature did not wish to distress her, why did it persist in this vein of thought?

"But one chooses one's companions?" Klandar Bayne regarded her with keen eyes. "Indeed, I have wondered: how is it a Starchild travels in the company of the Children of Kep. They have great reason to name you enemy."

She drew a slow, deep breath. So, this creature knew something of the world's current history beyond its borders, of events between Araxis and the Geffitzi. What should she say and how would it affect all of their fates?

"We have chosen to walk a path together against a common enemy," she sent at last.

"Have the Geffitzi clans become so civilized in twenty years that they can forget the murder of half their nation—"

"No!" The word tore from her. To hear the Wyxan say that about her companions, knowing the pain that ate at them every day, was to hear them accused of an unspeakable action.

As the silence drew out between them, she realized Klandar Bayne was waiting for her to elaborate on her reaction. How much did this creature know or suspect of the situation between her and the Geffitzi warriors, she wondered.

"They took me captive as I crossed the land they call Omurda," she admitted at last. "And yes, although I, personally, have not done them harm, they...they have great reason to hate me." Her chest felt tight, making it difficult to breathe. The image of Frax, filthy and weary but laughing at her muddy appearance, flitted across her mind, causing a curious, twisting pain inside her. She forced herself to continue. "They do not forget. But they agreed to lay aside their feelings for a while in the face of a greater danger."

"You are their prisoner? Why, then, did you not flee when they were no longer able to detain you? When their leader fell to the sigalithe' vine you might have escaped. Perhaps you might have even evaded us."

Again, she felt a chill at the Wyxa's seemingly callous disregard for life. Frax said they did not kill, but they didn't seem to suffer any pangs at the thought of the demise of others, either. "If I had abandoned the Geffitz lord he might have died. It may be the Wyxan way to abandon others to death, but it is not mine," she replied sharply.

"It is not the Wyxan way to abandon any living thing to death," Klandar Bayne sent calmly. "You are here. The Geffitzi are here. But you must realize this peculiar sense of commitment to these Geffitzi has placed you in a grave situation. Was it the wisest choice you could have made?"

The wisest choice? This time she was not as swift in her reply. What he said was true; she could have run when Frax was injured. But to abandon him? What would she have gained? Thoughts of that betrayal would've haunted her, waking and sleeping. That would have been a much worse evil than what pursued her, for she would see it as having a source inside of her. In the Wyxan's words, she had put herself in a grave situation by staying with a fallen companion and placing herself within their power. It was too late to look back now on what alternatives might have once been open to her. She looked up at the Wyxan chieftain resentfully, feeling a twinge of frustration as she met the calm eyes of her new captor. "I made my choice. Only time will tell the wisdom of it. What of Wyxan wisdom and compassion? What will you do with us? Our small force offers no threat to you."

"There are many of my people who disagree with you." Klandar Bayne gestured with its long-fingered, delicate hand. "Sit, Starchild Kaphri. Be comfortable. I would speak with you further."

The drifting vapors around her feet scattered in a small circle to reveal a mossy surface. Much to Kaphri's surprise, the area was soft and dry despite the vanished mist. She took a cross-legged position facing the creature, the Wyxan waiting patiently until she settled before continuing.

"*It is the contention of many in the Ankar Mekt that you and the Geffitzi warriors sought out and removed the object you carried, the thing you call the 'crystal', from its resting place for your own purposes.*"

Kaphri stared at the creature, surprise rippling through her. "*But that isn't true.*" She hesitated for the barest breath. The Wyxa were obviously familiar with the crystal, so there seemed no harm in speaking candidly. It might even be better for their cause. "*As we fled the Balandra—an evil force they say is returning to the tower on the edge of Omurda—the Geffitz commander and I passed through a vast underground temple of darkness. Something in that darkness sought to lure me into its power. But even before I touched it, the crystal was working to protect me. It also worked to remove a foul piece of spelling someone had used on me. And it broke the barrier to the south, which one of the Ly Kai erected upon this world. I had no memory of picking the thing up until Uri Caspani found it clinging to my breeches in a mass of dried blood. Afterward I remembered something clinging to my fingers when I touched a sticky smear on the floor of the temple. But I did not knowingly take the crystal. It came to me of its own accord.*"

"*You freely admit you and the Geffitz leader passed through the Black Temple. And you bear the scars of the evil that dwells there inside of you. Perhaps you acted, whether knowingly or innocently, in the service of that darkness.*"

"*I did not go into the place seeking anything. Too many things already want to use me for their own purpose, Klandar Bayne. No. We were fleeing pursuit by the creatures the Geffitzi call the Balandra. Neither the warriors nor I had any idea I carried the crystal until a full day after we escaped the temple.*

"*What you say is true: the evil that lurks beneath the Black Tower has* touched me. Many days ago, in the lake tower far in the north, someone tried to use it to ensnare me, but I eluded it. The force attacked me again at the barrier. At this moment, the evil being that used it against me is seeking me. What your people felt on the border of your land a few nights ago was the crystal, acting on its own to defend me. I have no idea what the thing is, but it works to protect me. If your people can tell me about it, I beg you to share what you know.

"There's an evil force gaining strength beyond your land. The crystal has shielded me from it. In the past, I rejected it; even going so far as to hide it away, but now I recognize I need the protection it offers me. Return it to me before disaster strikes us all. And please, release me and my companions so we can continue in our attempt to defeat the evil that pursues me." Did they have any idea of what would happen to them all if she lost the protection of the crystal? She was sweating with fear and desperation.

"The evil that is seeking a return to the Maugrock once held rule over this world. If I share with you those days of horror you would understand why we react the way we do." The Wyxan ignored her pleas as he picked up the conversation. "It was a time of such cruelty and death! Our only defense was an action which came close to completing the destruction of our world. The thought of falling into those times again strikes terror into the hearts of us all. We will not allow that darkness to gain a hold on this world again at any cost.

"The nature of the crystal is not important to you. The purpose it serves—sealing against re-entry of that evil into our world—is everything to us. When you removed it from its resting place, you removed that protection."

A terrible coldness sank into her. This creature did not care how or why the crystal had come to her. Memory of the cold, emotionless mental sea of the Ankar Mekt finally forced the true danger of her situation upon her: the warriors had let her live and even helped further her cause in the hope they might reclaim their lands through her struggle. The Wyxa had no such concern. What Frax had warned was true: for the perceived safety of their world, the Wyxa would look beyond her and her companions.

Denying she had taken the crystal was useless: Klandar Bayne did not care. It's protection was gone. They did not intend to return it to her. The only thing that remained was the question of what would become of her and her companions.

*"And what will the Wyxa do with us?"* She managed the barest mental whisper.

*"Nothing, yet,"* Klandar Bayne replied. *"The severity of the situation demands a full assembly of the Wyxa. Many of the Ankar Mekt have slept long and are slow in their awakening. There is much of which they must be made aware."*

*"Such as?"* Of what must the long-sleeping Wyxa become aware? How long had they slept and how much did they know of the Ly Kai intrusion into their world? This one called her Starchild, which meant he knew something about it, but did he know the threat her mere existence presented with Araxis about? How would that affect his, their, reactions if they discovered that? She watched the chieftain of the Wyxa closely but she could discern nothing of the creature's thoughts.

*"It will all be revealed in time."*

Kaphri's hands tightened into small fists of frustration and fear. And when would that be? Within moments? Days? How long did sleeping Wyxa take to awaken? To become aware of what they deemed necessary details? Did they realize that in the meantime Araxis was growing stronger as he sought another way to set his hold upon her, and that they had taken her only protection. Would their course of action be as clear-cut as Frax predicted? Would they eliminate everything they deemed a threat?

Perhaps there was another way. *"Please, tell me. Where is Gemma?"*

Gemma could explain the situation. Gemma might be able to persuade them where she could not.

"*What is Gemma?*"

It didn't know? "*I—*" a sudden sensation of confusion washed over her. She paused, struggling to organize her thoughts. She needed to...what? "*I need to see the Geffitzi warriors. I want to talk to them now. Please.*"

"*The Ankar Mekt does not believe that wise.*"

Kaphri bit back her protest, knowing she would not influence the Wyxa. For the moment, she and the warriors were under the total control of these creatures. For how long? Her heart began a slow thud of fear. Frax would save them. With Uri and Seuliac as allies, he would devise some plan of escape.

Maybe so, but even if the Geffitzi succeeded in escaping, would they have the time or ability to find and rescue her? As she sat in the dimness staring at her clenched hands, doubt ate its way through her. A terrible emptiness replaced her panic. Was there nothing more to her life than for her existence to threaten every other creature on this world? Was that the sum of her life?

Perhaps that was the way things must be for her. But not for the warriors. She looked up at Klandar Bayne. "*Before the Wyxa decide anyone's fate I would have them know one thing: the Geffitz warriors with me are innocent of any wrongdoing. Their leader, Frax Kitahn, was only in the temple because he rescued me from the Balandra. Although it has never been my intention, perhaps I am a threat, but not them. Promise me you will not harm them, and I will agree to cooperate with the Wyxa. I will do whatever is necessary to help defeat the evil that threatens this world because of my actions—if you will agree to return the Geffitzi safely to their people.*"

"*Why would you do this?*"

"*Because what I've told you is the truth. The crystal came to me. And because I know that sooner or later I must face the evil that pursues me.*"

The Swampfather regarded her for a long moment with large, liquid eyes. *"There is much, indeed, the Ankar Mekt must hear. I cannot make such a promise, but I will present it for their consideration. Rest well, Starchild. We will talk again."* A wave of dizziness washed over her and Kaphri found herself once more in the green chamber.

Going to the sleep-platform, she picked up a coverlet, but she could not bring herself to lie down upon the bed. Its comfort somehow seemed a perversion of her purpose.

Wrapping the blanket around her shoulders, she settled on the floor and stared numbly at the pale green wall.

What had she done? Had she helped or harmed their situation?

A strange emptiness gripped her as she sat alone and miserable with her thoughts and doubts.

# 45

## Geffitzi and Wyxa

Klandar Bayne remained lost in thought for a long time after he returned the girl to her chamber.

The world was changing. The peace and tranquility of eons had shattered a few nights ago with a horrendous clash of powers in a place they should not be. Powers poised to rain disaster down upon them.

Did these creatures have any idea what they had brought here? What they had done?

The scale of it shook him. Despite that, a thought kept tugging at the edge of his mind. Two thousand years... Was it possible a Wyxan had foreseen this situation over two thousand years ago?

It sent his senses rushing. And yet...

His thoughts would not please those in the Ankar Mekt who had already passed on to the Ethereal Plain. Bad enough, the situation to begin with, but the idea, of them not being the key influence in a world-scale event would not fit their image of the role they should play. It would be even more difficult for them to accept that the

Geffitzi clans, with their emotional, reactive nature, might be the only hope of averting this renewed threat.

Many who comprised the Ankar Mekt were astoundingly ancient. In their vast age, so far removed from this current world, they had grown indifferent to the changing situation of this Plain. Klandar Bayne's resolve hardened. He was the Swampfather, representative for this Plain. His only interest was the safety of the Palenquemas, the Primordial Plain. His only interest must continue to be the security of this place and all its creatures, despite what those of the Ankar Mekt might choose to consider. He understood their temperament and their position, but they had moved beyond this world.

There would be—already was—disagreement, and not all of them, not the most ancient, had awakened yet.

The risks involved... But if this Plain was lost...! A shudder of agitation ran through his long, chitinous body, causing his tightly laced wings to rattle in a rapid, regular rhythm against the back of his thorax. He soothed himself with several slow, calming leg-strokes along his soft lower abdomen as he tried to slow his racing mind.

He had seen the girl. Felt her fear and the dangerous strength coiled inside her when the Ankar Mekt attempted to assimilate her. It had made him warn the others off, lest she react in some unpredictable way that might imperil them all. And he had noted the trace of a Geffitzi mental pattern in her mind. The details were too brief to distinguish, but enough for him to match with one of the five males they held in a chamber above.

He paused, forcing all other thoughts from his mind. For this short amount of time, he, the Swampfather, was the sole force in control of everything. He must make the best use of his time before the Ankar Mekt reassembled and he became only a fraction of the whole—one voice among many.

This moment in time was enough to concern him right now. He

must see the players. Then he would consider the rest. Let the war-rior come, to be considered. He reached out.

The Geffitz was indisputably a true-blood of Kitahn. Klandar Bayne recognized the distinguishing familial mane of thick, red-brown hair and the potent telepathic presence. It was almost in-evitable the pattern he found in the girl's mind would be one of Caer Cadarn.

Muscles rippling powerfully, the warrior dropped into a fighter's stance, knees bent, arms extended slightly. The Wyxan chieftain ob-served him from the obscurity of the shadows, knowing he would feel sickened after teleportation. It was a normal reaction for any species not accustomed to that method of movement. Ignoring the discomfort, however, the warrior searched out instantly, stirring Klandar Bayne's approval. The Kitahni warrior had recovered swiftly from his encounter with the sigalithe' vine. Fortunate: he would need to be at prime fitness if what the Wyxan chieftain suspected were true.

The Swampfather subtly increased the circle of illumination around the Geffitz until it dimly touched upon his own form. The warrior spun with a precision that would have been deadly if he held a weapon. His gray eyes locked with Klandar Bayne's, and he froze, silent and watchful. There was no sense of fear in him. No growls of fury, no aggressive movements, no threats.

The first stirrings of hope rippled in Klandar Bayne. Even he, a devout believer in the Winisp's skills at farseeing, had harbored se-vere doubts in the face of the Geffitzi peoples' volatile nature. He had not allowed himself the remotest hope he would find one of such control among their kind. But this one, standing so warily... Perhaps there might be a chance.

It was an added mercy that the warrior was Kitahni and a skilled telepath, an ability that ran particularly strong in his troublesome bloodline. Though not as powerful and adept as the girl, communication with him should not present a problem.

*"Blood Warrior."* Klandar Bayne kept his sending deliberately neutral as he gave greeting. He examined the Geffitz with close intensity, noting as much of its mental reaction as possible. The Wyxa had subjected the girl to Ankar Mekt. Even though she had disrupted the assimilation with her attempted use of the crystal, Klandar Bayne could, as a result of their limited success, touch her inner thoughts. That allowed him to read her mind and control some of her reactions. But the Geffitzi. They were so volatile of nature, so strong in temperament! The act of mentally incorporating one of them into the Ankar Mekt always risked a trauma to the collective mind. Just their physical presence in this place created a disruptive effect on the Wyxan hive. The thought of absorbing five of them was daunting—a near impossibility!

Meanwhile, Klandar Bayne must attempt the task he set for himself with access to the barest of mental readings from the creature before him, and with no buffer on its emotional reactions.

It was a situation ripe for miscommunication and disaster.

They regarded each other in silence, the Geffitz taking in every detail of him, likely comparing it with what he knew from older warriors of Cadarn. He was young, but he would know the Wyxa wielded mindskills beyond his people, including mindreading.

The warrior's eyes had narrowed at his greeting, but he did not speak. Klandar Bayne sensed a myriad of questions and reactions flowing through his mind, not the least of which was a sharp, gnawing concern for the distinguishable pattern of the girl.

That was good. That was very good.

The Swampfather nodded at him. *"I am Klandar Bayne, chieftain of the Wyxa that reside on this plane of existence."*

When the warrior still did not speak, he continued. *"We would extend courteous greetings to you, Frax Kitahn, Commander of the Cadarn-*

*ian Edge and contested heir to Azay Rhiad. Also, to your brother, Tobin Kitahn; and to Uri Caspani, grandson of Stelach, Elder of the Inner Circle, brother-son and heir to Lord Drayven Caspani of Windmer; and to the Warlord, Seuliac Aedec, of Caer Rhynog, and Lord Velacy Aedec, Grandson of Holderlord Hraben Aedec of Caer Rhynog. This is an impressive, though uninvited, representation of the Geffitzi clans. My sincere apologies that we have not treated you as well as we might choose to treat welcome guests, but, as you are also aware, you are not considered welcome guests."*

*"You'd be hard put to find a time in your peoples' collective memory when you welcomed the Children of Kep as guests in this place, Wyxan."* The reply came quick and cold. *"And we do not choose to be your "guests", welcomed or otherwise. You abducted us. You didn't bring me here to extend an empty greeting. What is it that you want?"*

Straight and to the point. As ever, these wild creatures lacked appreciation for subtlety or restraint. Still, that might be the best way to approach this. *"There are things afoot that have drawn our concern. We desire answers to questions."*

*"Answers to questions."* The Geffitz stared at him for a moment in disbelief before closing again to wariness. Klandar Bayne sensed a banked anger burning inside him. *"Answers to questions? Have the Wyxa never heard of just approaching someone and asking, the way other beings of this world do? And what makes you think I can—or will—answer your questions?"*

*"Because your life and the lives of your companions depend upon it."*

*"A threat? Is that supposed to make me cower in fear?"* The cold fury in the question struck Klandar Bayne like an icy lash.

*"The threat is not from the Wyxa."*

*"Really? Then explain your unprovoked attack on us. We moved in our own lands, beyond your borders, Wyxan. Borders established in ancient times. Or have you decided to alter those lines in our absence?"* His sending was clipped, precise. *"If you think to take our lands, be warned: the*

time is close for the Children of Kep to reclaim what is ours—from any who would take it."

Klandar Bayne sighed. The Children of Kep. Highly appropriate the Geffitzi chose the Earth Goddess as their own, their nature was so similar to her volatile whims. The Wyxa followed the doctrine of the Earth Mother also; yet their interpretation differed so much from the Geffitzi that they might have followed two different deities.

"No, Blood Warrior, we have not altered the boundaries, though the absence of a Geffitzi presence in the lands outside ours has given us a brief respite from the bold intrusions of your people, in particular those of Cadarn, into our land." He could not resist a small barb at this creature's bothersome people. "We are concerned. Concerned, because a few nights ago something we had not felt in ages—conflicting ancient forces—blazed on our border.

"We are not surprised to discover the Children of Kep involved. You have been at the heart of many disruptions to this world. We needed to secure you to discover your relationship to the sudden flare of powers, battling so far from where they should have rested. We tried to bring you into the Palenquemas in the least stressful way possible. At no time did we intend to put any member of your group in danger. Unfortunately, one of you managed to break the sleep-sending and rouse another two. That created several problems for us. You were at the heart of the Palenquemas. It would be difficult to explain our actions to you quickly enough. And we had no idea what your reaction might be—whether you might wreak havoc in our lands. In typical Geffitzi fashion, in the short time we hesitated to act, you took your situation from bad to worse.

"In the past you have been honorable allies to other races of this world, but how you manage to survive the day to day turmoil of your own existence is beyond our comprehension. True to form, you were able to attract the attention of the only kitsk in the area, and then succeeded in provoking it to attack. While we attempted to save both of the injured from that encounter, we lost the other two of you. By then you had thoroughly lost yourselves beyond our aid, within our own lands, no less! We were forced to await the inevitable disaster that would reveal your location and hope the damage it entailed would not be too severe. Happily, the sigalithe' vine will recover."

Hearing Frax's low hiss of outrage at his comment, Klandar Bayne hurried on. "We do not actually consider you and your comrades prisoners, but neither can we allow you to wander about freely. Besides, Blood Warrior, you are not the innocent victim in all of this, as you would pretend. We have the crystal and the Starchild, so, please, cease your posturing: it is useless and it wastes precious time."

\*\*\*

The Starchild? Frax didn't dare to blink as he stared at the Wyxan. At last, an answer to the question that had eaten away at him since his awakening a day ago. He'd been afraid to think about the Priestess for fear of betraying her presence, hoping, however unlikely, that she'd escaped the swamp dwellers' attention and remained free. So, now he knew: the Wyxa had her. They even had a name for her—one that seemed disturbingly appropriate.

He wanted to demand they release her to him, that the Wyxa free them all immediately and allow them to continue on their way. He remained silent, knowing it would be futile. Under ordinary circumstances, the Wyxa would set them free after an inconvenient delay and an encounter with their mindmeld.

Something told him that wasn't going to happen this time. This time, the situation was dangerously different.

"She is well?" he asked at last, cautiously.

"She is well. She expressed a great deal of concern for the safety of you and the others, which seems rather odd, does it not, considering you held her prisoner?"

"Indeed." Frax regarded Klandar Bayne warily. So, the swamp dwellers possessed the priestess and the crystal. And they knew he considered her a Geffitzi prisoner. That might not be bad. He could still extricate them from this situation. There was a chance it would cost them the crystal, a serious loss, if what events indicated were true, but nowhere near as bad as what might happen if the Wyxa continued to delay them. The deeper Araxis and the Balandra penetrated into the continent, the more difficult it would become to evade them.

Perhaps it was time to begin negotiations.

He chose his next words with care. *"It is the experience of my people that the Eldren of the Palenquemas are not ones to interfere in the affairs of others. Since you've agreed that we were not inside your borders and, therefore, not of concern to you, I'm sure you'll release our prisoner back to us and let us continue on our way. After we answer your questions, of course.*

***

A renewed sense of vindication flowed through Klandar Bayne when the Geffitz commander's first concern was for the girl and not the crystal. Now a genuine thrill of delight ran through him.

This one was clever. But was he clever enough for the task the Swampfather feared might lay before him?

*"Perhaps, Commander."*

***

Perhaps? Frax's mouth went dry. By all reason and nature, the creature should have agreed with him on that. At the least, his words should have secured a promise of their eventual release, even if the Wyxa intended—outrageously—to exact some punishment on them. This Klandar Bayne was deviating from normal behavior.

He had feared that might happen. The moment the Wyxa pulled them into the Palenquemas all the rules had changed. Something was dangerously different about their situation.

Any hope he harbored for an easy release evaporated. Staring past the Wyxan into the shadows, Frax Kitahn conceded the true, serious nature of their position: the Wyxa could interfere in their endeavor beyond anything he could ward off with bluff or manipulation.

If that were true, further posturing would be pointless. Best to get on with it in the hope an opportunity to turn this all to his advantage would present itself somewhere further along.

A shot of bitter frustration ran through him. Curse these damned creatures! They had done nothing to help his people twenty years ago, yet here they were now, interfering where they had no right to act.

He wanted to vent the fury and pain of a whole people upon this creature. But this was not the time for mindless reaction. If he believed in the things that had motivated him these last few weeks, if he believed they were true, then the future of his people depended on what happened here.

The surface of his skin grew chilled and his breathing tightened as the burden of his whole race pressed down on him, forcing him to cold reason. Frax flexed his fingers, then tightened them into fists. Now, more than ever, he must keep all his wits about him.

\*\*\*

The Wyxan chieftain could feel the bitter resentment emanating from the warrior of Cadarn. The shifting wash of emotions was horribly disorienting, but he dared not try to suppress them the way he had with the girl. Doing that might antagonize the Commander of the Edge beyond recovery, and he could not chance that. There were questions he must ask; things he must say. Things the warrior must hear. He could ill-afford anything to go wrong. He waited, knowing the Geffitz must vent some of the anger he'd accumulated over the years in order to achieve a mental state receptive to hearing the things that must be said. And perhaps his rage was justifiable, at least in the way the Geffitzi viewed their world.

Long moments dragged out as Klandar Bayne waited, battered

by the storm of emotions that raged in the other and wondering if, perhaps, his hopes were for naught. But, when the Geffitz commander finally looked back at him again, though his eyes smoldered with anger, he had clearly regained control of his thoughts.

*\*\**

The circle of light had gradually expanded to encompass them both. Frax stared at the strange, insect creature before him. This was one of the Eldren Races, superior and aloof in its dealings with the other creatures of this world since the beginnings of time. It cared nothing for events that did not affect its own little sphere.

And it brought him here for some purpose.

An image of the priestess, her expression carefully blank and hiding all reaction despite the seething emotions he sometimes knew raged beneath her fragile exterior, passed through his mind.

*"All right,"* he said. *"What do you want?"*

*\*\**

To see you. To speak with you. To discover if you are the one, the warrior of 'forest and blood', Klandar Bayne wanted to reply. Instead, he said, *"As I have told you, we desire answers to questions."*

He was encouraged and relieved by the Geffitz's return to a wary, controlled attitude. What he was attempting by a direct encounter with this warrior was risky enough without having to cope with the constant assault of tricky emotional waves that would confuse his thoughts.

*"You will answer fully and honestly?"* He watched the Geffitz give a single nod, knowing the warrior wondered how much he could disguise in his answers if he tried. Much, the Wyxan chieftain thought to himself, if he thinks he can.

Which had to be firmly discouraged. *"Be aware before we begin: we subjected the Starchild to Ankar Mekt. The collective mind has shared in her experiences."*

It was a half-truth. The second step, where they would have examined the girl's basic reasoning and motivations, had failed when she pulled two of their number into the joining with her. It clouded their action and forced the Ankar Mekt to release her prematurely. Then she moved to use the crystal against them, making them subdue her before they could re-attempt Ankar Mekt, depriving them of a deeper insight into her character.

This warrior of Cadarn did not need to know that, however. The Ankar Mekt held a certain amount of power over the girl now, and, for all intents and purposes, that was enough.

The commander gave him a shrewdly penetrating look. "*If, as you say, you joined her knowledge to your own, you already know our purpose.*"

So, the threat must be more immediate to secure his full cooperation. "*Just because we joined the Starchild in Ankar Mekt,*" Klandar Bayne warned, "*does not mean the Geffitzi are exempt. The Children of Kep are not known for their emotional restraint, and it would be difficult and unpleasant for both sides involved. However, incorporating you all into the Ankar Mekt is not ruled out as a means to get the answers we seek.*"

He saw a narrowing of gray eyes, but this time the Kitahni warrior held his tongue. Good. He recognized the threat: if they found him too evasive, he might be forced into a mental joining that he wished to avoid.

"*Then get on with your questions.*" The cold fury was back.

"*Did you go to the Black Temple seeking the thing you call the crystal?*"

"*No. How could we seek something we had no idea existed? We still don't know what the cursed thing is, except that it appears to be an object of power.*"

"*Why did you give the crystal to the Starchild?*"

"*Give it to her? Kep! Why would we give a thing of obvious power to our enemy? No, it came to her. She—we—didn't even know she carried it until after we passed into the south. By then it was impossible to put it back.*"

The surprise and appall in the Geffitz's responses made Klandar

Bayne inclined to believe him, but he would not dismiss a second possibility too quickly. The commander was a good warrior. Perhaps he was an adept liar, as well.

The Swampfather pressed on. *"You do admit that you went to the tower seeking something?"*

\*\*\*

*"We went to the southern tower, the Maugrock, seeking information on a potential threat to our people. We know the history of the place. A dangerous sense of evil leaks from it: that's why my people blocked the grand staircase to the Black Temple ages ago. When the Illya came to us with rumors of winged creatures attacking Illian families living along the north border of the Omurda we were all aware of what it might mean. We had to find out if the threat was real."*

For all the success the effort had gained them, Frax thought bitterly. The worst thing the Illya or the Geffitzi could imagine was true: Araxis had stirred an ancient power, resurrecting it and using it for his evil purposes. Yet here they were, trapped in the south with the Wyxa questioning their motives. Kep, why would this being think they had gone to the Maugrock searching for anything? Surely, not from the Priestess...

With a sinking feeling, he recalled how he admitted to her that their original destination had been the tower. But he hadn't told her why. Still, she couldn't believe they'd gone there to take the crystal. She couldn't! She found the crystal in the Black Temple after he, thinking the rock fall blocked access to the place, accidentally took them there. The Ankar Mekt must have picked at least a portion of the truth from her mind. More likely, Klandar Bayne was twisting information to suit his own purposes just to see his reaction.

He scowled. He had suspected—feared—the Wyxa would be interested in the crystal, but he never expected an accusation that he had schemed to take the thing from the temple. This Wyxan acted as if some serious damage had occurred. As if the thing was serving some purpose there. And that would mean the swamp dwellers knew something about it, like what it was and what it was doing there.

"*What is the damned crystal and what's your interest in it?*"

Klandar Bayne ignored his question. "*You were aware when you first set out on your journey, then, what the threat might be?*"

"*We're not ignorant of the old tales, Wyxan. An eyewitness described the attackers. The possibility they might be Balandran was mentioned amid a great stir of doubt and disbelief.*"

"*Were you prepared to address the threat?*"

"*We're a scouting party.*" Frax gave the Wyxan a sharp look of disbelief. "*We went to determine the truth to rumors the Illya brought us, and to report back to the Inner Circle before a scheduled meeting with the assembled leaders. We had no orders to act beyond that.*" With their small number, the Wyxan must see the truth in that.

"*A most impressive scouting party.*"

"*Not everyone is from the original party,*" he replied guardedly. "*The Circle chose Cadarn and Windmer for our knowledge of the tower. The Aedecs joined us after their party fell under attack.*"

\*\*\*

Klandar Bayne felt the stab of bitter resentment run through the warrior at the mention of his Aedec companions. So, they were not a united force, after all. These Earth Children still actively feuded. What of the girl? The warrior had named her enemy only moments ago. What was his true reaction to her? That was vitally important.

"*The Starchild. What is she to you?*" The images of the relationship he gleaned from the girl had been a confusing mixture of emotions from fury and hatred, to pain, and, oddly, even affection.

"*She is an enemy of my people and my prisoner,*" Frax declared flatly.

The cold, hard lack of emotion Klandar Bayne picked up from the Commander of the Edge of Cadarn was so unexpected that it left him momentarily disoriented. He struggled to regain his equilibrium. His next words were almost a protest. "Yet, Blood Warrior, you place high expectations upon her to aid your people."

\*\*\*

Frax stared at the Wyxan stonily. Why would he say that? Nothing in his own words or thoughts should lead the creature to believe he placed any such expectations on the Priestess. In fact, he had deep doubts about her ability to do anything, up to defending herself. She was simply the only hope they had in a bad situation. So far, in this whole inquisition the Swampfather had not asked the first question about what they had discovered in the tower. Why was the Wyxan's concern focused solely on the fact the Priestess possessed that cursed necklace?

And what was all the business with 'blood warrior'? The title sounded as archaic as these creatures.

Resentment followed close on the tail of suspicion. It must be easy for this creature to sit in this dark cavern, asking questions and passing judgments on others' endeavors. Was this where it sat, idle, twenty years ago while Araxis tore the Geffitzi from their lands?

Anger and bitter recriminations had no place here, Frax reminded himself.

He drew a slow, deep breath. *"We've experienced the power of these...Starchildren...before,"* he replied stiffly. *"It does not seem unreasonable to expect her to undo what her people did to us."*

\*\*\*

Klandar Bayne could plainly read the hostility in Frax, but he had no way of knowing its source, that thoughts of the Wyxa and their role in the Geffitzi past, rather than the girl's actions, precipitated it.

Consternation and confusion heightening, the Swampfather pushed on. *"But, even though you may hold her prisoner, you exercise no real control over her, you must know that. She could destroy you with a flick of her finger if she chose."*

\*\*\*

Memory of that thin, dirt-smudged face made the Wyxan's statement sound ridiculous. But, her defense against the ahmdulak on the trail in Omurda stole through his thoughts—yes. Yes, she could. The path he chose to follow the day he took her prisoner was a dangerous, treacherous one. He'd known that from the beginning. But he also recognized she was vulnerable, and he had seized upon that, too. He held some power and influence over her, and he was not ready to give that up to the Wyxa.

He shrugged with calculated indifference. *"Perhaps she could, Wyxan, but she hasn't. I know if she wants to survive, she must defeat the force that pursues her. Which means the one who exiled my people and stole our lands. After she does that, she can remove the barrier that bars our return to the south. I intend to see that happen."*

*"That is not enough! The threat is much greater."*

*"Oh? Why? Because you suddenly think there's a chance the evil pursuing her might touch you, too? Is that what this is all about? It didn't concern you twenty years ago. Stay out of the matter now! What we are doing does not concern the Wyxa."*

*"You are wrong. This matter greatly concerns us."*

*"No. It doesn't. This is a matter for the Geffitzi clans—an opportunity for us to reclaim our lands. Your people didn't help us when we lost them, don't interfere now!"*

*"You are clever, Blood Warrior. You moved as lightly as a spirit across the Palenquemas, and you succeeded admirably in eluding us. That is an impressive ability, and a bane to those that would seek you. But there are forces stirring around you and your companions that are more powerful than you can imagine. Do not make the mistake of thinking your skills will protect you against them. You have only the barest comprehension of what begins to move in this land. We encountered it before, and it strikes cold terror into the hearts of the Wyxa."*

"My people suffered during the Reign of the Darkness and the Great Cataclysm, too, Wyxan," Frax snapped.

"Yes. But the Children of Kep did not play a part in the final battle to defeat the Darkness. Only we had the power to do that. It called for a terrible, extreme action, but we thought our task done, and the matter ended for all time. Regrettably, it appears we were mistaken.

"We recognize you aspire to be the solution to this re-emerging problem, but the Ankar Mekt does not view you as the best solution."

"Not the best solution? Just what the hell...?" The rush of outrage that ran over Frax dizzied him. "You coldly ignored our struggles twenty years ago while a ruthless force massacred our people and drove us from our homes. Now we find ourselves once again in a battle for our survival and all of a sudden you are here, telling us we may or may not be the ones best suited to defend ourselves?"

"Our world is in peril, Frax Kitahn. The Geffitzi situation is only a minor portion of the problem. You have no idea what you face."

Minor? Frax's fury blazed.

"Restraint, please, Blood Warrior." The Swampfather's sending bordered on a plea. It raised an appendage as if to ward off some threat from him.

Frax stared at the creature, seeing for the first time how the Wyxan was struggling to continue the exchange between them. It was close to writhing in agony. I'm doing that, he thought remotely. Somehow, I'm causing the pain and confusion in him. But how? And if he was the source of the creature's pain, why should he care? Perhaps he should consider it a small bit of revenge for all the Geffitzi warriors captured and affected by these creatures in their cursed Ankar Mekt over the years.

But, again, it didn't solve anything. Grudgingly, Frax forced his anger away. "All right, Wyxan. Suppose you tell me what we face."

Before the Swampfather could respond, a ripple of telepathic activity fluttered at the edge of Frax's mental comprehension and Klandar Bayne's mental presence blanked for a moment.

The Swampfather abruptly refocused attention back to him. *"This interview is ended for now, Blood Warrior."*

Ended? Frax's heart froze. Too late, he wondered how much opportunity he'd lost here with his anger. *"Wait. Your questions. You haven't asked what we found in the Black Tower."*

*"We will speak again."*

*"I—"* a wave of lightheadedness washed over him. Damn the Wyxa and their teleportation! *"Wait! Tell me—"*

# 46

## Back in the Cell

"Frax!" Tobin caught him as he bent double with nausea. "Kep! What did they do to you? Are you hurt? Uri!"

Frax waved a hand in weak protest, but he did not push away as Tobin shouldered his weight. "Damn Wyxa." He cursed between quick, shallow breaths.

Tobin's expression twisted with helpless rage as he looked at him. *"I warned you."* He hissed mentally at his older brother. *"I told you this would happen. Did they—"*

"No. Not assimilation." Frax shuddered as a wave of pain twisted in his belly. "It's not as bad as it looks, Tobin, I swear." He gave a choked, bitter laugh. "I'm just sick from their damned teleportation." What a joke that would become in Rhynog!

The younger Kitahn growled in anger, but eased his grip.

"Take him over there and let him sit down," Uri motioned toward the inner wall of the chamber as the Aedecs moved to join them. "Velacy, get him some water."

Frax closed his eyes and eased to the floor, to lean against the wall as he waited for his stomach to settle. Kep, his reaction to the second teleport was stronger than the first one. Would it grow progressively worse with each trip? That would be bad. There was at least a third trip in his future, Klandar Bayne had sounded very clear about that.

The others stood about, holding their questions and giving him time to recover while he concentrated on the gourd cup Velacy placed in his hand. It took several shallow sips, interspersed with long pauses, before the nausea finally eased enough for him to speak. He glanced around the half-circle of troubled faces with a wan smile.

"Well?" Tobin no longer attempted to veil his impatience.

"You'd all better sit down. This will take a while."

What to say? His body screamed from weariness. If he could just snatch a little sleep ... But no time to drift, not right now. He pulled back to focus, composing his thoughts. He had spoken aloud when he told them to sit, a clear indication for them to follow his example. The Wyxa were more likely to eavesdrop on a mental exchange. Not that they couldn't listen in, no matter how they communicated, but no need to make it easier for them.

His stomach gave a twist, and he tightened his muscles to disguise a flinch of pain. It was too soon to have this discussion. He should wait, find out more, and present some type of perspective on the situation. But these warriors would never tolerate his silence, even if he explained that it was the best strategy. A Geffitz warrior would endure infinite hardship if he knew why he endured it. It gave him ownership of his situation, whether he approved of the reason or not.

Besides, any of the rest of them could be the next one taken. They had to know what to expect.

He straightened, drew a long, deep breath, and forced a smile as he took in the tight expressions. "It will comfort you to know we are classified as unwanted guests."

There were snorts and angry muttered curses all around. For once, the curl of scorn that lifted the warlord's lips pleased Frax: at least this time Cadarn wasn't on the receiving end of it.

"A Geffitz whose freedom is restricted is not a guest by any definition." As expected, Seuliac made a pointed, succinct observation.

Frax nodded. "We're prisoners, plain and simple." He was glad he'd had the foresight to avoid mindspeech: right now, he couldn't trust his own reaction toward some of the things the Wyxa chieftain had said to him. It was wiser to speak aloud, avoiding unintentional, telltale personal reactions telepathy might reveal, most particularly to the Warlord. "What's worse, I don't think they want to release us."

"What!" Uri looked stunned.

"But you said..." Velacy shot Uri an outraged look of accusation.

"Be silent and listen," Seuliac snapped at the younger Aedec.

Velacy ducked his head with a sullen expression as the Warlord turned attention back to Frax, his eyes hard and angry. "Why, not release us?"

"I'm not sure yet. Something different is going on with these Wyxa. They're not acting the way we've been taught to expect. I think it's tied to that damned crystal."

"They know about it?" The Caspani warrior frowned.

"They claim they have it in their possession."

"And the girl?"

"Her, too. They call her the 'Starchild,'" Frax added wryly.

"I don't like that," Uri shook his head in dismay. "It's too familiar, as if they know intimate details about her. Where is she? What have they done with her?"

"They say she's well and expressing concern for us. And yes, Uri, they know a great deal about her, if what I heard is true. They claim they subjected her to Ankar Mekt."

Uri and Tobin both swore, but for different reasons: Uri, in concern for the Priestess; Tobin, for the threat the situation posed for the rest of them.

"What do they want from us?"

Frax had to admire the Warlord's ability to get to and stay focused on the essence of a matter. "That's the strange part. The Wyxan I talked to said they wanted answers to questions. But the questions..." his troubled expression deepened with the recall. "He claimed they assimilated the Priestess, but, if I understand the way Ankar Mekt works, he was remarkably uninformed on certain things. They should know everything, down to the first word she spoke as an infant. That would include anything we said or did in her presence. Yet, the whole encounter centered on our relationship to the Priestess and why we went to the Maugrock. He just accused us of going there to steal the crystal and wanted to know why. He didn't ask what else we found. No concern. Nothing."

Uri and Seuliac frowned.

"You told them what happened?" Tobin leaned forward, his expression tight with concern.

"Him. I told him. To start from the beginning; they teleported me to this vast, dark, foggy, whispery place where I spoke with a creature name Klandar Bayne. He calls himself Swampfather, Keeper of this Plain of Existence."

Uri nodded. "The title for their leader on this world, yes. He leads the Wyxa who live in the Palenquemas, which they also call the Primordial Plain because they live the physical, first part of their lives here."

"He may rule here, but I don't think he has the final say in this situation. That may be bad. In spite of everything, I suspect he's actually a reasonable sort. As Wyxa go," he added. "Unfortunately, he's not the only one we must deal with. I'm sure the Ankar Mekt will definitely figure into the near future."

"The Ankar Mekt is their method of governing," Uri explained for the benefit of Seuliac and Velacy. "Think of it as a council conducted through mind sharing among the living and the dead. It can contain any number of Wyxa, but the major events include the essences of those that have died or passed on to what they call their Ethereal, or Spiritual, Plane. Those are the true Eldren. They are vastly ancient spirits or pure mental entities from a time long before the clans. And yes, you're right: they won't be kindly disposed toward Geffitzi in any capacity."

"So? What did you do?" Velacy demanded.

"I answered his questions, Velacy. He threatened me with assimilation if I didn't. He wanted to know if we went to the Maugrock seeking that damned crystal and if we gave it to the Priestess. I said no. I don't think he believed me."

Uri looked dismayed. "That's bad, Frax."

"Tobin can say 'I told you so.'" He gave his brother a tight smile.

The younger Kitahn's eyes narrowed in anger. "I'm not pleased to be right in this situation."

"So, what does it mean?" Velacy asked.

"It means they will take at least some of us into Ankar Mekt." Murmurs of dismay rippled around Frax. "I'm the logical first choice, since they established contact with me first, but it could be any of us. So, if you're the one who finds yourself suddenly in front of them, there are some things you should remember." Their attention locked on him. "First, many Geffitz warriors have been through the process. You will survive it. You probably won't want to enter the Palenquemas again as a result, but," he shrugged, "for some of you, it's no loss. Second: you will not die. The Wyxa do not kill. Maybe, with so many of us, they won't take us all. But you should all be aware: they'll take us, one at a time, until they think they've reached the truth, whatever they think that is, so we should prepare some type of strategy."

"Why didn't you just tell them the truth?" Velacy exclaimed angrily.

"Damn it, Velacy! I did tell them the truth. They don't want to believe it."

Velacy scowled.

"What strategy would you suggest?" Seuliac asked.

Frax looked from Uri to Tobin. "If anyone knows something about that legendary "trappers trick" you could help us avoid this future unpleasantness..."

"I've wracked my brain over it since I woke, Frax." Uri shook his head. "I haven't come up with anything. The ones that know about it are old grizzlies from Cadarn, and they refuse to talk about it. Twenty years, and they're still busy protecting their damned hunting turf."

Tobin sighed, his expression glum.

What had the successful Cadarnian trappers done to frustrate the Ankar Mekt? The Wyxa assimilated warriors that came back terrified, unable to even think of entering the Palenquemas again, or they came back seemingly unscathed, unrepentant, and defiantly returned to trap the swamp to the end of their days without further reprisal. The Wyxa never bothered them again. Why? If they could find the right thread to pull, they might unravel something. But Frax had no clue.

"I did observe that strong emotion affects them negatively,' he said. "Anger causes them confusion and disorientation."

"Every Geffitz they have ever encountered has been angry," Tobin observed tersely.

"Or belligerent," Uri added.

Frax felt a twist of grudging humor. "True." The swamp dwellers had certainly experienced Geffitz animosity on a grand scale and first hand in their past encounters with the trappers. They would be prepared for that reaction.

"So we think some warriors acted differently in the past," Seuliac said.

"Evidently some of them did. There are two drastically different responses to the experience."

"Which is most common?"

"Most never returned to the Palenquemas."

"And what is our most likely reaction?"

Uri laughed. "Anger, hostility, and aggression."

"What reaction would they least expect?" Seuliac asked.

"Cooperation." Uri was quick to respond.

"Perhaps your successful minority fought the situation less and suffered less adverse reaction." But Rhynog had no first-hand experience in this particular situation. He looked at Frax.

Frax thought back to some of those legendary old men. A few still lived. Most were reclusive, except one, who held a reputation for quick temper. They all kept to themselves more than average. He understood where Seuliac was leading them, but his limited experience showed him no pattern.

"Cooperation?" Tobin glared at the Warlord in disgust. "Are you insane? We have to give them the most difficult experience they've ever encountered."

"That's been done before," Seuliac told him. "Obviously it didn't work. There are five of us here, where they faced it alone. We have a chance to be more clever. Maybe we should seek our own answers."

As both Tobin and Velacy opened their mouths to protest, Frax laughed aloud. "Five different reactions! If the Ankar Mekt takes something from us, why shouldn't we take something in equal exchange?"

Uri had also caught on. "Can one remain focused enough to do it?" he wondered.

"What?" The two younger warriors frowned, puzzled.

"Let them have what they want without resistance, but see what you can take in return," Uri said.

"A sneak attack?" Tobin put the thought into blunt words. "What the hell would we want from the bugs?"

"Would it matter? Whatever you took might not be usable, but a hard focus, with a purpose, could be an effective counter to their assault," Seuliac said.

"If the Wyxa think you're attacking them you might draw an unpleasant defensive reaction out of them," Uri warned him sharply.

"Yet, it might be worth a try," Frax said.

*"Frax, Seuliac doesn't care if you come out of this encounter intact,"* Uri shot a fierce mental aside to his friend. "I urge strong caution," he said aloud to them all. "Be careful how aggressively you act."

Uri's warning made sense. The strategy would call for control and subtlety, things hard to maintain when one's brain was being pulled apart. But there were Geffitzi that had managed some type of trick to defeat the Ankar Mekt.

Frax looked at the uneasy, angry expressions around him and knew that, just like him, these warriors feared assimilation, but not nearly as much as they resented the thought of Wyxan trespass into their minds.

Seuliac leaned forward. "The Priestess was already subjected to this?"

"So this Klandar Bayne says."

"You don't believe him."

"Like I said, Warlord, the girl knows the truth. If they assimilated her, they would know what happened in the tower and how she got the crystal. Yet he insisted on questioning our motives and the actions behind this whole situation."

"So they don't believe her," Tobin said.

"Or they're cross-checking to be thorough," Uri suggested.

"Or maybe she has the skills to circumvent them, and they know or sense it," Seuliac said.

And that was a horrible, awesome thought they would be foolish not to consider. If she was that good... All Frax's earlier doubts swirled in around him. She had told Uri the Ly Kai couldn't lie in a sending. Caspani had tested her more than once to satisfy their suspicions and her responses had been pained or wary, but never disingenuous.

Could she block and deceive both the Wyxa and the Geffitzi?

"What is it about us that disturbs these creatures?"

The other four stared at Seuliac blankly, forcing the Warlord to repeat the question impatiently. "What is it about us that disturbs these Wyxa?"

Uri smiled with bitter humor. "For a starter, we kill things. They don't like that, especially here in their territory. And they think we're disruptive and way too emotional. They prefer calm and order."

Seuliac raised a fine eyebrow. "That can't be a surprise. With a group joining such as this Ankar Mekt there wouldn't be a place for wild emotion, would there?"

It was the same concept the Priestess had explained about the Ly Kai Council on that cold, rainy night in Omurda, A group joining demanded rigid self-control of the participants. Strong emotion was too disruptive to the whole. Which, Frax suspected, was a reason she was able to maintain calm most of the time, no matter what happened around her. Or what he did to her. Control of her emotions had been a primary and repeated lesson.

Which would make her an ideal candidate for successful assimilation. She knew how to behave in a mental joining. Still, he was not convinced Klandar Bayne had revealed the whole truth about her joining. Surely, she would resist.

"After they take you into this Ankar-thing, then what?" Velacy burst out.

Frax bit back frustration as the idea that hung on the edge of his thoughts vanished. Damn the younger Aedec! Was the young fool really third in the line of succession to lead Rhynog? Considering how treacherous life in a major hold could be, Frax found it amazing and baffling that the young Geffitz was still alive. Discreet comments over the years had intimated that he had character flaws, but one learned to treat such rumors judiciously, always conscious of them, but never taking them to heart in case they were false plants put out to catch an enemy off guard. A few days of close confinement had certainly exposed the truth. Surely, Seuliac must pray daily for the continued health of Hraben and his heir, Midsel. Frax almost felt sympathy for the Warlord.

Almost. But, anything that handicapped a foe—and Rhynog was a centuries-old foe—worked in Cadarn's favor.

"Well, whatever they do, they can't keep us here forever," Tobin said.

"No, they can't." Frax agreed, relieved as the shift in subject drained away some of his irritation with Velacy. The constant undercurrent of hostility and tension in this chamber wore on them all. The Wyxa must feel it, too. "This Klandar Bayne also seemed interested in our internal politics. I think he grew distressed when he discovered we were not together by mutual agreement or choice. I don't see why it should concern them."

"At least as long as we're not spilling each other's blood in their guest chamber."

Frax glanced up to see a gleam of ironic amusement in Seuliac's eyes. Was that just a caustic comment, or a threat aimed at him, or, possibly, Velacy? Beside him, Tobin gave a snort of hard agreement to the Warlord's comment, and Frax allowed a slight lift of his lips in a humorless acknowledgment. Kep, when did he start bristling at comments even his firebrand of a brother let pass?

"It would probably make it easier for them to let us go if they thought we worked as a cohesive force," Uri pointed out.

"Well, yes. He did seem concerned about that. But we are working together."

Uri looked as if he disagreed, but refrained from comment.

"So, what happens next?" Tobin asked.

"We wait. They're not finished with us yet, but there's nothing we can do until we know more." Frax yawned abruptly. "How long was I gone?"

"How long did it feel to you?" Uri said carefully.

"About an hour."

The big Geffitz nodded. "Yes."

"Kep, I'm tired." Frax leaned his head against the greenish wall and closed his eyes. Before the others could say another word, he fell asleep.

"That doesn't seem natural," Uri said uneasily.

Tobin prodded his brother in a cautious attempt to wake him. The commander did not even twitch in response.

"The Wyxa at work?" Seuliac asked quietly.

"Maybe." Uri stood. "I'll keep an eye on him in case he exhibits any signs of distress." He stared at Frax with a troubled frown. "He needs the rest. Whatever is happening, he has to be at his best. All our fates are in his hands."

\*\*\*

A short while later Velacy and Tobin's exercise session deteriorated from a wrestling match to a full-fledged fistfight.

Velacy's slip of thumb might have been an accident. But Tobin's responding throw was hard enough that the floor shuddered when Velacy struck it. Velacy came up with an outraged roar, Tobin met him head-on, and they locked in a battle with every intention of killing the other. It took everything Uri and Seuliac had to separate them.

Exiled to opposite ends of the chamber, the younger warriors continued their sniping and glowering until Uri ordered them to move so the central chamber blocked their view of each other. Velacy was not an adequate telepath to receive Tobin's mental comments at that distance, and they eventually realized that calling out taunts and insults to an unseen target sounded childish. Left alone like bad children, they slowly sulked back to reason.

*"Kep must have hated to see the Battle of Pryon,"* Uri sent to Seuliac in a disgusted tone, referring to one of the bloodiest periods of Geffitzi infighting in their long history. In their religion, all warriors slain in battle went before Kep immediately after death, so she could direct them to whatever level of afterlife paradise their valor had earned.

*"You mean all those surly, dead warriors waiting their turn at reward?"* Seuliac asked, amused.

*"Continuing the battle right in front of Her."* Uri shook his head morosely.

*"Brawl, you mean."* Seuliac laughed at the image his mind conjured, of a seething field of deceased Geffitzi warriors locked in battle before their amazed and impatient Goddess.

Uri heaved a troubled sigh. Not that he would admit it, but the younger warriors' fight had been a bit of a welcome distraction, giving them a vent for some of the pent-up frustration they all felt. But now that things had settled down, he felt as if he had forgotten something. Something important...

Seuliac caught his expression and sobered, perhaps catching a sense of the same thing. They sat in silence for a heartbeat.

"Frax!" "Kitahn!" It dawned on them both at the same moment.

The spot where Frax had been sleeping was empty.

# 47

## The Wyxa Gather

Something was amiss. Klandar Bayne sensed the tension and turmoil the moment his consciousness merged into the vast sea of shared mental existence that was the Ankar Mekt.

He was the sole member from the Primordial Plain inside the joining. All the rest belonged to the Ethereal Realm, and none of them attempted to join with him, to share the group mind.

He continued to hold separate, surmising his recent contact with the outsiders made the assembly wary of direct contact with him. With such a large amount of Wyxan consciousness tied up in the Ankar Mekt, the Wyxa would be nothing if not cautious.

When no other member living in the Palenquemas entered the joining, Klandar Bayne felt a mild stir of concern.

Abruptly Hafod-y-lan, speaker for the Ethereal Plain, focused attention upon him. *"Keeper of the First Plain, have you spoken with the intruders?"*

The tone of the presence that had spoken so imperiously to the Starchild was no less so to Klandar Bayne.

"*I have.*" The Swampfather was no more than a flicker of greenish light, separate, with thousands of beings surrounding him. If they joined with him, they would know all he knew instantaneously. Yet, they made no effort to take him into the greater mindlink.

Which meant whatever information they held disturbed them. His curiosity intensified.

"*What reason do they offer for their activities?*" Hafod-y-lan asked.

"*For the most part, ignorance.*"

"*They removed the Guardian Stone. They perpetrated a crime against this world.*"

"*The Starchild removed the Stone.*" He rebuked the other mildly. "*We deal with two distinct groups of individuals here: the Geffitzi and the Starchild. We must be specific.*"

"*It admits to taking the Stone?*"

"*She admits to taking the Stone in error.*"

"*Not likely, in all the vastness of this world, it would find and pick up such a thing in error. Why did this being seek out the Guardian Stone?*"

"*She does not admit to seeking the Stone. She claims it beckoned to her when she fled through the Black Temple. You know that much of her story.*" Klandar Bayne's curiosity shifted toward puzzlement. Why was the Ankar Mekt pursuing this topic in this manner, asking questions for which they already had answers? Even though their attempted assimilation of her memory was only partially successful, events she had experienced were accessible to them. Only her deeper thinking processes, her motivations and early life experiences, had eluded them.

"*Does she admit to tampering with the Stone?*"

The question caught him by surprise. His reaction sent a ripple through the other minds around him.

"*Swampfather. Perhaps your recent exposure to the Geffitz warrior inadvertently allowed you to absorb some of his savage behavior.*" Hafod-y-lan's rebuke was stern.

*"I offer sincere apologies to the joining. The implications of the question greatly startled and dismayed me."*

*"As it affected us, as well."*

*"But, tampering? How?"*

*"The protective force linked to the Guardian Stone is gone."*

*"But—that is impossible. The Wyxa created the Stone with the cooperation of that force. Nothing can break the binding."*

*"Yet, the force is gone."*

*"Is there any indication of what happened? Any damage? Any remnant traces of what might do such a thing?"*

*"None. The ward crystal's structure is undamaged; the power-workings laid upon it remain undisturbed. The protective force is gone. The Guardian Stone is so diminished it is barely effective at all. Small wonder our world has come under assault; there was nothing to stop the beginning trickle of invasion. And now, with this removal from its resting place, disaster is pushing to break through, unchecked."* At last, the greater mind opened to Klandar Bayne, allowing him access to what the others had discovered while he met with the Starchild and the Geffitz commander.

What he found made him tremble in tightly contained horror and dismay.

Klandar Bayne was well aware of the immense effort required to create the Guardian Stone. It would be equally difficult for something to disarm it. But they had not sensed any disturbance of that magnitude! With no evidence of tampering, there must be some other explanation.

*"The Starchild said the crystal protected her. Perhaps it used her to carry it to us, to make us aware of this development."* That would answer a question that had nagged at him since their first, abrupt awareness of the crystal in the south.

*"Then why did it lay silent in the Palenquemas, failing to alert us to its presence so we could retrieve it. And why did it respond to this Starchild*

*when she tried to summon it against us? Clearly the creature exercises some influence over it."*

Reasonable observations. Swiftly Klandar Bayne scanned through all the findings the Ankar Mekt had opened to him. The Guardian Stone was empty. How and why? What could make the force that had protected this world for ages choose to abandon its post—and it must have chosen to leave if there were no indications of violence against the Stone.

Had the Ankar Mekt considered any reason for this situation beyond faulting their hapless visitors? Klandar Bayne wished he were as confident in his thoughts as the Eldren. But he was not so old and wise.

Or so self-absorbed.

Hard and unbending in their thinking, the ancients of the Ethereal Plain based their conclusions on the facts laid before them, without feeling the need for further investigation. Age and the experience of countless years did, indeed, give them keen insight. And the evidence of time frequently supported them. The here and now of the Primordial Plain, however, held many subtleties and variables which influenced those greater spans of time in the near term. Difficult to deal with tiny details and subtleties when your view scaled ages, but sometimes necessary. That was the reason members of the two Plains joined in Ankar Mekt. The ancients did not question their own observations: if it appeared to be so, then it was. The Wyxa of the Primordial Plain had recognized that problem long ago and set a restriction in place: the ancients were forbidden to take autonomous action against the Primordial Plain. The Swampfather wielded final say on any resolution taken there. The Eldren must abide that most critical rule.

It did not prevent them trying to use their powerful influence over any decision.

Klandar Bayne could not shake his sense of foreboding. What

if the reason for the change in the Guardian Stone lay elsewhere? What if they were dismissing something too easily?

He had a sudden desire to withdraw from the group mind. He held the individuals that they discussed at hand. He could work toward finding answers. But the Ankar Mekt did not seem inclined to dismiss him. Neither did they seem inclined to move forward. They just hung around him, tense and silent. Full of expectation and reproach, as if they knew he had the answer and was just slow in presenting it.

"*Perhaps the Guardian Stone has aligned itself with the Starchild,*" he dared to suggest.

"*Aligned with one of them?*" A general stir of astonishment and disbelief rippled outward. "*Impossible. By her very nature the Starchild must be its enemy.*"

The Geffitzi were her reasoned enemies, also, he thought. But they recognized a mutual threat, and, if what their leader said was true, they were working with her. If the stormy-natured warriors could set their enmity aside after what had caused their exile from the south, then anything was possible, even to the Wyxa recognizing the need for help from outsiders. Klandar Bayne refrained from making the observation in order to pursue his point. "*And yet, the Guardian Stone came to her.*"

"*We do not recognize that for truth,*" Hafod-y-lan was quick to respond.

"*Yet, Honored Ancients, we touched this in her mind. Can we refuse to acknowledge that? She did not attempt to deceive—*"

"*We did not detect deceit. These are powerful, treacherous beings; we know this from past experience. Her memories might be false. What does she seek to do? Her mind was unclear. What did you discover in your contact with them?*"

Dutifully Klandar Bayne opened his mind to the rest of the

Ankar Mekt and shared the things he had observed and learned of Kaphri and the Geffitz commander.

"*Such clever creatures, these Geffitzi. What do they hope to achieve in their misalliance with this creature?*"

"*They want the Starchild to remove the barricade that prevents their access to their lands in the southern hemisphere.*"

"*Why do they think she would do that?*" A mild ripple of curiosity ran through the group mind. "*Is this some deception she uses to lure them into helping her?*"

Klandar Bayne could not say. "*Perhaps we missed something while evaluating the information we secured.*"

He sensed a general flurry of activity as the others rummaged through information they had acquired in their attempted mind-meld, searching for any critical bits that might shed some light on the situation.

"*Nothing. As we suspected.*"

Was it because the information did not exist, or had they missed it, along with other critical things, in their failure to join success-fully with the Starchild? "*Perhaps another attempt at a joining with her...*"

A ripple of trepidation ran through the group mind.

"*That is not an option.*" Hafod-y-lan dismissed the suggestion.

"*There is one other possibility. The Winisp's prophecy...*"

"*No, Swampfather,*" Hafod-y-lan sent sharply. "*We are not willing to discuss that as a possibility.*"

"*We must consider the possible repercussions if we interfere in this.*"

"*Interfere? We do not interfere; we act. What do you suggest we do?*"

"*Wait. Watch. These creatures are not wholly ignorant of the threat they face.*"

"*Are you suggesting we rely on unknown forces to discover unknown so-lutions at some inopportune moment?*"

"*The Winisp—*"

"No. Those are foolish stories only creatures like the Geffitzi find hope in, Klandar Bayne. Would you have us believe vaporous, insipid ideas will snatch us from disaster? No. That is unthinkable."

"Even if it is all we have? It may be our only path to saving this Plain."

Losing the Primordial Plain was unthinkable, yet this new discovery made that a distinct risk. The Ankar Mekt quivered and throbbed with a light of unhappy indecision. "What do these creatures offer us in this situation?"

"Offer us? They are willing to put their lives at risk."

"That is not enough."

No. It wasn't enough. But it was all they had. "What would you suggest? As you say, the ward-crystal is inadequate to the task for which we created it."

"This threat will not affect us." A whisper came from remote thoughts—ancients stirring from the distant past. "The force which invades is weak. It can never re-establish the power it once claimed. It will not touch us."

Some of them suggested the Wyxa should ignore this situation? Klandar Bayne's dismay deepened at the callous thought. "Once before, we ignored a problem until disaster struck and forced us to act. Do you think our foe will forget what we did? If evil regains power, it will not ignore us. It cannot. It will strike to protect itself and to seek revenge. If not right now, then sometime in the future, after its power grows. And it will grow in power. That is inevitable. That is its nature. This Plain will never be safe if that evil returns to this world."

Would the Wyxa of this Plain, the ones not present in this Ankar Mekt, be willing to live out the rest of their existence under such a threat? He did not believe so. Klandar Bayne did not mask his dismay at the direction their thoughts were trending. The ancients were a cautious lot. Time stretched infinitely for them and nothing of this world could harm the Ethereal Plain. The old threat still loomed over those living on the Primordial Plain, however. They must view things differently, and this assembly might be steering them in a direction for disaster.

*"We must be cautious in our actions: the Starchild is an unknown force, as we already witnessed. We don't know what role she is destined to play. It might be catastrophic for our world if we prevent her from acting. And these Geffitzi warriors..."* A sudden wave of emotion tore at Klandar Bayne's mind.

No! Not now! The young Geffitzi warriors were fighting. A swirl of confusion and dismay rippled across the group mind as Geffitzi anger and hostility radiated out through the Wyxan complex.

The foolish creatures! Klandar Bayne increased the intensity of his thoughts, attempting to draw the attention of the Ankar Mekt away from the disturbance. *"We cannot continue to hold them captive."* That was not what he had wanted to say, but the disruption had just rendered anything else foolish-sounding.

*"We cannot release them to continue forward."* Hafod-y-lan was firmly dominant again.

*"What do you propose, then?"*

*"Propose? No. That would intimate room for negotiation. There is not. They cannot continue on the path they follow. We will return them to their people. There is no other option."*

Not what he wanted to hear. Klandar Bayne pursued his course patiently. *"The risk is, indeed, great. Yet, we do have some insight into this situation: I remind you again of the Winisp's prophecy. His words were precise. He spoke of such a time and situation."*

*"We do not consider the Winisp's words applicable here."* Hafod-y-lan came to the forefront of the Ankar Mekt's shared consciousness again. *"We cannot wait in the hope a remedy for this situation will present itself. As you say, this is a Starchild we discuss. She is a gate-opener. Even if she is capable of constructive action, we cannot predict what the overall effects might be or how far-reaching. If she makes an error, it could jeopar-*

dize immortality for you and all those on the Primordial Plain. We must contain that now."

If Klandar Bayne had been in possession of his body, his wings would have rattled mightily with dismay and distress. Now he understood the ancients' aggressive position: any situation that put the link between the two Wyxan Plains in jeopardy became the jurisdiction of the ancients of the Ethereal Plain. The situation was no longer solely in the control of the Primordial Plain.

But could the ancients justify acting without consideration for the other denizens of this world? The Wyxa were not the only beings at risk here. Removing the Geffitzi and the Starchild from the equation still left far too many problems unresolved.

"The course of action you advocate will not resolve the threat hanging over this world. Other races will remain in jeopardy."

"Is that our concern? The lesser and the weak always pay a price beneath the heel of fate. Some will survive. They always do. We will protect the Primordial Plain. If it ceases to exist, all will be lost."

"It cannot cease to exist!" "It will continue. It always has!" "Dare we make such a judgment?" Arguments swirled in the green light.

"We dare." Spoken as harshly and coldly as Klandar Bayne expected. "But we digress from the issue. Again, why did these creatures remove the Guardian Stone and what did they do to it? What is their true purpose? We will speak with this Geffitz leader, on the unlikely prospect he might contribute something useful to this assembly.

"One further question, Swampfather. Do we know what "Gemma" is?"

"We do not. The image associated with the word eludes us."

"Then we will ask the Geffitz. Bring him now."

"In what manner?" Did they wish a joining or a physical encounter?

"Bring him here physically. We will speak with him. If more becomes necessary, then we will proceed from there."

"As you wish." Klandar Bayne reached out for Frax Kitahn.

# 48

## The Ankar Mekt

His brain screaming a warning, Frax shifted from asleep to wide-awake in a single heartbeat. He surged to his feet, green light illuminating trailers of fog as they wafted lazily in the wake of his panicked movement.

Teleportation sickness struck him hard, folding him over. He pressed his arms into his belly to fight a roiling stomach and a hammering heart. Amid all that he realized he was stark naked.

Damn the Wyxa to hell! He'd accepted the inevitability of another encounter, but they put him at an additional disadvantage by snatching him from sleep and stripping him bare. It was the type of thing he would do in order to throw hostile prisoner off balance. And he'd keep them off balance by putting them in a threatening environment. He could accept the darkness, with the glowing green ball that loomed before him, as nothing less.

It looked as if the Wyxa might have taken a page from the Geffitzi rulebook.

That did not bode well for him.

But, a naked body was a naked body: he had no particular modesty to offend. And more than a few of his people had been in this situation before him. Ignoring the chaos in his belly, he straightened and focused his attention on the thing hovering in front of him.

Thousands of tiny flecks of light floated gently within the clearly proscribed circumference of the glowing green ball. If he stretched his arms out from his sides, fingers extended, he might touch the walls across its diameter. Did it have some type of outer barrier or skin? He could not bring himself to reach out and satisfy his curiosity.

Was Klandar Bayne inside that thing? Thinking of the large creature, reduced to a tiny mote of light made his stomach lurch again. If he had been plunged directly into that, he shuddered inwardly, there would have been no accounting for his reaction. Which might be why he stood physically in this dark space. Maybe the Ankar Mekt had made that mistake before with some hapless trapper of Cadarn and paid a heavy price for the lesson learned.

So, things could be worse.

Hell, no need to feel overly confident: things could still get worse. But right now things were going nowhere and that bothered him, too. The Wyxa could probably remain inactive like this for days and never even notice the passage of time; they lived that long. Geffitzi did not.

"All right, you brought me here. What do you want?" He spoke aloud, his mind shielded, refusing to risk any sending from the massive mental presence hanging in front of him. His voice sounded harsh in the silence, but at least it didn't crack with fear. Jerked around like this, sleeping to waking, not knowing what to expect next, was unnerving, to say the least.

Just the way they meant it to be.

The whole globe pulsed once. "*Arrogant Geffitz.*" The response overwhelmed his mindshields like a wave slopping over a seawall. *"Curb your insolence."*

Curb his insolence? The rush of his fury dizzied him. He caught himself, forcing calm. Again, not the time, not the place. Something he was telling himself more and more frequently these last few days. With so much at stake, emotion had no place here.

It was still damn hard to fight it.

The chilled air of the chamber began to sink into his flesh. He waggled his fingers at his sides, trying to drive the cold away from them as he glanced about. The green light held back a vast darkness. Again, the thought: where was Klandar Bayne? The same gut feeling that told him the booming, imperious voice held absolutely no concern for the welfare of any Geffitz, alive or dead, told him Klandar Bayne was not so callous and insensitive. If he could maneuver the Wyxa into using the Swampfather to communicate with him, he might win a small but important concession. But, how to draw him out of that green ball? That would probably require a deft bit of manipulation on his part.

He should see how much they would work with him first. "What do you want?" he repeated.

*"You are Frax Kitahn, of the Caer Cadarn?"* The question boomed in his head with cold precision.

Just whom did they think they had? "I am." He spoke aloud again. "And as a representative of the Geffitzi clans I strongly protest your treatment of my party, and warn you that our continued detainment will be considered an act of war."

*"Your clan is adept at mindspeech. It is the preferred means of communication here."*

Very well, he would play it their way. *"Perhaps you did not understand what I said,"* he sent coldly. *"Yes, I am Frax Kitahn and as a—"*

*"We understood you, Commander. It is you who does not understand. Your paltry threats are nothing compared to what you set loose when you*

removed the ward-crystal from its place of guardianship. You have immersed our whole world into a battle for its continued survival."

What in Kep's Holy Name—? Frax stared at the glowing ball of light in disbelief. "First of all, we didn't remove anything; it came to the Priestess of its own free will. Second, we didn't do anything; whatever is happening at the Maugrock started before we ever got there. So, why don't you just give the thing back to the girl and let us go on our way."

"Foolish creature! Will your people never learn? You meddle in things you cannot begin to comprehend—"

"We aren't meddling. We are pursuing our own purpose. Then you interfered." Again, he checked the anger that surged up inside him. Cursed Wyxa! How could he reason with these creatures? But, reason he must. Faced with what he knew of Geffitz history and the persistent Wyxan claims of impending disaster, he could only accept the threat as real. He knew the inhabitants of the north were dying with every passing day, the number growing exponentially with the incursion of the Balandra. This encounter only confirmed what he suspected all along: the crystal was important.

He took a deep breath to calm his thoughts, and tried again. "Tell us what's happening. We can comprehend a lot—when we're given the information." No doubt, he wasted his sarcasm. "Maybe we can work together—"

"Make no mistake, Geffitz, we are not working together. You are only here to answer our questions, willingly or unwillingly, whichever mode you select. You are not involved in this decision-making process at any level."

So, the Ankar Mekt planned to move forward, in whatever manner they chose, without consideration for what the Geffitzi clans might want.

"Then, there is no further point to this encounter," he spoke aloud. "We have nothing to discuss."

"That is, of course, a choice, Geffitz Lord. You should know, however, we will do whatever we deem necessary to get our answers. Assimilating a

*Geffitz is not a pleasant task. We wish to avoid it as much, or more, than you do, but we are resolved to take the action if necessary."*

The fire of the challenge burned in Frax's veins. After centuries of these encounters, one would think the Wyxa would know Geffitzi did not bow to threats. "Fine." Frax raised his hands and splayed his fingers in a gesture of feigned resignation. "Do what you want. But I warn you, I won't make it easy."

The light that was the Ankar Mekt pulsed in agitation.

***

Ah, the Geffitzi! In mere moments, this one had reduced the Ankar Mekt to a sea of frustration and seething emotions it had not experienced in ages. And that was only on the first question, to establish the identity of the warrior. Asserting his position as leader of the Primordial Plain, Klandar Bayne moved to the fore of the joining. *"Will you resume telepathic communication, Blood Warrior? The spoken word is awkward. It is difficult for the Ankar Mekt to convert your language into a coherent response."*

***

Frax let the air out of his lungs slowly in order to hide his surprise. Perhaps their captors were more desperate than they were letting on, resorting to Klandar Bayne so quickly.

He relented, switching back to mindspeech. *"Fine. Tell me, Swampfather: why am I here? I know you can compare what I told you to what you already know from your encounter with the Priestess."*

He felt Klandar Bayne's mental sigh. *"It is not so simple. The disturbance on the edge of our lands in which you participated alerted us to a dire situation. An ancient threat we banished ages ago is seeking a return. Now the defense we placed against its re-emergence has arrived on our borders in the hands of an off-world girl, carried far from its post of guardianship."*

So, the crystal really served some purpose in the vast, foul darkness of the Black Temple. *"What ancient threat?"*

"*We set the crystal to guard the doorway through which we exiled the force that nearly shattered our world two thousand years ago.*"

Two thousand years? That could only mean one thing: Bithzielp. "*Nothing lives that long,*" he protested.

He dared say that in a chamber full of Wyxa?

"*It appears some things do. He—the evil—is seeking a return. The clashing forces at the edge of our land were the protective force in the ward crystal fighting the re-emergence of that evil into our world.*"

"*The crystal was protecting her—*"

"*Perhaps. The Starchild does bear the scars of his touch, something that concerns us, though how he might have gained access to her we cannot say. It does not explain what happened to the protective force.*"

Frax knew the origin of those scars: the girl had told them the same force that seized her at the barrier had attacked her in the north, contributing to her flight from the northern tower. Adding to the question: why didn't the Wyxa know that if they had joined the Priestess in Ankar Mekt as Klandar Bayne claimed? How could they miss such a thing?

That, however, was not the issue here. Frax realized there was a sense of something uncomfortably akin to fear in the chamber. It had been slowly but steadily growing, worrying at his nerve ends like the building edge of a lightning strike. Fear? From this strange ball of glowing light? Light offered no scent, and there was no emotion in Klandar Bayne's sending—but fear seeped from that ball of light, nonetheless.

Hidden deeply within the heart of their lands, these creatures were afraid.

If the Wyxa were afraid, how much more should the Geffitzi fear? During the dark times, when Bithzielp exercised reign over the land, the Geffitzi clans, along with many other creatures, had been hunted, tortured, and enslaved. Meanwhile, the Wyxa sat in their lands, untouched. They only rose up and drove Bithzielp and his minions out of the world after the actions of his followers threatened the destruction of the Palenquemas.

"What is this protective force you speak of?" Frax asked.

He sensed an even bigger flurry of activity inside the green globe this time.

Discord? Could there be some disagreement between Klandar Bayne and others in the Ankar Mekt over the information he was receiving? Frax waited.

The Swampfather returned. "We created and placed the amulet the Starchild carried into our land as a ward to seal the Goroth M'nget, the Circle of Sacrifices that lies in the heart of the Black Temple. That is the doorway through which we exiled Bithzielp from this world. Over the ages, he has worried at the corners of that seal, constantly seeking re-entry and revenge. With the emergence of the winged ones, he has obviously succeeded in weakening the seal. When the Starchild removed the crystal, she took away the last defense. Now, the only thing that guards against his reentry to our world is the sanctified blood our courier sacrificed to place the ward crystal. It is powerful in its own right, but a small defense against what seeks to regain entry to our world. It will not stand for long."

"So you want to take the crystal from her—"

"We already possess it."

"—and put it back in the Circle of Sacrifices." Unfortunately, from what he just heard, that seemed reasonable. In fact, it might be a good idea to encourage the action as quickly as possible.

"That would be the desired action. However, since recovering the crystal, we have discovered that the protective force we bound within it is gone. There is only a little power left to stand between this world and the invasion of Bithzielp. We must find the missing force and restore it before replacing it."

It sounded as if the Wyxa would be busy for a while and, since they said they didn't want Geffitzi help, they no longer needed to detain his group. Curiosity, however, pushed him another direction first. *"What happened to this force?"* he asked.

*"There is no sign of violence perpetrated against it. There is nothing to tell us why it is gone."*

*"Then I'm sure you want to focus your energies on solving that problem. We don't want to obstruct your efforts. Release us and we will go quietly on our way. And we will not approach the Palenquemas again."* He wanted to demand an apology for their treatment, but that might be too much.

*"Do not play innocent with us, Geffitz. What did you and your companions do to the crystal?"* The booming, hostile voice of the Ankar Mekt was back. *"Which of you handled it?"*

He could grow to hate that sender. *"I did. I looked at it and then put it around the girl's neck the first time; Uri Caspani removed it from the pack where she hid it and handed it back to her on the border of the Palenquemas right as the attack occurred. It was in the possession of the Priestess at all other times. She either wore it or carried it. No one else touched it that I am aware."*

*"Be warned, we can check the truthfulness of your words."*

He ignored the threat, his mind churning with a sudden, unpleasant possibility. Klandar Bayne just said the thing had lain in the depths of the Black Temple for ages, sealing that gate; yet, recently the Balandra had begun to re-emerge there, following a new leader. Araxis. Could the Evil One have affected the crystal in some way to start the incursion? If Kaphri could remove it from the circle of runes, perhaps he could, too. Neither of them belonged to this world. Was it possible the thing had ignored the Evil One as a threat?

That didn't make sense, however. If the Evil One was aware of the crystal and thought it held a strategic value, he would have found a way to use it instead of putting it back in place in a diminished form. Besides, the thing responded when Kaphri was under attack by Araxis at the edge of the swamp, the only time Frax had seen it actually do anything.

Perhaps the Evil One was using it in reverse, as a connection to track her movement. But he hadn't attacked while she wore it, only after she took it off, as if she was invisible to him while she had it on.

Harnessing his thoughts, he looked at the Ankar Mekt. *"How long has this force been missing?"* They still hadn't told him what it was.

*"It acted on the border of our lands a few nights ago,"* Klandar Bayne responded.

As he watched the lights in the globe pulse and drift with mental exchanges, Frax felt a deepening stir of suspicion; these creatures knew far more about this situation than they were telling him.

*"Perhaps the encounter injured it and it fled to heal."*

*"Unlikely."*

So sure. *"Maybe it left of its own choice."*

*"Impossible."* The pompous voice apparently intended to take control again. *"The Guardian willingly entered the agreement. It knew what that entailed. Enough of this, Klandar Bayne. This creature is here to answer our questions, not the reverse."*

The Guardian? He said the Guardian? Frax tried to disguise his shock behind a surge of irritation at the Ankar Mekt's dismissive tone.

Either he wasn't as effective as he hoped, or the Ankar Mekt was better at reading him than he thought. *"You know of this Guardian, Geffitz?"*

It was a strange and unpleasant sensation, feeling the attention of thousands of minds lock onto him with instantaneous intensity.

Frax drew a slow breath. What was the difference between sounding cautious and sounding evasive? *"I have seen a Guardian."* It couldn't be the same one! *"That doesn't mean it's the one you're looking for."* What could that damned little golden lizard have to do with all this? *"You make it sound as if one of those cursed things serves some special purpose in all this."*

He saw another flurry of activity, of lights darting about, brightening and dimming, in the ball in front of him. Whatever that was, he could live his whole life without knowing what that was about.

*"The protective force tied to the crystal is a Guardian, Geffitz. It is specifically charged with the protection of this world."*

Charged with—? Not the one he'd seen. Yet, it had said... His mind flashed back to that cold, wet, first encounter, which was the whole reason he stood here. His body suddenly filmed with sweat. Kep, all he wanted was the cursed barrier down and his people restored to their lands. He didn't need complications.

*"You claim you saw a Guardian. Where did it appear to you?"*

*"In Omurda."* The less elaborate his information, the fewer additional questions he would stir.

*"There is no Guardian in Omurda."*

*"That's where I saw it."*

*"There is no—"*

*"So you said! I saw it there."*

*"We know of no Guardian in Omurda."*

*"Why should you?"* He tried to sound dismissive of the whole situation. *"Do they report to you?"*

*"They influence many things in this world. We monitor their activity."*

*"Maybe they don't want you to know—"*

The green ball gave a pulse of light that sent a tingle of unpleasant sensation through his body. *"Do not parse words, Geffitz. Deception radiates from you."*

*"Just because you don't like what I say doesn't make it a lie."* That pulse hurt, damn them!

*"What were you doing at the time you claim you saw this Guardian in Omurda?"*

*"Taking the Ly Kai Priestess prisoner."* Let them wrestle with the significance of that.

*"What did it do?"*

Tell them that it spoke to him? They wouldn't want to hear, or believe, that. *"It sat on a stone, watching us."* That was truth.

Again, if this was as critical as they acted, why didn't they know about the link between the Priestess and Gemma?

Holy Kep! That was an excellent question. The realization almost sent Frax scurrying behind mindshields. He caught himself just in time.

As close as the girl and that lizard were, it seemed impossible the Ankar Mekt would miss it. He swallowed hard and sent a shot of mildly hostile reaction at whatever the pompous Wyxan voice of the Ankar Mekt was saying, just for effect, while he thought.

Maybe Seuliac was right; maybe she could hide things during a mind meld.

But that serpent was such an influential part of her life. How could she disguise that? It would be a monumental task, and he didn't believe she could do it.

Then how? How could the Wyxa miss the relationship between Gemma and Kaphri? It was impossible. Unless... Maybe she couldn't hide it, but maybe that damned little serpent could! Frax's heart gave another painful lurch as the implications of what he was thinking struck home. What if Gemma was the Guardian linked to the crystal?

But, reason argued, she had been with Kaphri for years. Why would she leave her charge of protecting their world to companion a lonely child? Unless... Gemma had told them that killing the Priestess could destroy their only hope of returning to their lands.

If the Wyxa could monitor the changes in his body, they must know how he was reacting to their information, even if they couldn't know his thoughts. Not good.

His mind was already leaping forward again. If Gemma was with the girl and Gemma was the Guardian—and the Wyxa had tied the Guardian to the crystal and set it to guard their world from Bithzielp's invasion... Gemma said the girl might be their only hope...

Holy Kep, she really might be the key to it all!

And it appeared the Guardian had chosen some new allies. He almost laughed aloud at the irony of the situation. Uri had warned him on their first encounter that the creature was not behaving the way it should. He chose not to listen—and him being the one who hated and mistrusted the creature the most!

How much had been going on around them that they missed in their ignorance? He pushed down a surge of fury at the suspicion of being used. But—no. They were in the south. The things they had encountered, including standing here now, in front of the Wyxa, were not a wasted effort. It gave them vital information.

He and the others must move forward with this task.

Standing here, facing the Wyxa, that seemed a rapidly fading prospect. Damn that serpent! What was he supposed to say to advance their case against these ancient, single-minded creatures who thought they held the right to be the sole, deciding factor in this?

Did the Priestess know about her tiny companion's link to the crystal? Gut instinct told him she was as unsuspecting as they were. Did she know it now, after arriving here? He needed to talk to her.

These Wyxa would never allow it.

In place of that, he must convince them there was greater advantage in releasing them to go forward than in holding them captive. Or worse.

Was possession of the crystal critical to their going forward? Perhaps the Priestess had fulfilled her role by bringing it here. There was certainly no way the swamp dwellers would turn loose of the thing based on anything he could say. He was back to the beginning again, with a focus on just getting their freedom so that they could move on.

To what? How much was he willing to entwine his fate and the whole of the Geffitzi clans, to the cursed little Guardian's machinations?

Like it or not, they were either all in or out. No half-measures. And completely out, turning his back and walking away, living with the eternal question of what should, or might, have been, was not something he could live with.

His obligation lay in the return of his people to their lands. Let the Wyxa cope with the other problem. They had succeeded before. His sole purpose was to get that barrier removed.

But the bigger question still would not leave his head: why hadn't Gemma seen fit to enlighten her old allies of this change in the situation? His words in the swamp, his speculation on how much Gemma was trying to influence their situation, came back to haunt him now.

Whatever the serpent's reason, why should he upset her plans? Nothing had changed in his attitude toward the Guardian: he still did not like or trust Gemma. But he didn't like or trust the Wyxa, either, and they were his immediate obstacle. Whether or not he appreciated the way Gemma went about it, it looked as if the serpent had made them a part of her action.

Besides, the Wyxa would know the truth soon enough. It chilled him to the bone, but he knew the situation was moving toward his assimilation into the Ankar Mekt.

Tamping down his dread, he forced his attention back to the present situation.

What was the obnoxious voice of the Ankar Mekt saying? "*Your pardon.*" He sent forced courtesy, hoping it would smooth over his obvious inattention, "*I was trying to recall any details of the encounter* with the Guardian I might give you. The creature just sat there looking at us. Then it sort of blended into the background."

It didn't work.

"Do not attempt to deceive us, Geffitz." The sending was thunderous in his head. "Memory of the Guardian stirs in your recent memory."

There was no way they could know what he thought. Yet, at least. "Not your Guardian," he responded.

"Enough of this obfuscation and deception, Geffitz." The focus of thousands of minds hit him like a punch.

When he could finally organize his thoughts again, he was on his knees, with two Wyxa gripping his arms. They pulled him to his feet.

"Let me go!" He lashed out defensively with his elbows.

They released him and took a step away as he struggled to stand under his own strength.

"Don't touch me!" He flashed warning.

The three-fingered hands drew back further from the threat of a blow from a muscular Geffitz arm.

"There is no need for violence, Geffitz Lord. They are only here to keep you from harming yourself." The Ankar Mekt made a thinly disguised attempt to shove a false sense of calm into his mind along with the comment.

He evaded it. "There is great need for violence if you think you are going to invade my mind."

"We have need and you will not cooperate."

"You refuse to consider us as a part of this situation, and you refuse to give us critical information—"

"Five Geffitz warriors and a Starchild? You are insignificant to this problem."

Bastards. "Then I will do whatever I can to move forward without you."

"As you wish. We have encountered resistance in your people before. If

*you struggle you risk doing yourself physical harm, but you will not suc-
ceed in resisting the process."*

What had the others—the old trappers—done? How had they
defeated this pompous gathering? He shivered, feeling so
alone—ironic, considering the thousands upon thousands of minds
around him, all waiting to tear into his brain. He swallowed hard,
trying to stall the situation while he worked frantically for a solution. *"Then compromise. Tell me what you know and I'll tell you what we
know."*

*"There is no compromise: something you consider insignificant could be
vital to us. The time for games is over."*

His time had run out. What Tobin said a short time ago was true:
many Geffitzi had passed through this process and none of them had
ever cooperated. Did that mean he should surrender to a predictable
pattern and, ultimately, failure? Or was Seuliac right?

There was always another way. Sometimes one just failed to see
it in time to make use of it. What if he didn't resist? Could that give
him an advantage?

With the Wyxa? No. But what if, as Seuliac suggested, he focused
on getting something in exchange? If he had to submit to their incursion, shouldn't he get something in return?

But what? And how to go about it? Would calm cooperation and
non-resistance, enable him to hold his thoughts and brain together
long enough, and well enough against their assault to take something?

His eyes went to the Ankar Mekt. How many thousands—mil-
lions—of minds where in that thing? It would demand a hard focus.
Pick a point and go with it. He couldn't target the speaker; they
might consider that an attack. And he couldn't target Klandar
Bayne. That left all the rest of those points of light as fair game.
Geffitzi warriors rallied around the women and children or their
leaders. Which of those sheltered at the center of this gathering?

Perhaps Geffitzi logic did not hold here. His only other option was the brightest of the lights: it stood to reason that feature must represent something.

Pushing down terror, he lowered his shoulders and braced his legs. *"Let's get on with it."*

The joining hit Frax's mind like a shuddering wave of vibration. The first to snatch at him were the doubters, the ones who thought he lied. Their aggression scattered like leaves on the wind as he surged toward them. Then came the curiosity seekers, the ones who wanted to compare him to their previous encounters. He dove into them as they engulfed him.

Recognizing what he attempted, they fell back, giving way to the darker ones—the ones who hated and mistrusted the Geffitzi. Organized thought crumbled as they shredded his brain. His momentum slowed, stopped, and his mind shattered into a million tiny bits before their onslaught.

# 49

## Paradoxical Choices

A cry ripped from his lungs as the Ankar Mekt vanished from his mind. The sound was barely a rasp in his raw throat. Memories and thoughts, torn loose in a churning, mad whirl fought to resolve into order. Frax's body seized in a spasm, then he was heaving air in great gasps, his body shaking and wet with sweat.

Physical awareness came more slowly: he was on his knees and elbows in the mist. Still in that vast, cursed chamber, then. He had no idea when he'd collapsed, or how long he remained that way now, body tucked, and arms cradling his head protectively as he trembled and prayed it was over. The only sound was the thunder of his heart, rocking him with the strength of its beat.

Slowly his heartbeat settled and he became aware of the silence around him. But he wasn't alone. Turning his head, he looked past his shielding upper arm.

Just as on their first encounter, Klandar Bayne sat at the edge of the light circle, watching him.

The Swampfather was here, staring at him. After what they had just done to him? The anger surging through him did more to bring life back into him than anything else he'd felt.

"You. What do you wan—?" His throat grabbed, painfully choking off his question. He shuddered at the pain. Kep, he must have screamed his throat raw.

"*I am concerned for your well-being.*"

"My—!" He gave a hoarse, broken laugh at the irony of the statement. The sound caught in his throat again, throwing him into a fit of coughing. His head throbbed with every jar of his body.

Telepathy was easier. "*Your people just tore my brain apart and rammed it back together, and now you say you're concerned for my well-being? That's funny. Too bad I don't feel like laughing.*" The coughing spell had forced him up into a crouching position. He clenched his teeth to keep them from chattering as a shiver ran over him from head to toe. "*Shit.*"

"*You are bordering on shock, a dangerous physical state to your people,*" Klandar Bayne observed calmly. "*It would be better if I moved you to a warmer environ, but your reaction to the transport procedure is so negative...*"

"No! Let me be." He'd seen shock in injured warriors. It was not good, but he didn't think he could survive the Wyxan method of movement at this point.

He settled on his knees and wrapped his arms around his body to fight the chill. If he hoped to survive this, he needed help. The Wyxa chieftain was his only resource. "*I could use a blanket.*" He would have preferred his clothes, but he was too weak to pull them on.

"*Of course.*"

Within a few heartbeats, another Wyxan materialized beside him, the requested object in hand.

"*Tell him to put it down and get the hell away. I don't want him near me.*"

"*Very well,*" Klandar Bayne's sending held a note of dry amusement. The Wyxan dropped the cloth within Frax's reach and vanished.

"*Do you require assistance?*" The Swampfather watched with an air of mild concern as Frax snagged the blanket with a shaking hand and pulled it toward him.

"No." The Wyxa had done enough, putting him in this state. Clumsily, shivering violently, Frax fought the folds open and tugged the soft, clingy material over his shoulders. Instantly the fabric blocked the chill of the chamber and sealed his body heat around him. Several more violent shudders racked his body as he struggled awkwardly to pull his legs up beneath the folds. His movements were slow and disjointed. Curse the Wyxa! How long would this last? Was there permanent damage?

"*You must drink this to make a full recovery.*" The Swampfather held out a small green cylinder, a cup hollowed from the stem of a plant.

Frax turned his head away in silent refusal.

"*This is not an option, Blood Warrior. You are in a precarious state. I would rather you drink willingly, but I will call for assistance if necessary.*"

Sometime during his ordeal, the leather tie that bound his hair back had come loose, letting his heavy mane separate in a curtain of dark, sweaty strands. One heavy tendril fell over his left eye as he looked up at the Wyxan. Any movement of his head to toss it out of his eyes would result in thundering agony, and he couldn't bring himself to take his arm from beneath the blessed warmth of the blanket to brush it back. He must look as wretched a pile of flesh as any Geffitz who had ever encountered the Ankar Mekt.

But they had not beaten him yet.

All the same, he knew he had to drink the proffered cup. The humiliation of being forced into another situation with these creatures was more than he could accept and he was too weak to resist.

"*What is it?*"

"*A restorative to strengthen your body, clear your mind, and ease the pain in your head."* Klandar Bayne put a sense of force behind his sending. *"It is medicine, Blood Warrior. Nothing more than a healing draft."*

His head was definitely a pounding agony that made clear thinking difficult. If the Wyxan insisted on prolonging this encounter—and it looked as if the Swampfather did—then he needed something to stop the pain.

Wearily, Frax extended a hand into the cold air.

\*\*\*

Klandar Bayne passed the cylinder of fluid, making sure of the Geffitz's grip before releasing it. He watched Frax drink the mixture with a sense of curiosity and regret.

What he told the warrior was a partial truth. The cup did contain a mild sedative with healing properties. During the joining, the warrior's struggles had been powerful and violent, making firm restraint necessary. His senses had not recovered enough yet to see or feel the bruises developing on his body. The Wyxa would have administered the potion while the warrior was unconscious, but he had fought back to wakefulness too quickly. Now there would be an inconvenient delay in their communication while the drug took effect. Time was of the essence here. As Keeper of the First Plain, the Ankar Mekt could not refuse his request for this meeting, but they could severely limit the length of the encounter. If the warrior lapsed into a state of shock and had to be rushed into a diffwys bath, Klandar Bayne would lose this precious opportunity forever.

More importantly, the draft contained a powder to aid in fading the warrior's memory of his experience with the Ankar Mekt, a routine treatment for all Geffitzi forced into the joining. The encounter was a violation of mind and body against which they were helpless to defend, and the creatures, with their wild, explosive nature and fierce pride, required help to get through that trauma. It would make him forget the worst of the encounter, but how much, no one could say.

It would be best for them all if it erased it completely.

The Geffitz half-heartedly pitched the cup away. As the fog drifted over it, Klandar Bayne whisked it from the chamber with a mental flick.

*"Shouldn't this be over? Shouldn't you be releasing us at the edge of the swamp right now?"*

*"Allow your body and mind a moment to recover, and then we will talk."*

*"Talk. Talk about what?"* Frax closed his eyes, waiting for the promised relief from the pain in his head. *"You know everything about me now, don't you?"*

No. Not quite everything. There were complications. Again.

Difficulties during the assimilation of Geffitzi were not uncommon. Sometimes the warriors became mad with fear, blanking all comprehensible activity from their thought process and making assimilation too dangerous to pursue. In those encounters, the Ankar Mekt was forced to withdraw without inserting the desired fear-flight reflex they sought to install. Those failures always returned to Wyxan lands and the Ankar Mekt, reluctant to pursue another stressful encounter, unhappily ignored them.

This warrior had behaved differently.

Where previous warriors wrapped themselves in terror, hostility, and rage—or even fainted—none of them, no matter how desperate, had ever attempted to take the mindmeld head-on. This one had waited, accepting the invasion, then shoved out through the joining, ruthlessly snatching up memories.

He had taken things away from the encounter.

Klandar Bayne would not tell him that his headlong attack had proven a dangerous, if somewhat effective, defense. The assaulted Wyxan minds had panicked and retreated, disrupting the joining until the more aggressive participants could move forward and get him under control. Many of the less forceful members declined to participate further, eliminating some of the most experienced, thoughtful Eldren, leaving the process to the more hardcore.

Of course, no one, especially the warrior, could have any idea what he'd done by wildly seizing on memories and thoughts of creatures vastly more ancient than his whole race. The Wyxa shared a generational memory and their mental joining in Ankar Mekt enabled them to share everything that had come before.

A tempestuous Geffitz, retaining bits of their information, was a horrendous prospect.

Memories and thoughts from ages past; how might they affect him? Klandar Bayne could not suppress a shudder, half in fear, and half in intrigue. Geffitzi were so mentally fragile. How effective would the potion he'd just administered be at taking away what the warrior had stolen?

This one presented so much potential if only the Ankar Mekt would make use of him. But they refused to consider, much less believe in, the Winisp's prophecy.

Fortunately, their shortened assimilation was not a complete failure; the Ankar Mekt had gleaned the information they sought. Unfortunately, the information was as horrifying as it was enlightening. The joining had nearly collapsed in seething turmoil, unable to understand the Guardian's betrayal. Some were demanding the immediate termination of their captives' lives as a solution to the situation, an astounding, uncharacteristically harsh reaction for even the most radical of the ancients.

Their final solution had been swift and rational. Though it did not please him, as the representative of this Plain he could not find reason to disagree. He could only demand this brief encounter in exchange for his acquiescence.

They knew what he would do. They did not agree with him,

but they could not forbid his action. The path he pursued was part of Wyxan history and did not directly conflict with their decision. They, too, had acquiesced, allowing him this brief encounter.

This time, however, might be all he required.

"*You got what you wanted.*" The warrior had managed to brush the strand of hair from his eyes and was watching him resentfully.

"*We know of the Guardian, Gemma's, activities, yes.*"

"*So, what do you want from me now?*"

Klandar Bayne sighed. How quickly these creatures regained their belligerent attitude. It was eternally irritating. Yet, in this situation, it might be their most promising trait. They would need every ounce of confidence and swagger they could muster if they were going to succeed in the task they were fighting to assume—and the thing the Ankar Mekt so stridently opposed. What the group joining said was true: these Geffitzi had no idea what they proposed to go up against.

He doubted knowing would deter or intimidate them.

The joining had given Klandar Bayne direct access to the warrior's mind. He could feel the pain and confusion fading as the healing drought began to work, clearing the warrior's thoughts and normalizing his physical state. Allowing the return of those horrible, treacherous emotions.

The Wyxa chieftain was no longer a helpless victim to them, however. He reached out, lightly suppressing their return. Gently, always gently—the warrior must never suspect manipulation—he pressed a sense of calm, dulling his reactions and making him more manageable while he still recovered, when it would be least noticeable.

Then Klandar Bayne began his work. "*There is war in the north, Blood Warrior. Your people, and all the other races there, are sorely pressed to defend themselves. Each of those winged creatures emerging from the Goroth M'nget passes through on the blood of a creature from this world.*"

*The death pit in the darkness beneath the Black Tower fills with the bodies. The very life force of our world is being used to draw our death from beyond."*

\*\*\*

War in the north. And he, Seuliac Aedec, and the Caspani heir were all here, trapped in the south. Although he had accepted from the beginning that a battle might be inevitable, the reality overwhelmed him with horror and dismay. Without vanity, he knew the Geffitzi forces were weaker in leadership without the three of them.

All because of his decision to aid the enemy of his people, the Ly Kai Priestess.

Had he been shortsighted in his dogged pursuit of that?

Tobin would say so.

But, no—the moment of doubt slipped away as swiftly as it came. This was not an issue for quick, gut reaction. He had weighed it all out coldly, judiciously. Many times. Even if they had slain the Priestess that first, fateful day in Omurda, the battle would have come. It was inevitable. He had to look beyond that, to how much they would gain if she were successful: an end to this threat, a return to their lands and life as it once was. This was a risk he must take for them all.

The petty bickering and bloodshed of his peoples' history flashed before his mind's eye. He felt a flush of anger and sadness as he pushed it away. He was seeking a return of something much higher than that.

Pulling the blanket tighter around his shoulders, Frax shrugged. *"The clans will do what they must to defeat the threat."*

\*\*\*

*"As must we all,"* the Swampfather agreed, mystified that the threat to the clans did not evoke the expected sizzle of fierce reaction he was prepared to suppress.

Now for the next step. "*And so the Ankar Mekt has come to a decision.*"

"*And that is?*" The warrior's wariness intensified.

Klandar Bayne felt a stir of satisfaction. Things were going well. The warrior's focus was singularly on the role his small group played in this situation. He attempted to draw Frax further in the direction he wished to lead him. "*The Ankar Mekt believes replacing the Guardian Stone on the Goroth M'nget, the Circle of Sacrifice, will slow this invasion to a manageable level that the northern races can defeat, now that they are aware of the situation. To implement this, the joining has decided to return you and your fellow warriors to the north. We will send you to the Black Temple with the Guardian Stone, the crystal, so you can replace it in the blood on the Rune of Amassing Power, thus preventing Bithzielp's re-emergence into our world. Once you have done that, you will be free to join your people in the battle to rid our world of the invasive force.*"

The flash of outrage shriveled before it fully formed. Going still, the warrior stared at him. "*You know damned well we can't survive the Black Temple. By your own admission, you know the place is full of the enemy. We'll be killed instantly.*"

"*You do not seem to understand, Blood Warrior: all the Ankar Mekt deems necessary is the return of the ward crystal to its resting place, to stop Bithzielp's re-emergence. All else is extraneous. They know if this is your only choice, you will do your best to succeed. To them, your loss is unfortunate, but necessary. It might even be hoped that such a blow to the Geffitzi high houses would become a rallying point, a sharing of mutual sorrow that would unite them in this battle.*"

"*That's all you can say? That maybe some good will come of our deaths as you callously send us to them? This Guardian Stone of yours, whatever it is, wasn't working when the Priestess picked it up. The Balandra were invading Omurda before we ever thought of going to the Black Tower. That thing is doomed to failure if it's used the same way again.*"

The warrior struggled to find anger, to lash him with fury the way he had during their first encounter. Klandar Bayne could feel his rising agitation.

* * *

"*What was in that cup?*" Frax asked abruptly. Frustration withered before it bloomed. "*It's effecting my reactions, isn't it?*"

"*The mixture dulls the reactions a bit,*" Klandar Bayne admitted. "*But the healing benefits outweigh the negative. It has pulled you back from the edge of danger and given us this opportunity to speak.*" He could feel Frax fighting to push off the heavy sensation encumbering his reactions and he eased back on his control to avoid revealing his own interference.

The Geffitz seized on the flicker of rising emotion to form a protest. "*You saved us just to throw us away in a useless endeavor?*"

The Ankar Mekt's solution saddened Klandar Bayne but he could not change it. He could only do this one other thing that he was building toward. "*The Ankar Mekt believes it will save our world, and that is all that matters to them. You have borne the burden of command, Frax Kitahn. You have sent warriors to their death for a greater cause.*"

"*I've led men into battle who did not survive to come out again. And every one of those deaths still pains me, which I know the Wyxa would never say of our demise.*" Frax coughed, tasted blood, and swallowed, refusing to spit. Body fluid, particularly blood, held power, and he would not give these creatures an opportunity at anything else they could use against him. "*What gives you the sole right to decide how to meet this threat? To decide who lives and who dies, who fights and who stands by? Do you honestly believe everything will go away when we put the crystal back? That Kep's Children and the Illya will clean up the north and you can stay down here, all safe and cozy and untouched?*"

"*Once the gateway is sealed and the invading Balandra are destroyed there will no longer be a threat.*"

No longer be a threat? How could they possibly think their solution would end this? What about Araxis and the barrier?

Cold insight flashed inside Frax: these creatures did not intend to take on that problem.

It took all his energy to summon up the slightest bit of outrage. *"We are dealing with more than the threat of Bithzielp's return. There's another force at work here. The same one you chose to ignore twenty years ago. This other one... This other one from the stars."* He couldn't use the same word for Kaphri and Araxis. *"He's leading these Balandra. He brought them into the south the night you felt that clash of forces. He's responsible for starting all this up again. You can't ignore him a second time!"* Araxis would always be a threat as long as Kaphri lived.

A dart of terrible realization shot through him at that last thought. Klandar Bayne said they were returning the warriors to the temple. What about the Priestess? Was the Ankar Mekt aware of the reason for Araxis' interest in her—that he was trying to restore himself to his full power through her?

After tearing his brain apart? Of course they were.

Were they preparing to kill her, to end the threat the same way he had prepared to act? Was that the other half of their solution to deal with Araxis?

If Gemma's warning that the Priestess was the Geffitzi people's best hope for a return to their lands was true, he could not let his prediction that the Wyxa would destroy her come true.

Besides, they still might escape this situation, no matter how bad things looked right now. *"What about the Starchild known as Kaphri? What has your cursed Ankar Mekt decided will become of her?"*

*"We are now aware of the threat she presents this world, though neither of you saw fit to speak of it. I tell you this to relieve any inner conflict you might experience over that omission."*

Inner conflict? Klandar Bayne could have no idea of the inner conflict he was experiencing! And none of it came from a sense of guilt at depriving the Wyxa of information. Frax stared stonily into the darkness past the Swampfather's shoulder, thin slivers of dread driving into his heart as he waited for its next words.

# 50

## What You Cannot Do

Klandar Bayne studied the silent, unmoving warrior. Despite the numbing potion he'd taken, the Geffitz remained awash with myriad conflicting emotions. How did these creatures ever maintain focus and sanity? Small wonder they were so volatile and unpredictable. *"Despite what you believe of us, Forest Lord, the Ankar Mekt is not needlessly cruel. The Starchild, Kaphri, is a danger to our world. A powerful evil pursues her and an even greater evil has touched her. The Wyxa, however, do not kill. We will put her into a prolonged sleep and hide her safely away. When the threat is passed, we will reawaken and return her to her own world."*

\*\*\*

That would end everything they were working for beyond recovery!

*"No. The Evil One no longer controls the power fueling the barrier. Only the Priestess can put and end to it. Your actions would destroy any hope of our ever returning to our lands."*

*"There is more at stake here than a return of the Second Children of Kep to their lands. Our whole world is at risk."*

*"The Geffitzi world is already at risk!"*

*"The Geffitzi perspective is only one way of viewing the problem, Blood Warrior. The situation calls for a broader response. The Starchild recognizes that. She has agreed to do whatever is necessary to protect you and this world."*

Frax sagged as if he'd been struck a horrible blow.

She couldn't. Yet, he knew she would. She'd already made one shortsighted, well-intentioned attempt at self-sacrifice at the barrier, when they were under attack by the Balandra. No doubt, the Wyxa took those feelings of guilt and twisted them to the fullest effect on her. He cursed under his breath in bitter frustration. *"I want to talk to the Ly Kai Priestess."*

*"That is forbidden."*

*"You haven't told her what the Ankar Mekt is planning to do. She won't agree if she knows."* He refused to accept the Wyxan solution as absolute. The warriors would find a way out of this situation f they could get a chance.

There was a way he might cut their losses and negotiate a change in their situation. *"I'll take the crystal back to the temple,"* he sent abruptly. *"Send the Priestess and the others somewhere else, so they can get back to our people."* They could bear the loss of one of their number as long as someone made it back to the Circles with the truth and the girl. Besides, he knew the code to access the passage under the minor altar. If he moved fast, he might escape again.

*"The Ankar Mekt 's course is decided. They will not alter it."*

*"Then why did you bother with this encounter?"*

\*\*\*

Klandar Bayne picked up Frax's despair with a sense of vindication. At last. The warrior was at the stage of near defeat that would force him to listen to what he really wanted to say. "*What do you know of the Wyxa, Lord Kitahn?*"

The warrior huddled under the blanket did not respond.

"*We are old, Forest Warrior, old beyond your imagining, and we have some, called prophets, who can see far into the future. At the time of the Great Cataclysm there lived a revered prophet, the Winisp, who predicted all our actions would come to naught: that the battle would not be completely won at that time despite the horrific destruction and loss our defense wrought on this World Plain. That it would be up to certain others to strike the final blow to ultimately secure our world. Although the Winisp is a revered prophet, his words do not please many of the Wyxa. They refused to acknowledge them. Instead, they push them aside in the collective memory and try to forget them.*

"*But a prophet's words will not cease to exist simply because a people do not wish to acknowledge them. If such things are meant to come to pass, they will come to pass.*"

Frax's eyes locked on him. "*What are you saying?*"

"*It is possible the Winisp foresaw your coming.*"

"*Oh no, we are not a part of your prophets and manipulation! If that's why you brought me here...*" The warrior fought his way out of the blanket and struggled to his feet.

"*You are wrong, Blood Warrior. It is possible your role in all this is preordained and that you are well on the path to fulfilling it.*" At last, the truth was out.

\*\*\*

Was this creature mad? The Children of Kep would never be part of any insane Wyxan prophet's prediction! Yet, his mind worked feverishly, perhaps this was the way for him to get them out of this mess. Ridiculous as the words were, he would be a fool to let them pass without consideration. Whatever these creatures wanted to believe was their concern. If he could use it to his advantage, however...

He sank to the floor and shrugged back into the folds of the blanket. *"What is this prediction?"* he asked resignedly.

*"It is in ambiguous verse that defied interpretation until these last few days. I repeat it:*

*The darkness will rise again,*

*To spread on swift, dark wings of night.*

*Then, out of the north, the warriors will come.*

*Exiles, seeking a doorway home.*

*The Children of the Earth, capturing*

*The Star that flees the even' sky.*

*Gold-clad star, seeking a path through darkness,*

*And warrior of forest and blood.*

*Earth and sky shall bind,*

*A union forged,*

*That will span all worlds and time."*

Frax heard the words with an increasing sense of cold, remote disbelief. Kep, if he understood them to speak of this point in time, they did not seem ambiguous at all! Evil had, indeed, come, spreading on the dark, grey wings of the Balandra. The warriors—Children of the Earth Mother and exiles—had returned to their land with their captive, who carried that damned golden lizard of a Guardian twined about her neck. The cold drove deeper as he recalled the night in the swamp when he discovered the star the Priestess had feared so greatly at their first encounter was also the Geffitzi evening star. But the rest? Warrior of forest and blood? Was that why the Wyxa persisted in calling him by the archaic titles of Blood Warrior and Forest Lord? Was Klandar Bayne trying to build a case for the green and red of Cadarn by weaving a mental snare of words around him?

Was he finally discovering the trap he had sensed in his first encounter with the Swampfather? Anger and suspicion roared through him like a flood, briefly dizzying him with its force before dissolving away. *"This is all a vile attempt to manipulate us!"*

*"Not so. A revered prophet spoke the words many years ago."*

*"Liar! You composed them to suit your own purposes after you forced me into your joining."*

*"No. Forest Lord—"*

*"Stop calling me that! Stop calling me Blood Warrior. This is all part of some scheme you creatures cooked up. You think you can just twist us to your own purpose. Well, we will not be pawns in any Wyxan game!"*

*"These are words the Ankar Mekt does not wish to acknowledge. They would disavow them if they dared. But that will not abolish their existence. You must see that these words designate your small group as the real solution to this threat, just as you seek."*

*"What does that mean? Define it."*

Klandar Bayne shook his long, delicately tapered head. *"I cannot. We can only speculate."*

*"Why don't you just ask him what he meant? He's in that ball of light, isn't he?"*

*"We cannot. The Winisp did not pass on to the Second Plain."*

*"He—"* Frax paused. Of course, two thousand years was nothing.

*"You misunderstand,"* Klandar Bayne sent quietly. *"The Winisp carried the Guardian Stone into the circle of the Goroth M'nget, where they struck him down. His blood helps seal the gate. Because he lost his physical self beyond the borders of the Palenquemas he did not pass on to the Second Plain."*

*"Holy Kep."* The blood on the Priestess' hand...

*"It is unfortunate,"* the Swampfather continued. *"However, a prophecy is only a collection of words, no matter how poignant it sounds. Even if you asked the Winisp, face to face, he could not tell you more than I have."*

*"What's your angle on this, Wyxan?"*

"*I only wish to make you aware of something that is a piece of our ancient history. It does not change anything in your current situation.*"

So, what was the point in telling him? "*I told you, we will not be pawns in any Wyxan game, no matter how ancient. I don't know what you're playing at here, but I refuse to listen any longer.*"

"*You must listen. Too much depends upon it. The Ankar Mekt has disclaimed the Winisp's prophecy, even in the obvious face of the present situation. Their solution, of changing the focus of your task, could bring disaster to this world.*"

Indeed, it could. But why should this Wyxan be the only one to see it? "*Why would you go against your own people?*"

"*I do not go against my own people. I only tell you the Winisp's words offer an alternative.*"

"*An alternative?*" The Swampfather was trying to convey something to him. He had to sort it out. "*How? You say they've made their decision. How are we supposed to make something else come about?*"

"*You cannot.*"

Frax stared at the creature. "*Is this some ridiculous riddle?*"

"*Listen, Lord Kitahn. It is in the words of the Winisp. The prophecy requires a different path than the Ankar Mekt would choose. But the Geffitzi cannot move against the Ankar Mekt to make that happen. You are not capable of it. But, there is another individual involved in this.*"

Another? Frax continued to stare at the Swampfather, his mind locked on trying to unravel the creature's words.

Kaphri?

"*The Starchild.*" Klandar Bayne did not have to read his thoughts to see the dawning comprehension in his eyes. "*Only she has the ability to change the course of things. Only she can do it. She must be capable of seeing and seizing the possibility or it will not happen.*

"*As the Swampfather of the Primordial Plain, I am charged with the protection of this world, which is the physical Plain of our existence. Our life cycle begins here. If we fail in this, all Wyxa will cease to exist. I* brought you here to speak with you against the declared wishes of the Ankar Mekt, because I must consider all possibilities, regardless of what they, or you, may think. I have told you all this to ensure that you will be prepared if an opportunity presents itself, regardless of what else might come to pass. It is all I can do. You cannot aid the Starchild or influence her: not you or any other. At this point the Geffitzi, as you bitterly recognize, are only hapless players in this game of warring powers, to be lost, as we all will be, if she is not worthy of the task before her."

"All that amounts to is a Wyxan shrug. What am I supposed to tell my people? That if she can she will, if she can't she won't?"

"You may tell them whatever you wish. But remember this: should the Starchild discover some alternative course of action to change what the Ankar Mekt would do, the balance of the Winisp's prophecy will remain on you. This is only one step along the path."

* * *

Klandar Bayne watched as the warrior mentally ran over the words of the prophecy in his head.

"What about the Guardian? You tore my brain apart to find some hidden truth you thought I carried. What about that?"

"Your joining revealed little on the issue we did not already know." Lie. Now they knew the Guardian was the being the Starchild called Gemma, and that it had left its post in the depths of in Black Temple years ago in order to reside with the girl in the far north. An inexplicable action in relation to the charge the ancients had lain upon it. The Ankar Mekt was searching for a way to find and force it back into its link with the Guardian Stone even as this exchange took place.

The warrior did not believe him. Klandar Bayne actually drew some comfort from that: the creature was not a fool.

"This is all just a game of words."

"Perhaps. Perhaps the Winisp was in error and the Starchild will not find a way to deliver you from the destiny my people have chosen for you.

*Perhaps the Ankar Mekt's solution will prove the best one. Or, perhaps she will succeed at these tasks some time in the future, with the assistance of other Geffitzi. Only time will tell. But what is meant to be will be."* And he had done all he could do. *"Now I must return you to the others. Think on what you have heard and make the best plan for the outcome you find yourselves facing. Swift action is of the essence. I will not speak with you again before the Ankar Mekt enacts their judgment.*

*"And, Commander, may Kep not accept your worthy soul into her bosom for a very long time to come."*

Frax felt the inevitable knot of discomfort in his gut.

# 51

## Truths

"*We are unable to summon the Guardian.*" The Ankar Mekt seethed with frustration.

Klandar Bayne waited for the moment when their annoyance resolved into organized thought once more. There was no reason to rush them; the Geffitz warrior would need time to recover and begin making plans. He also suspected that, in the strength of the Ankar Mekt's own emotions, they were not aware of how the fury of the young Geffitz scout was worsening their agitation. It was certainly affecting the Wyxa of this Primordial Plain. Many of them had retreated to the outlying swamp, beyond its range.

The young warrior's attention abruptly shifted to the return of his brother and the Ankar Mekt began to calm. After a moment, they finally sought out the only member capable of taking action on the Plain where the problem existed.

"*You must bring the Guardian to us so we can reunite it with the Ward Stone,*" Hafod-y-lan told him.

"Again, I caution you against this action. We do not understand why the Guardian shifted its attention to the Starchild."

"Its reasoning does not matter. Its charge is the protection of this world."

"Perhaps it still maintains the mission, but in a different manner."

"It protects our world by abandoning its task? Ridiculous."

"I fear it may see its mission as having evolved beyond simply guarding the doorway into our world against Bithzielp's return."

"There is no greater threat to this world than his return."

"Agreed."

"Then the Guardian must be restored to its post. This diversion, whatever its small purpose, will be ended."

"What if this particular guardianship is no longer valid," Klandar Bayne persisted.

The green orb swirled in the silence. "He does not lead the exiled winged ones." "They are here to reestablish his hold." "We see no indication of his presence." "He will come. We must stop him. Now."

"Perhaps the Starchild—"

"She is nothing!" Hafod-y-lan cut him off.

She was the Even' Star, a part of an immense power they had learned to block ages ago for their domain's protection.

"The Guardian must return to the defense of this world, Klandar Bayne. As Swampfather, you will make that happen."

He did not want the Ankar Mekt to lock the Guardian into a situation where it was unable to act, but to fulfill his plan he must take the risk. "There may be a way to bring the Guardian to us. If we put the Starchild in jeopardy..."

Agitation surged. "We did that. The Stone responded to her will, dangerously. Which is why we do not act more aggressively against her now. The Guardian did not come. "

"If we place the thing it interprets as its mission in peril the Guardian must respond."

"How?"

"The Guardian has chosen to focus its attention on the Starchild. Perhaps if we were to put their connection in jeopardy..."

"Putting her into a prolonged sleep is not a significant threat to her."

"No," he agreed. "She must be taken further, to the Ethereal Plain, where the Guardian cannot follow her."

"We do not kill."

"She is a Starchild," the Swampfather pointed out. "She can physically move to the Ethereal Plain without ill-effect. Despite the fact the ancients do not require such things for their own use, food, water and shelter exists there.

"When the Guardian senses the threat of this separation, it will come to her. Once it is inside the Palenquemas, the Ankar Mekt can exert its will and restore the link between the Guardian and the Stone. You can then return it to its place on the Goroth M'nget and secure the Starchild in a place where the Ankar Mekt can maintain a protective vigil over her."

Concern swirled. "Can this work?"

"What is the Guardian's mandate?" Klandar Bayne asked them.

"Protect this world against this ancient threat."

"Somehow, the Guardian considers her a part of that mandate. Whatever change we make in her status will bring it to us."

"Then we should move now, without delay."

Klandar Bayne agreed, but not for the same reason as the ancients of the Ethereal Plane.

\*\*\*

Frax Kitahn was a true blood of Cadarn, Commander of the Edge, a royal son of the oldest family on this world, but it was not arrogance that made him feel, in every situation he had ever encountered, that his feet were firmly on the ground. That he had some control. It was a part of who he was. What he was. A Geffitz warrior.

When the Hrsst captured him as the young captain of a scouting party and held him almost a full moon-cycle, he'd been forced to hunker, naked and starving, in a sapling cage too small for him to stand upright. Even through the repeated, savage beatings the Hrsst seemed to take such pleasure in inflicting on him, he'd always known one thing; the opportunity for escape would present itself and he must be prepared to take it. He'd been right—and he had made sure the Hrsst paid dearly for what they'd done to him.

But as Klandar Bayne sent Frax back to his cell, the warrior felt nothing but helpless frustration. Trapped inside a living thing, moved about by the mere whim of his captors' mental powers, there might not be a timely mistake, a moment of unguarded distraction, for him to snatch and change to triumph.

That even a warrior of Cadarn might have to accept defeat.

However, there was a bitterer twist to the situation. If an opportunity to escape did present, it would probably be useless. Without the Priestess, escape was a moot issue. Again, when it mattered the most, he was totally powerless. The Wyxa held full control over their situation.

*"Will you tell them?"*

*"Tell them what, Uri? That if she can, she can and if she can't, she can't? What kind of prophecy is that?"* Anger tinged his sending.

*"You are not resigned to it."* Uri studied him gravely. He'd sat patient vigil over Frax after his nauseous return from the Ankar Mekt while Tobin had done his best to let their captors know his displeasure over their situation. Seuliac and Velacy had discreetly withdrawn out of the way while the younger Kitahn stormed up and down the length of the chamber in a respectable display of fury. If the Wyxa ever felt discomfort from their presence, Tobin Kitahn had surely given them distress.

Now the other three sat together at the far end of the chamber, silently waiting.

"No." Frax sighed. "Let's get them over here, Uri. We have to come up with a plan."

It took little time to formulate a strategy after he apprised the others of the situation. It took considerably longer to educate them on how to exercise the few options they had. They went over the child's rhyme Frax had used on the minor altar back in the temple to ensure everyone remembered it, and, with a little tweaking, he was able to give them an acceptable image of the bas-relief on its side. Anyone who got that far might have a chance at escape.

If they could get there in the pitch black beneath the Maugrock—they had no light source and could not depend on anything from the Wyxa. If the swamp dwellers withheld their boots, it would be impossible to cross the shard-strewn floor without serious injury. They debated the tactic of crawling, but the black splinters Frax remembered had looked as dangerous to hands as they did to feet.

Memory of the vast blackness inside the temple and the pressing sense of evil that had gathered around him and the girl made the muscles of his shoulders tense, as if the darkness touched his skin again.

"I know this looks bad, but it's not over. Just be prepared. There's always a chance something might present itself." He did not tell them Klandar Bayne had said everything was in the hands of the Priestess, if she had wits enough to thwart the Ankar Mekt and make his ridiculous prophecy come to pass. The prophecy was bad enough.

The others withdrew to consider what he'd told them, leaving Frax to wonder what the outcome of all this would have been if Gemma had not abandoned Kaphri. Would the pompous swamp dwellers have been more willing to listen to reason with the tiny Guardian's presence? Might she have directed all this into a different outcome?

An image came into his mind, of the Priestess' thin, smudged face as she sat across the fire, struggling to understand, her question full of pain and anger despite her calm exterior. "You mean, what is she trying not to influence?"

Again, the question that seemed to go hand in hand with the damned Guardian: what was it trying—or not trying—to influence?

A mixture of horror and triumph shot through him. Was it that simple? Did the scheming, wretched little serpent abandon Kaphri so she would have to work out her own action here, just as the Swampfather said must happen?

It was ridiculous, and acknowledging such a thought would only give further credence to Klandar Bayne's babble about the Winisp's prophecy. He would not fall into that trap. Still...

His thoughts returned to the girl, this time seeing her, mud-smeared, weary and thin as she tramped beside him through the heat and filth of the swamp. Never complaining, never completely giving in to the despair gripping them. The tilt of the delicate chin, the quick flash of anger, defiance, or pain in her dark eyes. The rare glimpse of smile that could light her with an inner glow, and was, unhappily, precipitated all too often by his cousin, Uri.

The ordeal in the Palenquemas had nearly undone him, yet she had fought on beside him without complaint. Now he thought on it, he realized it was more than he could have expected of some warriors he knew.

She was definitely beginning to develop in the right direction. He had the sudden vision of her standing before him, filled with horror and determination, the knife poised in her hand, while agony tore at him and his bones groaned in the crushing grip of the sigalithe' vine. She had attacked the thing ruthlessly and efficiently, severing its grip on him without hesitation.

So different from the resigned little waif, running from everything and ready to die under a geffitz blade rather than defend herself, that they had stumbled upon in Omurda.

His heart raced.

Was it true? Was there something inside her—beyond the Guardian, beyond the Geffitzi, the Wyxa, and even beyond

Bithzielp and Araxis? Could the thin, fire-haired wisp of a girl actually deliver their world of the threat hanging over it?

He had always wanted to believe she could succeed, even though doubts constantly plagued him. In the swamp, he'd stared at her peaceful, delicate features while she slept, and wondered if she could defeat what pursued her, or if he was a fool walking them all into disaster.

All he knew as he suddenly found himself bathed in cold moonlight was that he was not willing to accept the Ankar Mekt's solution to this problem.

# 52

## The Moonplain

*"You are summoned before the Ankar Mekt."* Klandar Bayne's sudden mental presence brought Kaphri scrambling to her feet, her heart hammering.

For two days since her encounter with the Swampfather, she had been isolated in the Wyxan cell. Two days in which to sleep, eat and rest. To think, worry about the warriors and what would happen to them all. To feel a strange and agonizing sense of loss she could not define.

It appeared the wait was over.

What would happen now?

*"It is the time for decisions to be implemented."* Klandar Bayne's answer came softly into her mind.

Kaphri stiffened. For two days she'd mulled her conversation with the Wyxan. Something had nagged at her, a sense something had not been right. Now, suddenly, there it was. *"I did not send you a question. You read my thoughts."* Horror and outrage began to build in her. *"Is that how you control my emotions?"*

"*You must understand, Starchild, we do not communicate in the same manner as you,*" Klandar Bayne came back soothingly. He could not reveal his pleasure that she had finally recognized the power his people held over her. The more she was aware of what she dealt with, the more likely she was to cope with it.

But, he didn't want her to delve too deeply into their skill at manipulating her thought processes, or how much they had fallen short with her, at this point. "*We communicate at the origin of the thought process. It makes everything calm and precise for us. Emotion makes dealing with a volatile species like yourself or the Geffitzi slow and difficult. It takes time for us to sort the information we need from the disruptive flow of emotions wrapped around it. Communicating directly with your inner mind enables us to better understand your basic thoughts and motivations.*"

Although she might have remotely suspected it, the actual idea of these creatures rummaging about in her brain without her consent infuriated her. Telepathy was an exchange of thoughts. This went far deeper, into mind reading. How much did they know about her?

Perhaps more than she knew of herself. Cold apprehension twisted inside her. Did their ability make them think they were wiser and more capable of making the judgments that affected her future than she was?

"*Not more wise,*" Klandar Bayne said. "*Just more objective.*"

This new display of obvious trespass into her thoughts sent her tension soaring even higher. "*That is not enough to justify invading my mind! I do not want you or your Ankar Mekt in my head, or in my life.*"

"*What do you want, Starchild?*" The question was soft.

"*What? Can it be that something is hidden beyond your uninvited reach?*" Her retort was sharp and bitter, a swift cover for an answer she did not have.

"*The answer is unclear.*"

The reply caught her by surprise, cutting through her resentment. She hesitated, knowing he spoke true. What she wanted out of this whole situation, from this world, from the Geffitzi warriors, or from the Wyxa, was unclear, even to her. A long, heavy silence hung between them.

"*I want to live free of the manipulation of others,*" she responded at last.

"*Then you must make it so.*"

Before she could reply, a wave of dizziness swept over her. Hredroth! Teleportation again!

Her anger and frustration faded at the touch of cold, damp air on her skin. She was standing on a grassy plane, lit by a jagged moon in a black, starry sky.

Her heart leapt. Stars. Was it possible...?

The Ankar Mekt's warning, that she held no power in this place, flashed in her memory. Still, she reached out.

Star response remained blocked from her. The swamp dwellers must possess immense power to block the Stars so completely. Small wonder the geas did not plague her here.

Hope faded to wariness. She swept out, trying to sense any nearby life, but found only a vast emptiness. The wind, again moaning sad and low in the distance, made her acutely aware of her stark surroundings. There was just sky, moon and a flat landscape broken by small plumes of fog that rose slowly from the marshy ground to drift on the chilled air. Wyxa from their other Plain? She shivered, partly from the cold and partly from apprehension.

Even as she watched, things were changing, however. The wafts of the vapor that floated over the surface began to concentrate, clinging together, until she was standing in a large, grassy circle enclosed in a wall of silent white vapor that glowed in the moonlight.

Was that a shadow of dark movement within the fog wall? Kaphri frowned as she strained to see. Had it been the form of a

Wyxan, or just her imagination? But there were more shadows now: tall, thin, elusive hints of things she was unable to lock on in mist encircling her.

Abruptly she realized the space was tinting with green light. Tiny green motes streamed, swirling as they flowed past her to assemble in a huge globe of pale, murky light that hung above the ground a short distance away.

Her stomach went queasy. Was that the Ankar Mekt? She'd been inside that? Memory of the cold, merciless mental sea shot of panic through her.

She would not go back into that thing again.

The green lights of the Ankar Mekt roiled faintly in agitation.

"*Beneath the all-seeing eyes of the Earth Mother, and begging her wisdom and guidance, this Ankar Mekt is joined.*" Kaphri recognized the cold, aloft presence from her first encounter with the Wyxa. "*Summon forth the others.*"

The others? Her hope surged. She twisted about, almost colliding with a Wyxan she had not realized was standing beside her.

Klandar Bayne? She gave it a quick mental brush. This one was a stranger.

Another of the creatures materialized out of the air on her other side and another at her back. There was no misinterpreting their appearance—they were guards—but their presence did not dampen her eagerness as she looked around.

The air across the clearing shimmered like heat rising from stone on a hot summer day and five familiar forms materialized in the moonlight. They were scattered, caught unexpectedly in the odd poses of whatever they'd been doing seconds before, but a single word, spoken low and sharp, brought them together, facing outward, their backs protected in a defensive formation.

The word, carrying across the silence, sent her heart racing. Her eyes searched the group, to find and lock on the tall figure standing at their forefront. He looked tired and his movements seemed slow, as if he had not totally recovered his strength, but that did not reflect in the haughty, fierce expression of defiance that tightened his features as he scanned the moonlit circle about him.

Then his eyes found her and she saw his body stiffen.

\*\*\*

"Ho-lee Kep!"

Tobin's exclamation went barely noticed as Frax stood, frozen in a mixture of relief, shock, and dismay. Then he was mentally cursing himself for a fool.

He should have known. If the Wyxa had restored him and the others to health, they would restore her, too. But who could have anticipated the changes wrought with that restoration? Dressed in gleaming white, the female that met his eyes across the clearing, her lips parted, half in appeal, half in fear, was not the skinny, mud-covered waif that had struggled beside him in the swamp. She was still slender, but now she was obviously and pleasantly curved. And the infuriating strip of red hair glowed like a soft flame in the moonlight.

He heard Seuliac's mocking laugh on his other side. "Fire and ice," the Aedec warlord murmured, admiration unmistakable in his tone.

A surge of irritation at the others' reactions ran through Frax Kitahn and he knew, with a sudden, depressing clarity, that if they succeeded in escaping this tangle his life had just become more complicated. Who would have thought it? She was lovely. And, enemy or not, with four other healthy males around him, the Winisp's prophecy suddenly took on a more real, much more immediate reality.

But that was not what mattered right now. Regardless of whether he believed in the Winisp's words, the intentions of Klandar Bayne, or the wisdom of the Ankar Mekt, if the Wyxan plan prevailed, there would be no future for any of them, difficult or otherwise.

A sudden realization struck him. Of course! Thanks to Klandar Bayne, he knew where this thing was leading. The Swampfather had given him freedom to act here.

Was the Ankar Mekt aware he knew its plan? Did it matter? They had already chosen their solution. It was up to the Priestess and the rest of them—he refused to relinquish control of his fate regardless of what Klandar Bayne claimed—to change the course of things here. The sense of helplessness that had gripped him over the past few days fell away to renewed confidence.

First, he had to assess their ability to communicate. A quick check confirmed the Wyxa had severed all telepathic links between him and the other warriors. The move confined them to speaking aloud in Geffitzi, with minimal hope of the girl understanding their words. Inconvenient, but not unexpected.

He took another look around, taking note of the vague shadows that moved in the seething veil of white surrounding them. Then his eyes went to the green sphere of the Ankar Mekt and back to the girl. So this was it? The tension inside of him, born of his greatest fear, that Kaphri might not be present when the time for this encounter came, released.

Did she know what was going to transpire here? At such a distance, he was unable to separate anything from the obvious tension in her posture. He could only interpret it to mean that, even if she did know the projected outcome of their situation, she had found no solution. He was all too familiar with that frustration; he'd run the thing in his head repeatedly, feeling the terrible sting of his own helplessness.

But as long as the girl was here, they still had a chance she might find a way.

He could feel the others at his back, tense and uneasy, but ready.

Waiting. He hadn't told anyone but Uri about the ancient Wyxan's prediction the Geffitzi and the Starchild might have a role in this crisis—how the Ankar Mekt refused to accept it. Or how she might save them all, or send them to their deaths.

"Stay calm," he murmured. They had one weapon here—the strength of their emotions. They must be very careful how they used it.

The next thing he must do was test the boundaries their captors had set. The girl was standing about thirty feet away, flanked by three Wyxa. He sent out a cautious mental probe, trying to touch her mind. The attempt was blocked.

Could he get her back within their group? He doubted the Ankar Mekt would allow physical contact, but he had to try. He stepped forward.

*"You will not approach the Starchild, Geffitz Lord."*

"She travels with us. She is part of this group." He was careful not to make the claim more specific for fear of drawing a negative reaction from Tobin or the Aedecs. Dividing his small force in any way right now would be a terrible mistake. "You will not interfere in Geffitzi business."

*"She is no longer your concern."*

It was time to risk a small action. He directed his anger at the orb like a small and vicious blade, pricking it lightly. "You dare...!"

The seething white perimeter came alive with dark and looming forms. Suddenly there were Wyxa standing all around them.

"What the hell, Kitahn?" Seuliac snarled as he took a step backward to avoid brushing against one of the creatures. On Frax's left side, Tobin also took a startled step back, nearly trampling Uri. From one of the others—Uri or Velacy, he could not determine which—there was the sound of outrage as their tightening circle forced them all to jostle elbows.

"Relax," he hissed. His test for a reaction had proven swiftly and unpleasantly informative. Now nine, no ten, of the creatures surrounded them. Two for each of them. And Frax had the bruises to prove that, despite their frail appearance, any two of the swamp dwellers towering so tall around them would be enough to control any one of them physically. And yet, three hovered over the Priestess and she was certainly no physical challenge for them. His eyes swung back to her, narrowing speculatively.

Tobin muttered a vehement curse beside him and Frax repeated his cautioning command.

The imperious mental voice of the Ankar Mekt began again.

*"We dare to do whatever we deem necessary to bring this matter to the quickest, safest resolution for our world, Geffitz Lord. Be warned, any further aggression on your part will result in your complete isolation from your companions. Our folk stationed around you will ensure this encounter progresses in a quick and orderly manner. They will take whatever actions you make necessary. We understand this must be difficult for you, but we insist you remain controlled and objective in your reactions. No further outbursts will be tolerated."*

Complete isolation? He kept a tight rein on a chill of dismay. A separation from the others at this point would be very ill timed.

The quick and harsh reaction from the Ankar Mekt had caught him off guard. Klandar Bayne had writhed in pain beneath the emotional intensity of his reactions during their first encounter but had made no attempt to check him. The Ankar Mekt obviously did not intend to endure the same thing. Which was more in keeping with the image of the swamp dwellers his life had given him up to this point.

Maybe he should re-consider his suspicion of the Swampfather's motives. Klandar Bayne must have been very dedicated to his purpose, to subject himself to the emotional punishment Frax knew he'd endured to present his case.

The Wyxa had severely curtailed his ability to maneuver in this current situation and he still had to find a way to convey a message to the Priestess. He could not let her believe they accepted this solution.

He tried to catch Kaphri's attention across the moonlight, but she had turned toward the great globe of green light as the Ankar Mekt continued.

*"By now you are all aware you have been telepathically isolated from your companions. Be assured: it is a temporary thing. You may still send to the Ankar Mekt and, although your companions will not hear your question, they will hear our reply."*

"I wish to speak aloud." Frax broke in. "Is that acceptable?"

The Priestess could not understand Geffitzi any more than he understood Ly Kai, but she could deduce something from the tone of his questions and the Ankar Mekt's responses. He simply had to lead them in the right direction.

There was a long pause as the Ankar Mekt considered the request.

*"You may speak, as long as you do not seek to disrupt. You are warned: no emotional outbursts will be tolerated."*

"Then I wish to say something before this gathering." He spoke quickly, before they could stop him, but he was careful to keep his tone calm. "We do not recognize your right to interfere with us, or to make decisions regarding the fate of our people." He put a heavy emphasis on the word 'not'. Surely, the Wyxa did not expect them to endure all this without some protest. "A decision had been made, and action was being taken, before you interfered."

*"We were not a part of that decision."*

"It was not, and is not, your decision to make."

*"This is our world, too, Geffitz. Your actions in this matter have already brought us all to the brink of disaster."*

"Our..." Frax bit back a flash of anger. He heard the corresponding rumbles of reaction from the warriors at his back.

The Ankar Mekt continued over his exclamation. "*Frax Kitahn, you wish the Starchild to do battle with the one who erected the barrier in the hope that, with his defeat, the wall barring the way to your lands will fall. But, think of the consequences if she fails. She will suffer. You will suffer, your people, our people. Our whole world, will suffer. We cannot take the risk. With our solution, the threat to our world will end. That is all that is important.*"

For a moment, Frax stood pale and speechless at the cold simplicity of the Ankar Mekt's speech.

"You think putting the thing you call the Guardian Stone back will fix things." His tone was fierce. "You're wrong. The thing stopped working years ago. Putting it back is a frayed patch at best. And even if we temporarily succeed in closing the way and destroying the Balandra, the one who drove us from the south remains a problem for us.

"Our people want our lands back. She is our one and only, our best hope. As you've said, this is our world, too. We know our history; we know—she knows—the risks involved. Take the damned Guardian Stone. Do with it as you will. But release us, so we can continue our task." Frax felt the awesome burden of the task he was fighting to assume. For a fleeting moment, he wondered if he was insane to argue so bitterly for it. "We will not refuse your aid, but if you won't help us, then at least don't interfere."

"*You have no plan of action. You are not a cohesive force.*"

"You forced me into your joining. You know what the Guardian said."

"*The Guardian abandoned its post and is nowhere to be found. No, the price of your failure is too high. It is our judgment your company, as the solution, is inadequate. The Wyxa must take action to preserve us all.*"

"It won't work!"

"*It will suffice until we can devise a permanent solution to the threat that lies beyond the Goroth M'nget. That is the true danger to this world.*"

*"The time has come to implement the decisions we have made. We will return the Geffitzi warriors to the north so they may deal with the problem that threatens there. The Starchild will remain here. We will secure her on the Ethereal Plain, beyond any threat from this world."*

The Ankar Mekt said they all would hear its response. Frax watched Kaphri across the clearing intently, trying to interpret her expression. She was staring at the green globe of the Ankar Mekt, her face turned in profile to him, and he could not read her reaction. Had she known their fates before this moment? Was she speaking to the Ankar Mekt? Protesting?

She looked over at him again and his whole being jolted in horror. She forced the small, quiet smile—he knew her that well—and her face was pale. But the message was clear: go to your people. Do not worry about me. I accept this.

Curse the streak of noble sacrifice in her! She could not believe the Wyxan promise to return them to the north had brought them around to agreeing to this! He must do something to dispel that thought. But, isolation from the others would be a disastrous result if he reacted wrongly.

The Wyxa had severed all mental and verbal communication between them, but they overlooked one thing. Telepathy might convey a full message of emotion and intent, but beings that used speech were sometimes forced to rely on things other than words. He had one thing left he could do. If it failed to dissuade her from her foolish course of self-sacrifice, there was nothing for them except to accept the Ankar Mekt's solution.

He had her eye. Glaring furiously, willing every ounce of defiant refusal he could muster into it, he gave a single slow, emphatic shake of his head.

# 53

## Taking Control

Frax's reaction shook her to the quick. He was flatly refusing to accept the Wyxa's plan to return them to the north. But why? The Balandra were killing his people. Did the fall of the barrier mean so much to him that he was willing to risk not having anyone left to go back to?

No, the Geffitzi valued their people. Which meant there was some other reason. The warriors across the clearing were rigid with tightly contained anger and defiance, but she could only stand, frozen, her mind churning with sudden uncertainty as the Ankar Mekt continued with its decree.

*"Listen well, Children of Kep. The fate of our world and its people lies upon you. You must do exactly as we instruct. At the heart of the Black Temple lies the Goroth M'nget, the Circle of Sacrifices. At its center is the Rune of Amassing Power, the doorway through which this evil insinuates itself, assisted by the blood of our world. We will transport you there, where you must replace the Guardian Stone directly upon the Rune to seal the*

*way and reestablish its guardianship. Then your people may destroy his servants. Do not fail."*

Kaphri's knees tried to crumple beneath her. The Wyxa were sending the warriors into the depths of the Black Temple! This wasn't an act of justice. This was a death sentence!

She knew Frax's eyes had never left her face when she looked back at him. The anger and accusation she feared seeing was not there. There was no doubt, no appeal, no question. His expression was a simple, clear giving over of this whole situation to her. And somehow she understood, as if he pressed a weapon into her hand. As she had feared all along; whatever happened here, she must be the one to carry it.

The Ankar Mekt was already proceeding with its decree, the gathering of their power prickling her skin.

With a choked cry, she took a step forward, only to find herself caught between two of the Wyxa guards as they gripped her arms.

Across the clearing, heated sounds of protest erupted as those Wyxan guards forced the warriors even closer together. The emotions they held in restraint up to this point burned heavy in the air now as they divided their fury between the green glow of the Ankar Mekt, the Wyxa surrounding them, and the ones restraining her.

\*\*\*

"Is this Wyxan justice, to send us to our death without even a weapon to defend ourselves?" Frax shouted. He clenched his fists in desperation as the girl stopped and stared at him. Did she comprehend what was happening here?

*"It is not our intention to send you to your death. We are returning your weapons and other possessions to you."*

Their packs materialized on the grass before them.

Frax noted with chilled irony that they bulged heavily with provisions, as if they would need them after the next few moments.

A heartbeat later their weapons appeared.

*"Take up your things, Warriors, but do not think to use your weapons here."* The Wyxa hovering around them stepped aside, allowing them access to their packs and weapons.

"Everyone get a canna nut open," he ordered. Light would increase their chances of getting to the minor altar and into the caverns below. "I'll take the crystal. The rest of you follow Tobin to the altar."

They surged forward, pulling on clothes and boots, then digging for the precious nuts that might be the key to their survival. They snatched their weapons last, Frax warning them to keep them lowered. No one wanted to find themself in the darkness beneath the Maugrock without a weapon, thing which the swamp dwellers were entirely capable of doing if they failed to cooperate in this last step.

*** 

She watched as the warriors shrugged into their heavy packs, slid blades into boots and belts, and slipped bows and quivers of arrows on their backs. Frax straightened to glare at her again across the moonlight. Beside him, Uri cracked a canna nut and hastily spread the blue sap on a small disc that Tobin handed him. A brief glimmer of blue highlighted their grim features before disks, net and all, disappeared into beltpouchs to hide the glow.

"What are you doing?" She twisted toward the Ankar Mekt. "You can't send them back to that place. They'll die!" She never agreed to this!

*"Remove the Starchild for transfer to the Ethereal Plain."*

A wave of confusion rolled through her. Ethereal Plain? What did that mean? She said she would help them, but not this! What was happening? This—everything—was wrong. Something was missing here.

Hands tugged her arms as the Wyxa tried to draw her toward the seething wall of fog. Anger and desperation choked her. She kicked out at the Wyxan on her right. Missed. Her foot slid and she fell to one knee. They continued to pull her.

From beneath her outstretched arm, she saw a movement. A Wyxan emerged from the fog, the tall, insectoid form advancing on the warriors across the moonlit space. It carried something carefully in its clasped hands.

She recognized the mental signature. Klandar Bayne.

The crystal! He held the crystal! Realization was an ice dagger shoved into her heart. They were sending the warriors into the darkness of the Black Temple, to return the Guardian Stone—no!—the crystal!—to the place where she had found it. That was certain death! Everything would end here and she would never be able to help them reclaim their lands.

"Frax, don't take it! You will all die!" She screamed, knowing he would hear the warning in her cry even if he didn't understand the words.

Wyxan power continued to build as the Ankar Mekt worked to carry through the final stage of its decision.

She fought against the Wyxa dragging her between them. She must stop this. But... She didn't understand. They called it the Guardian Stone. Frax had said... What? He used the word Guardian. She remembered that, but not the context. It had made her feel angry and sad. Now the Wyxa were sending him and the others to take this Guardian Stone back into the darkness. They were going to destroy everything.

She must stop this, but she couldn't do this alone. There should be someone else to help her. Where was the help she needed? Her thoughts were slow, as if a heavy veil shrouded a part of her brain. But, memory argued, there was someone she should call on! Someone who was always there...

Gemma!

The veil in her brain burst, shredding and sending her mind

reeling. How could she have forgotten her tiny companion? How could she forget the one stable thing in her life, the being that was her mentor. Her friend. Her guardian...? Horror locked her body as more memory flooded in. Frax said the Guardian... Oh, Hredroth! He said the tiny golden dragon...

She didn't care about the truth. She needed her tiny friend.

But Gemma had vanished at the edge of the swamp.

Gemma! Her mental cry of desperation spiraled out across the Palenquemas.

Light blazed from the object cupped in the Swampfather's hands.

An answering flash of gold flared at the far edge of the fog circle and Gemma bloomed into existence.

Before Kaphri could cry out in joy, the tiny golden body seemed to distort and lengthen. The dragon flared her wings, as if to stop in midair, but her momentum did not slow. The gold thinned and drew out into a fine strand that sliced across the circle toward Klandar Bayne.

A trap, Kaphri's brain screamed. This was a trap!

Gemma became a thin stream of gold that flowed toward the Swampfather's cupped hands, thinning to the barest thread.

She vanished.

A soft touch brushed inside her mind, as if Gemma gave her a tender farewell, and Kaphri finally understood. The little dragon had moved beyond her reach.

"No..." What had she done? How could she be so stupid and selfish? He had warned her: the Wyxa did not care about the other beings of this world. He had told her Gemma was a Guardian. And now the Ankar Mekt had bound her companion to the thing they called the Guardian Stone—the crystal—to force the dragon to protect this world.

But, she suddenly realized, their interpretation of the task wasn't the same as Gemma's. The tiny dragon had sought her out years ago for a reason. She had a role to play in this, whether she, the Geffitzi, or the Wyxa wanted it or not.

Kaphri was the one who must set this right or they would all die. She didn't know how! Fear and sorrow twisted her heart. Without Gemma, she was helpless.

Of one thing, she was sure: Gemma did not belong in the darkness and neither did the warriors.

When it finally came, it was as easy as merely taking what she wanted. The crystal answered, feeding her need as she reached out and firmly stopped the Ankar Mekt's working.

Across the clearing, a brilliant whiteness flared and the crystal suddenly hung by its chain at her breast. As its glow slowly dimmed she grasped it—Gemma—in her right hand and in the midst of the stunned silence, she finished her statement. "...you will not do this."

The controls the Wyxa exerted over her mind evaporated.

The warriors' expressions mirrored the disbelief that held the circle of Wyxa motionless. Tobin stared at her in amazement, then, as the stunned silence continued, he relaxed his stance and tilted his head with a new defiance as he glanced about.

Frax regarded her steadily across the space and she realized she knew his thoughts: you have control, now finish it.

Finish it, yes. But how? Already she'd accomplished something she never thought possible by thwarting the plans of the Ankar Mekt. As the question tore through her mind, realization struck her: she had known teleportation before Klandar Bayne used it on her. Every day in Kryie Karth she moved water to the kitchens and baskets of food to the larder.

The Wyxa moved living things—groups of living things in the case of her and the warriors. Could she do it, too? Not by using starpower: the swamp dwellers still blocked that from this place. But she had the crystal clutched in her hand. It had just proven so easy to use.

All these thoughts ran through her mind in the course of a heart-beat, while she stood at the center of a fog-hemmed circle, moon-light flooding over her.

With the outrage of thousands of minds rising around her she took a deep breath and drew on the crystal.

"Kep!"

She was just as startled as Tobin, Uri, Velacy, and Seuliac when she appeared in front of them, but Frax caught her arm, as if he'd been expecting her.

"*Return the Guardian Stone to us!*"

Kaphri staggered under the wave of the Ankar Mekt's fury.

"*Take that thing and get out of here!*" Frax's command drove deep into her brain as the confusion inside the green ball of churning light broke down its control.

"*But you—*"

"*Once the crystal is gone they'll have no interest in us. Go!*"

"*Where?*" She was sure she needed a clear image of a place to move to it.

"*Anywhere! Just do it!*"

"*Windmer,*" Uri exclaimed. "*We'll find you there.*"

Frax nodded. "*Go there. Follow the eastern road out from the hold gate, through the mountains. We'll find you. But you must be prepared to do whatever you have to do without us.*"

"*You should go now.*" The Warlord's calm observation brought them all about. Seuliac was staring at the sky. For the first time, Kaphri became aware of the low sound that had been clawing at the edges of her hearing. She followed his gaze to a strange, mottled darkness spreading across the starry sky. It was advancing on the place of the Ankar Mekt with astounding speed. The irritating sound was rising in volume.

"*A storm?*" Uri asked doubtfully.

Seuliac shook his head. "*Too fast.*"

Was it something the Wyxa had called up to stop them?

But the terrible Wyxan rage had vanished. She looked around to find the swamp dwellers staring upward, also.

The keening sound rose another pitch and realization sent horror shooting through her. *"It's the Balandra! Araxis has sent his forces into the Palenquemas."*

Frax spun her away from the darkness sweeping the sky. *"We can take cover in the fog, then you can spirit yourself out of here."* He spat a few words of Geffitzi at the others and they ran, charging through the scattering glow of the Ankar Mekt, toward the thinning wall of fog that only moments before had been an imprisoning barrier.

There was something terrifying in seeing Wyxa vanish into the air.

*"Gods of—"* Tobin, in the lead, shied sharply, causing Kaphri to stumble as she tried to avoid him.

A Wyxan stood in their path.

"Swampfather!" Shocked recognition tore the word from her. Why was he standing here while the others fled? Did he still want the crystal?

Her eyes locked with his, and she felt a jolt of realization. Of course, why were they running?

Frax's grip on her arm was so tight that it jerked him backward when she stopped moving. He came about, quick fury ripping through him. *"It's over, Wyxan. Leave her alone and flee with the rest of your lot."*

*"My people do not flee, Blood Warrior."* Klandar Bayne sent calmly. *"They go to weave their powers into a weapon of battle. We will not defeat this evil tonight. That remains for you. But we will succeed in destroying a portion of it, severely crippling the force that seeks you."*

*"You knew this would happen?"* Frax stared at him, aghast.

Klandar Bayne's head inclined in acknowledgment. *"The Winisp foresaw many things."* He looked down at Kaphri. *"You must leave this battlefield now, to find your own way."*

She wanted to scream in frustration. Demand that they release Gemma. But the cloud of Balandra was fast descending upon them. Her hand tightened defensively around the crystal. *"I cannot give this back to you."*

*"You commanded and it responded. Now you must go."*

*"Tonight the glory of the Palenquemas will shine like the Little Daughter."* Uri sent to Klandar Bayne as Frax pulled her away.

*"This once a Geffitzi battle blessing is appropriate and welcome. Tell this tale well, Storyteller."* The delicately tapered head gave a nod of acknowledgment. The light about them dimmed as the cloud of invading Balandra swept over the path of the moon and dropped toward them. *"Go now."*

*"Join hands,"* Kaphri ordered. Focusing was difficult with the tooth-grinding shriek of the Balandra tearing at her ears. *"Everyone concentrate on the holdhall—"*

*"Inside is too dangerous."* Frax snatched her hand. *"Go for the plaza in front of the main gate."*

The image flooded her mind from five other sources. The gate, with the stone placard hung on the crossway, blazed clearly. But as she drew on the crystal, sweeping its strength over the six of them and willing them away, the sensation of another will, seeking to insert its influence over hers, snatched at her.

She fought to wrest back control.

*"May your Gods speed you, for the survival of us all."* Klandar Bayne's sending went barely noticed as the air changed around them.

# 54

## Treachery on Another Front

The moonlight dimmed then brightened again.

"Oh, Kep!" A wave of shock and confusion boiled up from the warriors around Kaphri. Connecting hands broke grips as they scattered.

Before Kaphri could react, everything changed.

She was on her back in darkness, her clothes soaking wet, the air around her cold. A shrill scream of rage replaced the sound of Geffitz dismay. Something large and powerfully heavy struck the ground near her head, sending an icy spray of mud and leaves against the side of her face.

Hredroth! She was under attack! But from what? Where was she?

A savage sense of loss and fear wrenched her gut. Something had happened. The Geffitzi warriors...

She saw a distant flicker of light her, a sense of movement. She rolled sideways, barely avoiding a blow that sliced the air above her head. In that same instant, everything shifted again.

Silence struck her senses like a negative thunderclap and she was standing, the air on her skin clean and cool. She—

All the muscles in Kaphri's body went rigid as the long-absent geas crashed in to the spaces the Wyxa had held empty in the Palenquemas.

"*I said get down!*" A hand caught her arm, and she felt the impact of her body hitting a rough stone surface, but there was no room for more pain inside the torment of the geas.

Danger! Her mind screamed, fighting back. Something had gone wrong! A heartbeat ago, normally calm, calculating Geffitzi warriors had panicked. Were still panicked.

But a Geffitz warrior had pulled her down beside him. A Geffitz warrior still held some control even if she did not. She rolled onto her side, burrowing against the hard body next to her, and drew her knees up tight and curled into a ball.

Such pain!

"*We can't sit here,*" Tobin's mental hiss sliced through her agony. "*We have to take cover.*"

"*Damn it, Kitahn, where? There's nothing but open plaza in every direction.*"

"*Kep, I don't believe this,*" Frax snapped. "*Of all the... Uri! The gate's up. Grab her and move inside! Tobin, take the lead.*"

What was happening? The flood of shock, panic, and, from Frax, outrage, tore at her. She fought her way to the surface of conscious thought, but what she received from the warriors' minds only added to her confusion and mounting terror. It said the danger was real. Imminent. She managed to force the geas away long enough to see it was still nighttime before it wrapped her in its grip again.

Remotely, she felt Uri snatch her up.

"*Damn it, Priestess, uncurl!*" A hard thumb found a pressure point, and she gasped with fresh physical pain, her limbs loosening.

"*The rest of you. Go! Go!*"

In a mad scurry they charged across a space and plunged through an opening into the deeper darkness of an enclosure.

"*Get your feet under you.*" Uri thrust her against a stone wall and slammed into place beside her. Beyond the havoc the geas was wreaking on her perceptions, the sound of heavy breathing told her the others had followed close behind them.

The rough stone was a distant scrape against her spine as she slid down the wall, but it was nothing compared to the pain that wracked her body. Hredroth! The agony! She tried to raise a hand to her forehead and realized Uri's fingers still clasped her wrist.

Too much was happening. It was pushing her into a sensory overload. Defensively, she began to retreat into a mental darkness.

"*How could this happen?*" Frax mentally grappled about for her. "*How could you know...? No! Uri, don't let her shut down. We need answers.*"

"*This was all a trap! You treacherous bastards—*"

"*Shut up, Velacy!*"

"*Come on, Willow.*" Uri's sending was tight with concern and fear as his big hands chafed her wrists. "*We need you.*"

They were under some kind of attack. From a distance she could hear her companions and feel the panic and outrage in them, but the geas burned with a terrible, all-engulfing need that would devour her if she did not gain control of it.

Desperately, she fought against it.

But what could be more important than succumbing to its demand? The geas ate through her thoughts, trying to eliminate anything that would conflict with its purpose. Nothing must delay her any longer. Nothing must stop her from answering that call. Not even...

"Gemma!" she gasped.

The image of her tiny companion disintegrating into a stream of golden dust finally broke the geas; grasped and force it back into perspective. She drew another ragged breath and caught Uri's hand to tell him she was regaining control. His fingers closed about her wrist again.

The sudden easing of the geas left her disoriented. She groped out telepathically, trying to distinguish something of their surroundings. They were hunkered inside a stone, square-walled space, enveloped in darkness. She located Frax, Velacy and Seuliac pressed close against the wall beyond Uri. Past them, Tobin laid, belly to the floor, peering out the tall, narrow opening through which they had entered. The tension hanging over them was nearly physical.

*"Where's Gemma?"* She would have surged away from the wall but Uri held her in place. She didn't notice. Instead, she searched about the space frantically with her mind.

*"She's not here."* Frax's answer was heavy with caution.

*"But I saw her..."* Confusion rippled across her brain.

Kaphri didn't need the answering silence of five warriors to tell her the little dragon was not with them. She'd seen her precious companion appear inside the fog-ringed circle and distort into a stream of gold that flowed through the air to the Swampfather's hands and the crystal he held. The crystal that now hung around her neck. The Ankar Mekt had locked Gemma inside a talisman that no longer served the purpose for which they created it and Kaphri had no idea how to free her. The realization, after her wild surge of hope, left her shattered.

A tear slipped down her cheek. Reality ratcheted into a shaking torrent of loss in a few short breaths.

A slap stung her. Stunned back into the present, she raised her free hand to her cheek.

*"All right now?"*

She gave Uri a brush of acknowledgment but his grip on her other wrist stayed tight as he broadened his sending. *"Frax. She's back with us."*

*"How could you bring us here? How could you know?"* The Geffitz commander's questions were a blaze of anger and suspicion in her head.

*"I..."*

Using the crystal to teleport them out of the Wyxan swamp had been a risk. She thought she knew what to do, but the thing was not a part of her starpower. It was simply the only means she had to stop the Ankar Mekt from sending the warriors to their death in the Black Temple.

Now, as she regained a grip on immediate reality, it became obvious from the surrounding reactions that they were not at Windmer Hold.

*"I pictured Windmer—"*

*"This is not Windmer!"*

In the tense silence that followed, she tore through her memory, replaying what she remembered. The jump was a new thing, but she'd known how to do it. There'd been no doubt. The image was clear, the others' minds attuned to hers. Everything was right. Everything was...

*"Something else, outside our image. It tried to take control,"* she said.

The warriors' curses went unheard as she took up the crystal in her free hand. In the darkness the clear droplet with the tiny fleck of gold at its center was firm and comforting beneath her fingers. Twice it had saved her. She would not believe it betrayed her now. Especially if Gemma...

Her hand shook so hard she released the crystal to fall back into place.

*"So something or someone overrode the image in your mind,"* Uri said.

"Why?" Seuliac demanded. "What purpose would bringing us here serve?"

Where were they? The warriors obviously recognized it. Their reactions raced with shock and the fearful expectation of danger, even though her sense of the surrounding structure was distinctly Geffitzi. Before she was able to form the question, Frax's anger and concern burned inside her head again.

"Who would want to send us here?"

It had been too swift for a clear impression, but she knew what it had not been: it was not anything related to Araxis or the evil force in the Black Temple. Which eliminated two very dangerous sources.

The image of the Swampfather crept into her mind. He stood been there, calm despite the drastic disruption to the Wyxa's plans her retaking of the crystal had caused, as if he anticipated it all along. He even wished them Godspeed.

Frax's measured evaluation pricked her outer mind.

"Klandar Bayne." He shifted his attention. "Uri? Could he do this?"

"Possibly. After so many years of Kitahni trespass they are sure to be familiar with this place from your peoples' mind-images." Uri's fingers relaxed from around her wrist at last. "But why?"

"How do we know this isn't some plan you worked up with those creatures, Kitahn?" Velacy snapped. "You were the only one they talked to. Maybe this is your plot..."

"To bring us here?" Tobin broke in angrily. "Are you out of your mind? Do you know what—?"

"Not now, Tobin!" Frax cut him off. He turned his attention back to Kaphri. "Priestess, is there anyone in this place with us?"

She responded instinctively to his question, reaching out and up. Hredroth, they were on the ground floor of a tower! If they were not at Windmer, they were somewhere very similar. "No," she said.

"Keep in mind, these might be Geffitzi warriors."

Why would that cause them so much distress? Where were they, that thoughts of their own people would strike such a panic? But his warning was a sobering reminder of how she had missed their presence on her first encounter with Geffitzi in Omurda.

She was very familiar with that subtle mental essence now, however. She searched out again, concentrating heavily. *"Nothing."*

An almost tangible tension seemed to flow out of the others.

"By the Goddess!" Frax sagged against the wall with a shaky sigh of relief. "Finding myself suddenly at the land gate of Rhynog couldn't be any worse than these last few minutes."

Uri gave a fervent snort of agreement beside her.

"You can have no idea." Seuliac's voice, heavy with irony, came softly out of the darkness.

There was a startled silence, then Tobin gave a sudden, hysteria-edged hoot of laughter. Uri chuckled as low sounds of amusement rippled from the others. "It's alright, Willow. Somehow you shifted us to Caer Cadarn."

Which might or might not be wonderful for them. But what had overridden their image of Windmer, and attacked her on arrival? And what about Gemma?

Sorrow choked her.

End Part 2

THE STORY CONTINUES in Part 3, Taking the World

# ACKNOWLEDGEMENTS

My writing journey began a long time ago, and though there were times when I could not devote time to the process, it was always present at the edge of my mind, like puzzle pieces turning to fit the whole. There are people that kept me moving forward along the way, from my high school friend, Brenda Kirk, to Joan Summers, to the members of our local writing critique group, past and present, the SKY Writers. I would not have been so bold as to believe I could do this without your inspiration, especially those of you who published before me. And then there's Sam, my loving husband who has always been here to support me with anything I needed to get the job done.

Also I'd like to credit Dave Hoefler at Unsplash for the cover background art.

I sincerely thank you all.

Bobbie Falin lives in Bowling Green, KY with her husband and four stray cats that stop by for breakfast and dinner every day. She began to write novels on cocktail napkins as a waitress while earning a BA in art education from Western KY University. Now she spends her time writing science fiction and fantasy. She reads voraciously, dabbles in 3D art, gardens and collects beautiful images of all sorts on Pinterest. If there was a space program to explore the stars, she'd be first in line.